AF397598

# The last white witch

A Novel by Nalle Windahl

The first book in the Saga Quadrology

Second edition

© 2020 Nalle Windahl

**Förlag:** BoD – Books on Demand, Stockholm, Sverige
**Tryck:** BoD – Books on Demand, Norderstedt, Tyskland

ISBN: 978-91-7969-589-7

**Did you like the art-work on the cover?**

Cover image by **Patrik Åkervinda**. He is incredibly talented, please use your google-fu or any other search-engine-powers to find more of his work online!


**Do you like the writing?** (perhaps better answer that question after you have read the book!)

For more information about me (the writer) and my work, please visit my webpage: http://jnw.se/


^..^


**Disclaimer**

This book is self-published and has not gone through any editorial nor linguistic process. Any weird language or wording is purely because my native language is not English. I leave it to your imagination to see the language as part of this fantasy world and its story.

Please enjoy this story. I have enjoyed creating it and I hope you will love it as much as I do! Feel free to contact me through my web page.

**one.**

Let us challenge your imagination.

What if you were standing on a small path in a forest near the ocean. What if a heavy mist conceals the surrounding environment? The soft light from the dawn can almost not penetrate the mist, giving what could be a milky, white, and soft mist a rather cold and grey appearance.

Adding the morning cold from a typical autumn day by the ocean, makes all the tiny hairs on your body standing on edge. The chilly morning breeze runs straight through your clothes.

Your eyes are trying to adapt to the environment, but it is just too hard to do, the mist keeps moving and changing, and it is not enough light to separate the mist from actual things. Trees, the path itself, rocks, branches, bushes, everything is molded together to one unity.

Since your vision is clouded by the mist you are solely dependent on your ears. But every single sound you hear around you are hard to identify.

Is it a huge wolf or bear sneaking in the forest, looking for breakfast, or is it any kind of monster, a vampire that has an extended hunting night due to the heavy mist? An undead or a werewolf? Or could it just be cute and tiny birds jumping around on the ground making all these little noises? Your wild imagination makes you pulse rise high, so high that you can almost hear each heartbeat. Your chest is struggling heavy to fill your lungs with the cool and damp morning air without making a sound.

All your senses are impaired. Your imagination has triggered every warning signal in your entire body. You want to run, as fast as you can, down the path to reach the harbour camp and safety. Or turn back to the village. Either way as fast as you can to get out of where you are at the moment. Alone. In the forest. On the unmanned path between the village and the harbour camp. No help nearby, no rescue. Just you. And whatever is out there in the mist with you.

Lucky for you that it is not you on that path, this very moment. Unfortunately, Dee is not that lucky, because she is the one standing on the path this very moment. On the edge of panicking, which she knows is the worst thing she could do right now. If she keeps her calm, she might be able to sneak her way to the harbour camp undetected. Any being out here this morning will struggle with the mist. In a way the mist is her best friend right now. It will partly cover her smell. Both the smell of her flesh that attracts animals, werewolves and the undead, and the smell of her blood that attracts the vampires.

Dee tried not to think of any of the thousand horrible things she could meet out here. She focused on Rick. If she were lucky, today would be the day when his ship returned from the long voyage. She hoped of all her heart that today would still be that day, and that he would be on the ship.

She had not seen her brother in over a year, since he was chosen for that horrible mission by the elders.

She kept her focus. Tried to calm her breathing. Slowly started to move again along the path, trying not to make a single sound. Or at least, as little noise as humanly possible when moving along a narrow path in the middle of the forest that is rarely used.

With all senses tense and on edge she took one small step, then another, without making a single noise. All surrounding sounds kept to their pace and did not seem disturbed by her movement. Then suddenly, after ten steps or so, a branch cracked under her foot. After that, total silence. She could not tell if it was the raising panic dulling her senses, or if the forest in fact had gone silent.

Completely silent. Did she dare to stand still? Or did she dare not to stand still?

From nowhere she heard a faint whisper, so thin she could barely hear it.

"This is my mist. I wish you no harm. Go! I will protect you!"

She could not see who ever was talking to her, she dared not reply. She started to move forward again, slowly, still not able to hear a thing from the surroundings. There was indeed something supernatural about this. Who was it that whispered through the mist? It must be someone with great power. Good or evil? Her thoughts started to spin.

"One day I might call upon your help, but not now. Go my child! Hurry!"

Whoever whispered to her was obviously close, had some kind of power and could protect her from the danger in the forest. From the urgency in the voice the danger could be close. That could explain why she did not hear anything. Anyone close to her would hopefully experience the same. She started to run. Then again. Could she be running into a trap? How could she know that whoever was responsible for the mist had good intentions towards her? The world here outside the cities are cold and hard, full of evil. The villages are fairly safe. Even the various camps, like the harbour camp. But outside of that, especially at night, not a very friendly place. Especially not if you like your life and have planned to stay alive a bit longer.

Being out here was insane, Dee knew that, and by defying her father like this would have painful consequences, she knew that as well. But if there was the slightest chance that Rick was on that ship, she just had to be there when it arrived. She ran as fast as she could.

A million thoughts rushed through her head. Who had whispered in the mist? Who was powerful enough to create it? The wizards were almost extinct. And as far as she knew the few who survived the great war was hiding far south, way past the coldblooded. What service could she possibly provide to someone with powers like this? Maybe it was brilliant hunting maneuver by one of vampires of the old? But could they create the illusion of a whisper with no apparent source?

"Hurry Diane, I cannot hold them much longer! You are getting too far away! Soon you will start to hear small sounds again, then I can protect you no longer."

Now she was in great trouble! Whoever it was knew her name! She did not know of anyone capable of doing that! What power was that?

But the voice was right. She started to hear tiny noises again. It started with her pounding heart. Her heavy breathing. Then something beside her. She kept running on the path without knowing where on the path she was. If it had been daylight and no mist, she would have recognized the surroundings, but now. No idea. How far was it to the harbour camp? Had she passed the small bridge yet? No, she did not think so, or had she? Hard to say. If she had passed the bridge, she had about a twenty-minute walk to reach the outskirts of the harbour camp. How long would that take to run? She could hear more now, she started to hear her steps on the path as she was struggling forward. For how long could she keep running? Her heart was already pounding hard in her chest, and her breathing was already fast and heavy. Could she make it?

What was that? It sounded like a werewolf howl, pretty close. There were more sounds as well. And was she imagining, or was the mist getting thinner? Yes, it was getting thinner, she could see more of the trees around the path now. She kept running, following the path left and right, up, and down. Had she taken a wrong turn somewhere? Where is that bridge? It felt like she had been out a lot longer than an hour. Normally she would have arrived at the harbour camp by that time. This mist had slowed her down, no doubt, but had she already passed the bridge?

There was the howling again. She stopped. She could see about five feet ahead now. All sounds had turned normal again, she could hear everything around her. Even see small movements in a bush here and there. Probably just the wind. Or maybe a small animal. She hoped anyway.

She started to move slow again, ears focused on every single sound, mostly scanning for the howl. It was hard to move slow again, but she dared not keep running and find herself running in to the arms of a hostile creature.

Finally, the bridge! She was on the right path! But still, a long way to go. About twenty-minute walk from safety. That would be a lot longer in this mist. Maybe an hour longer with this pace.

There was that howl again, very close this time. Chills went down her spine. She almost stopped, only to move very, very slow. Then, a sudden shift in the mist, and a silhouette of the huge werewolf, standing with its back towards her. An equally sudden shift in the mist and the silhouette was gone. She froze. Unfortunately, the werewolf would not disappear that easily.

**two.**

The ship rolled from side to side, this storm hit them from nowhere. Even if it was not that rough it affected them all. Probably because they were so close to home. It was far from the worst storm they have seen for the past year, compared to what they had been through, this was almost a nice little Sunday trip with the family, but most other people would either shout their prayers to or curse the creator by now.

The captain had order minimal staff on deck due to the storm, so most of the crew remained under deck in their bunks, listening to all the quirks and quarks of the ship, bending to the ocean's ever-changing will.

There were forty-eight of them as the Glory left port over a year ago. Only twenty-seven of the original crew members remained. Along the way they had gained thirteen new members, of which they already had lost four, so all in all, it was a crew of thirty-six souls that brought the Glory home. The cargo they carried could not be counted in gold or silver, nor in man hours. So, a price of twenty-five lives was a small price to pay. For all that had survived that is. For the twenty-five lost souls and their families the cargo was of little comfort.

Many wives, fathers, mothers, brothers, and sisters would soon be told that their loved ones would not return.

Yesterday the captain held a short speech, stating that this would be the final day offshore, and that they would return to port either late today or tomorrow at the latest.

That was before the storm hit.

The Hawk-man on duty dared only to send out his hawk once during the storm and it seemed the storm had made them drift off course considerably, not to mention that their goal was straight into the eye of the wind. No matter how hard the sails-men worked those sails they could never take the Glory straight into the eye of the wind, they would always deviate from course. It was only natural that the steersman would choose to drift offshore rather than risking collides with underwater rocks near the coastline and it would be a terrible thing to lose both ship and cargo when the journey almost had reached its end.

They had already survived many storms, some of them far worse than this, and also a good share of sea monsters and attacks both from pirates and cold bloods.

The Hawk-man on duty glazed out in the horrid weather front. No end in sight. He dared not send his hawk on scouting mission under these terrible conditions, yet the ship was in great need of guidance. This journey had already costed him three hawks, and only two remained. Granted, this was a risk all Hawks-man took when they signed aboard a ship, but he was not too keen to lose another one, not when they were so close to home.

The steersman called to him over the hard wind, in desperate need of guidance.

Well, leave it in the hands of the creator, off with the hawk, he thought.

The hawk sprung from the Glory like an arrow straight up to the sky. It took only seconds for the Hawk man too loose it out of sight. Like always he felt a certain pride. His hawks were among the fastest and strongest. They came from a long line of hawks bred and trained by his family.

Now all he could do was wait. There was great risk in this, the biggest was for the hawk to lose track of the ship while scouting in all directions to see what lays ahead. Not only was the hawk moving, the ship was also moving and could easily be lost between the clouds and big waves. But he was confident that the hawk would return with status in a short while. He knew that the steersman was depending on him in storms and on cloudy days when they were cut off from the sun, moons and the stars. He eagerly awaited the return of his hawk.

About five more minutes passed before he heard the familiar shriek from his hawk. It had made it! He held out his hand to greet it and to give it a place to land.

He saw the steersman looking in his direction, eagerly waiting for word of status.

He began his debrief of the hawk as usual. First of was land sighting. The hawk cried and shook his head once. No land to the north. Repeated the same for south. And east. But for west the hawk nodded. Ok.

"Land due west!" he yelled to the steersman though the hard wind.

Distance? Five cries with wings to its side.

"Five short distances." he continued.

Next was hostile movements. The hawk cried and nodded its head for all directions.

"Hostiles in all directions" he yelled, and the steersman immediately sounded the alarm.

This was a bad situation, so close to land and hostile movements in all directions. Storms was known to make sea monsters surface, but it was very unusual with sea monsters in these waters.

He did not envy the decision the steersman had to take now.

It was clear that they needed to steer off from shore to avoid stranding the ship or risk damaging it on underwater cliffs. But with sea monsters in all directions they risked being detected and attacked.

The Hawks man gave the hawk its reward, a shiny silverfish. They just loved them and could not get enough of them.

All crew on shift had now taken their stations on deck. All was armed and ready to fight.

The sails men were on station awaiting any orders from the steersman. The crew was very disciplined and drilled to perfection. The captain was very demanding but very generous when it came to share the prize money.

Suddenly there was an alarm signal coming from the rear left men, and the men arming the arrows turned their towers to meet the threat.

**three.**

Even if she just got a glimpse of the werewolf and it was standing with its back towards her, she knew that it could smell her presence. This was it. The end of her life. In any second, she would be torn into pieces. If she were lucky, she would be killed by the first attack, if not they would probably hear her scream of pain and agony all the way down to the harbour camp.

She braced herself, expecting the attack any moment now. There was no way she could escape this. No one could outrun a werewolf at close range. She had no weapons of any kind, no security detail, and no backup. She was alone. A howl cut through the mist, followed by a growl and heavy movement. She could hear the beast's feet scratch the surface of the path, breaking several branches with each step.

Out of nowhere there came a howl to the left of her, and then another from the right and a little behind her. There were three of them!

Even if thoughts appear in microseconds and are processed by the brain instantly, I doubt that anyone has had so many thoughts rushing through the mind as Dee had in that moment.

The strangest thing of it all, she reflected on later, is that among all the million thoughts that rushed through her head at that moment, the most intense was the thought on how to escape. What direction was the best to try and run for it.

When there was only one, the most intense was that she was going to die and imagining the many ways it could happen. But with three monsters so close, the escape was the strongest.

Even if her body froze, and the blood in her veins along with it, and every single hair on her body, no matter how tiny or small, was standing straight out and her skin was covered with goosebumps everywhere, even then her brain was struggling to send signals to every muscle in her body to move, to run, to put up a fight. The only thing in her conscious mind was to survive.

Even if there are zero stories of any human surviving a meeting with more than one werewolf, she was determined to survive a meeting with three at close range.

The mist was still thick and concealed all the werewolves. They still howled. And even if each second lasted longer than most days, she could still register them, wondering why they did not attack. The more seconds that passed, the more she realized that the howls were not in aggression, rather of agony.

She could hear movements from all three fronts and did still not dare to move.

As time passed, she had to choke a bubble of laughter, she realized that she had not been breathing for a very long time, and for some reason it seemed fun at the moment.

Several minutes passed, or lifetimes as Dee felt it, and then the mist started to clear.

She found herself trapped between the three werewolves, all rising twice as high as herself. They were standing in a triangle with their backs towards each other, and almost in the middle of them was Dee. Seconds later she grasped why they were standing like this. In front of each monster stood five or six Vampires. All of them with silver armor plates covering almost the entire body. Only their feet, hands and face were uncovered by silver. Their armor was so beautifully crafted that they had to be crafted by the dwarf masters in the old mountain. Dee acted instantly and started to run. She could see in the corner of her eye that one of the Vampire hunters changed his focus from the beast to her, but his commander screamed something in Vampirski. Should she know Vampirski she would have understood the commanders order to keep focus on the mark. But the order came just a split second too late and the beast attacked the hunting party in front of it. At the same time, the other two attacked as well.

As Dee fled in panic straight into the forest, leaving the fighting parties behind her the mist got thicker again. She could barely see where she was going but kept on moving forward as fast as she could, trying to get as far away from all the horrible creatures behind her.

Had she met either one of them, or at least only one kind of them, she would have been dead by now. Fortunate for her that they were focusing on each other.

When thinking back, she has no idea how long she was running in the mist, or in what direction she ran. Distance, time, and direction was consumed by the mist. What she does remember was the fall. Suddenly, the ground disappeared beneath her feet. She fell, without bouncing into anything on the way down, then an equally sudden stop and she got cold and wet. Not just cold, but almost numb. Then everything faded away.

**four**

Close behind them, the crew of the Glory saw one of the largest sea monsters they had seen on their entire journey. It was a new kind they had not encountered before, but they recognized its type from descriptions of other seamen.

A large whaleish fish with four long arms around the face, and a wide mouth filled with teeth. It swam fast towards them, getting ready to ram them from behind, but as it came closer, the arrow-men fired their arrows with great precision, forcing the monster to dive. As soon as it had submerged, the alarm came from the front of the ship. Another monster was about to attack from the front. It was of a kind they had seen before. A great squid with its tentacles ready to grab the ship. The arrow men hurried to rotate their towers and aimed at the new threat and at the same time the entire ship made a sudden lurch to the left, almost pushing the rail below water. That must have been the first monster that attacked from beneath.

Now the captain joined on deck. Not hesitating once to give order to the towers to divide their attention on both monsters. He'd also woken the men off duty to be part in the battle and ordered one of them to take scout, something that we all knew was risky in the storm, which was why it was unmanned at the moment.

The Glory took another heavy lurch, still to the left, as if the monster knew what it was doing and calculated its attack to get the ship to take in water from one side. But then the attack came from right and at the same time the giant squid had almost reached the ship and had gotten its first wave of arrows. The arrow men quickly reloaded and was ready for a second round towards it, but now it seemed that the two monsters had seen each other and started to battle over the ship. This was a terrible situation, two big sea monsters to the right of the ship, land somewhere close to the left and a raging storm all over the place.

The captain ordered the arrow men to stand down and save arrows for further encounters but keep a high alert since the two monsters was fighting so close. At any sign of the battle coming closer, they should fire all they got to try and force the monsters away from the ship.

The scout shouted from the top of the mast, barely hearable.

"Land due left, two short distances."

That meant that they had drifted three short distances in a very short while, partly due to the attacks of the sea monster, but even so, very close to the shore with no possibility to steer out to open water again. At least not now.

Captain and the steersman talked about turning the ship around, but it was dangerous to turn either way in this storm not taking the land nor sea monsters into account.

"Hawk man, send the hawk to scout for hostiles, I want numbers and directions", the captain shouted and continued to the scout in the top of the mast:

"Scout, let me know of any incoming hostiles, and keep continues updates on land due west!"

Both the Hawk man and the Scout confirmed their orders.

The Hawks man released his hawk, and it flew straight as an arrow up in the sky, equally fast as the last time, only never to return to the Glory again.

"Incoming hostile due left!" shouted the Scout and the captain ordered the towers to split focus, two remained on the two fighting monsters and two towers facing the new threat.

"Incoming hostile due aft!" The captain was just about to give a new set of orders when the Scout continued:

"Two incoming hostiles due aft, one incoming due left and another one due left! Land due left, one short distance."

The crew all gasped. Six sea monsters on one location, even if it were wise to assume that they would engage each other in battle, it was rare to see two at one time, now they were surrounded by six! And they were drifting very close to shore with no possibility to steer out to open water again.

The entire situation was a nightmare.

"Anchors! Get down below and secure the cargo!" the captain ordered and both anchors left their position at once, leaving the sails men unanchored.

The arrow men fired round after round, all concentrating on the threat closest to them. It looked like they kept the monsters at bay, but a sudden hit to the right of the ship made everybody stumble and with a terrifying scream the Scout fell of the ship into the raging water and disappeared.

Then there was another bump, and yet another, now they could all see the coastline, covered in razor sharp graphite cliffs, less than two hundred feet away. They all knew that underwater cliffs were very common outside of graphite mountains.

Then their attention got called again, a great sea snake came directly from right and opened its wide mouth.

**five.**

When Dee opened her eyes, she was disoriented. Had no idea where she was. She could not feel her body at first. All she could see was the treetops and the blue sky high above. When she slowly turned her head from side to side, she saw the steep mountain sides on each side of her. It took a while before her mind could process all the things she had just experienced. As far as she knew no one had survived an encounter with more than one werewolf nor with a more than a couple of vampires. And from what she could recall from all the stories and rumors from travelers and traders, she had never heard of a clash between the two clans.

As her head and brain slowly processed everything, she started to feel her body again. First, she felt cold, really cold and she shivered all the way into her bones, if that is even possible. Then she felt wet. Cold and wet, and horribly stiff. As she rose her head she could suddenly hear again. She had landed in water, slow running water, not very deep, face up. Face up. Escaped death at least twice she thought to herself as she tried to move her stiff body. It was a struggle to rise, but soon she was sitting in the water and got a good look around her. She had fallen into a ravine, probably created by this tiny water-flow, eroding the mountain through time, eating its way down. Almost no vegetation had made its way down here, could be due to lack of sunlight. It was not dark, but there was no direct sunlight coming down, and it would not be able to do so, unless the sun were standing straight above the ravine. And that would not occur more than a short while each day.

She looked up. The steep mountainside was at least 50 feet from the edge to the bottom. She was lucky to have survived that fall, so make that at least three times she had cheated death by now. She did not feel any pain in her body, only stiff and cold. She struggled a bit to get on her knees and then stood up, stretching her limbs as best as she could.

She could not hear anything but the pouring of the water. She looked back to where the water came from. A long way back, in an almost straight line, no end in sight. She turned the other way. Equally long and straight. But she figured, if the water is going somewhere, it is probably heading for the ocean, and so was she. So, if she could not climb up here, she might be able to find another way closer to the ocean. Thus she started to walk along the creek.

Every inch of her body was aching, more and more for each step it seemed. She was stiff and sore all over, and if anyone had seen her, they would either pity her or laugh at her.

In fact, there was one watching. And following. Someone who did not pity her and did not laugh.

The eyes that had captured her followed her on a distance, making sure not to be revealed.

As Dee walked on in this endless eroded corridor, she thought about many things. Both the nature of the creek, how long had it taken the water to cut out a ravine like this, and how was it even possible? Where did the water come from and was she right in her assumption that the water was leading to the ocean?

She also thought about fear. It had paralyzed her, made her blood freeze, and yet, her mind had been quite calm. It was as if the fear and the entire situation had sharpened her mind, at least in that moment. She could see details like never before, even if the mist had clouded everything, she could almost recall every hair on the body of the beasts, their movement to detail and all the little sounds they were making. Odd. Or was it just her imagination that filled in the blanks and compensated for the failure of all her senses.

Since the view did not change no matter how many steps she was taking, she kind of drifted away in her own thoughts at first, and as the number of steps grew, she moved on autopilot and the steady stream of thoughts had faded to a still nothingness.

The eyes that followed her did not miss a single step. Even if the daylight had faded and the darkness would embrace the ravine entirely any minute now, the eyes did not get tired of watching. Waiting.

When Dee came back to reality, it was completely dark around her. She did not know how long she had been walking in the dark, only that it was dark. Dark and cold. She looked up towards the sky, but either it was cloudy or the light from the stars was too weak to reach down this ravine.

She suddenly felt tired. She had not eaten anything since this morning, and it had been an eventful day, even if she had walked along the creek for the most part of the day, with no end in sight. She sat down, feeling a bit sorry for herself. Wondered if her dad missed her, if he was worried. She wondered if Rick had returned only to find his sister missing. What a disaster. She should have listened to her father. He was very clear when they discussed the matter at the breakfast table, no leaving the village in this mist. But she did not listen. As always. Why, oh why, did she have to be so stubborn?

The eyes kept close watch over the human. Waited patiently. Soon.

Dee leaned toward the mountain wall. Even if it was a bit cold, it was better to lean towards the wall than to sleep on the wet ground with her entire body. It did not take long before she fell asleep.

Now the human was asleep. Now it was time.

**Six.**

As the sea snake attacked with full speed from the right and closed its enormous jaws around the rails of the Glory, she squeaked in every single piece of the wood that she was crafted from. The stress from the raging ocean, the storm and the sea snake tested her strength to the limit. But even with big chunks of the ship missing from the snake attack, she was still in the game.

The captain counted the men on deck. Only one sails man left at its position, all arrow men still hanging strong, his scout missing from before, the steersman still at his post. Maybe they had a chance, but it was not a big one. His only option was to leave everything in the hand of the creator. May his will be executed on this day.

With little hope he started to give orders to the remaining crew on deck. All but the steersman and the arrow men were ordered below deck, preparing for the worst. He himself stayed on deck, as a captain should, no matter what his ship was facing.

He wondered if the Anchormen had secured the cargo, and what would happen if the Glory did not make it through this. Should all his own sacrifices and the sacrifices of the men be in vain, or was there a slight chance that the cargo would reach its destination?

He often took pride in being a man of faith, but at this moment his faith was not very strong. Even so, he tried to find it. His faith had always been a source of strength, but where it used to be, he only found distrust and despair.

As the sea snake came around for a second attack he turned to the steersman and saluted him in a traditional honor salute. Hand raised with three fingers up, one for himself, one for the one he saluted and the third for the creator. Old habits were not affected by his current loss of faith.

The snake took another big bite of the Glory, leaving her severely crippled in the water. Almost nothing remained of the deck and everybody that was on deck was gone. Either they fell into the water or they were on their way down the snake's stomach.

The Glory started to take in water and the remainder of the crew started to evacuate. They all knew that the cargo was their main priority, those who made it back alive with the cargo would be well rewarded. Should any one of them return without the cargo, or at least its whereabouts, they might as well not return at all.

The Glory had been built to sustain a certain amount of attacks from pirates and sea creatures, there was a special compartment two decks below the main deck. This compartment was built to be sealed off entirely, and even if the ship were going down it could still be ejected in any direction, given that the ship was fairly intact. The only two persons that was in that compartment was the Anchormen that had gotten the order to secure the cargo. Some men were standing outside of the compartment banging its walls and, now closed openings, wanting to get in. Some tried threatening their way in, calling the two cowards and many other names I will not recite here. Others begged and prayed. All was aware that the Glory was lost. There was only one last journey for her, and none of them would like to accompany her down to the bottom of the sea.

All around the compartment the two men heard the sound of breaking wood, water flooding in, screams from their fellow shipmates, growl from the sea snake and the rage of the storm outside. The two had no clear picture of what part of the ship was less affected, so they did not know which direction they should try to release the compartment, nor when they should attempt to do so. It was always meant for the captain to be here with the cargo in case of emergency. Neither understood the captain's choice to go down with the vessel unless he had no hope of any survivors.

Both looked to the other for encouragement and advice on what to do. Neither said anything and from the compartment came not a single sound. A ghostlike safe spot in the middle of everything. Like sitting inside a tomb while it was sealed by a disaster outside its walls.

As the sea snake engaged with the other monsters in battle the Glory took its last breath of fresh air before submerging entirely, never to return to the surface again. More good souls lost in its cause. More families that would mourn their sacrifice.

## seven

Dee slept uneasy, it was hard and cold, but then again, something felt warm. And there was something bright. She was uncertain whether it all was a dream or if it was real. She felt like she was on the edge between dream and reality, where the two met and blended, unable to separate from each other. It was hard to tell what was real and what was dream. Maybe it all was a dream. Maybe she was still in her bed at home, just anxious over the possibility to meet her brother the next day, and somehow it all turned into a weird nightmare.

She could hear little noises that she did not recognize. And something that might be a fire. But more like a still fire in the fireplace than a raging fire that consumed a building. She desperately wanted to wake up to see what reality she woke up to, but she just could not force her body to wake up. Her eyes remained shut and she was still balancing on the thin edge between the two worlds. She remained there until something captured her attention. Something in the real world. A noise or a voice. She was uncertain of which.

It was still dark. But she was warm and dry. She could hear the sparking of a fire, there was no doubt in her mind. It took a while to realize she was laying down, not sitting up as when she fell asleep. Above was the darkness of the ravine and the dark, starless night-sky.

It felt strange, it was not hard and cold stone beneath her, and all the moist from the tiny creek seemed to be gone. She turned her head to the right, and there was the mountain wall, vaguely visible. She turned her head to the left and to her surprise, there was a tiny fire, almost burned out. The sound she that woke her up, and as she still was hearing, was coming from the dark, somewhere downstream from where she was. She could not see anything in the dark, only hear.

It was some kind of muttering and something else to, she could not make out what it was, but almost like someone was dragging something.

She sat up, turned her head towards the sound, but still could not see anything. Beneath her was a bed of old leaves and dry moss. The fire was located on the other riverbank, well, on the other side of the tiny stream. Even if it was tiny, the fire that is, it was still giving a lot of heat.

But what was that noise? Dee focused on the sound again, gazed out in the dark.

In a split of a second, she thought she saw a pair of shiny dots in the dark in the direction of the sound. Perhaps a pair of eyes? But she could not see them anymore, and the longer she thought about it, the more unsure she was. It could have been anything, then again, nothing at all. But the sound was there, even if it was faint at times.

As she gazed out in the dark, time seemed to stand still, but the source of the sound was not. She was sure that it kept coming closer. But time and again, she was uncertain from what direction it came. The echoes in the ravine confused her.

She sat there, wondering what made the sound. Or rather, who made the sound. Every now and then she could make out a clear word. Not necessary a word she knew, but clearly a word, which meant that it came from a sentient being. The other evidence that supported that was that she was left on a primitive bed, and that he/she/it/they had made her a fire. Not only a fire, but a fire at a safe distance. The creature(s) probably did not mean her any harm, which was a comforting thought.

She turned her head from side to side. Trying to determine what way the sound originated from. At this point, it was probably her mind playing tricks with her.

Suddenly Dee could hear a full sentence. Even if it made her feel uneasy, she welcomed it.

”Oh great! Now it is awake, stupid human!” was the muttering words she could make out. Shortly thereafter she saw a little creature coming from downstream, dragging something behind. She could not make out what it was, but it looked like something in a sack.

The creature was walking on the other side of the little stream, towards the fire. Well, since the riverbank was so small, there was not really room to walk towards something else.

The mutter continued and as it kept growing in strength, Dee felt less and less hopeful.

”Stupid, stupid human, coming down here and disturbing Groll. Like the old days. Always same filthy humans. Cannot do anything right. Leaving their stinky paths, wandering of in the great forest like they owned it. Never something good came from those filthy creatures. Arrogant and stupid. Helpless like animal babies. And stupid. That is what Groll hates the most, the stupidity! Cannot see anything for what it is, always need to evaluate everything, giving it a price. Stinking humans! Dividing, categorizing, assigning value… Should be extinct the lot of them, they should!”

**Eight.**


The two anchormen sat in silence. From what they could understand the Glory was already submerged, the last desperate calls from their shipmates had faded a little while ago. They wondered for how long they could survive in this compartment without air. They wondered what way they should choose to try and exit the compartment from the ship. Would it float?

It is strange how the small compartment so quickly could change from a safe harbour in a raging fight for life outside of it, only to become a prison that seemed to get smaller and smaller for each passing second.

They looked at each other, and then on all the hatches and ropes and little wheels that they could turn. Only one was marked, and it was the aft release path. The other walls on in the small compartment had the same operations panel, but they figured that only one needed to be marked, in case of getting disoriented while in the compartment. The cargo was secure in the middle of the small chamber. They had no food nor water and felt an urge to make a quick escape from the ship for several reasons. They did not know how long the breathable air would last in there, and they preferred not to follow the Glory all the way down to the bottom. Sure, the risk of them getting detected by the sea monsters was still huge, not to mention the raging storm.

Neither of the two had been in this compartment before so they carefully studied all available things on each wall. One of them took an interest in a handle that was located in the middle of each wall, just above the floor. A voice inside his head told him to pull it, and before the other could stop him, he leaned over to the wall that stated aft, and pulled the handle. They could hear something happening beneath the compartment. And then nothing. No movement, no sounds, nothing. The other repeated the same for the left wall. Again, something happened below them, and then nothing. Then they both pulled the two remaining handles, almost at the same time. Still nothing after the sound was over.

What would be the next logical thing to do? And what had the handles done? Both desperately started to pull other smaller handles, turned some wheels, tried to pull in a random rope. It sounded a lot, but nothing really happened.

They still had not said anything to each other so when one of them broke their silence it was almost like the fragile moment cracked and some kind of reality entered their small compartment.

They both agreed that their mechanical skills were limited, but figured since they still were onboard a ship, ropes would be the most logical thing to use, since the entire sail system was built on dragging ropes in very complex path's.

Each wall had four ropes coming down from the ceiling. As they started to pull those ropes the compartment started to move. Best result they got from pulling all four ropes simultaneously.

It felt like ages before something actually happened, and when it finally did, they both could feel the compartment rise to the surface. It was like when the Glory had been lifted high on a wave that suddenly hit them. Same tickling feeling in the stomach.

Soon they felt the familiar movements from the large waves from the storm. They did not have any windows, so they could not see what was going on around them, they could only pray to the creator that the sea monsters did not detect them. Could they stay undetected they had a chance to survive, but it was still a great risk to drift the sea in this weird vessel, with no way to control its direction.

The only thing the two were grateful for at the moment was that they actually could feel fresh air again. It took a while to get used to their new vessels water properties. It moved very different compared to the Glory, but it was not very strange, since the Glory was several times bigger and heavier than this little flat and compact wooden barrel.

At least the cargo was safe for now. Better they had a chance to deliver it, than it being stuck on the bottom of the ocean.

They discussed their possibilities. Either they would drift for a very long time, which was most likely, and when someone found the vessel, they would probably be dead by then, since they didn't have any food nor water. The other option was that since they were so close to shore, the storm might drive them towards land. Maybe even strand them. Should that be the case, the most likely scenario would be that the force of the wave would crush their vessel against the sharp graphite cliffs, or if they drifted further north, against a steep mountain wall. Should that happen, they would most likely die. If they did, and the cargo was not damaged by the impact, someone else would find it and claim it. But there was a slim chance, and they prayed to the creator to make it so, that the storm pushed the vessel towards land and stranded them smooth and easy. If that happened, they'd have to figure out a way to get out of the compartment, and then figure out how to bring the cargo back to safety, without getting robbed along the way, or eaten by a werewolf, or by vampire, or getting caught in a horde of undead, and along the way find enough food and water to sustain them all the way back. Since the captain had said that it was a one-day journey with the Glory, it would be two or three by foot in flat terrain. But from what they had seen when still aboard the Glory, the terrain was everything but flat and friendly. They estimated rather seven to ten days. And they had to carry the cargo by hand all the way. And to be completely honest, whatever end their journey in this little vessel would provide them, it looked like a pretty good chance that they would not make it out alive.

As all anchormen they always carried knives, so they started to carve their possible last words to family and friends, in the hops that if they did not survive, at least their words would have a chance to reach home and their loved ones. Given that the vessel was not completely destroyed by the impact with the coastline, or that the vessel simply would sink and join the rest of the Glory. Well, they had not got much else to do, so they might as well keep carving. And hoping. And praying…

**Nine.**

The little creature arrived muttering to the fire and it did not pay Dee much attention at first. It was a very small creature, rising only about two feet above the ground. Should Dee stand up, she was uncertain whether it would reach her knees or not. As she watched him put more wood on the fire, she tried to make out what kind of creature he was. He must not had liked her watching, because he turned to her and yelled:

"Why are you awake, you filthy human? And what are you doing here in Groll's ravine? Do not just sit there and look like the fool you are! Speak human!"

Dee did not know where to start.

"I do not know why I'm here… I was running in the forest and then…"

Before she could continue the little creature exploded again.

"Running in the forest you say? Typical behavior of a lesser being that only uses a small portion of its big brain. Waste of space and energy I say! Only filling between those funny looking ears of yours. And you do not even use them. Say you hear, you do, but listen - oh, no, you do not! Never listen to what Groll says, or anybody else for that matter. Thinking you are better and smarter. But you are only taller and take up more space."

The creature tossed a piece of something wrapped in cloth to Dee. It was a piece of bread. Or something that very much looked like bread.

Dee whispered a short 'thank you' and took a big bite of the bread since she was very hungry. The creature on the opposite side of the little stream sat down by the fire, muttering something Dee did not catch. She was chewing too loud.

"Who are you, and what are you?" she asked.

The creature exploded and started to yell again.

"What an insult of a troll! What am I? I would tell you if it wasn't such a waste of time talking to a human! No shame in that large body of yours. But what to expect from a filthy creature like you? Waste of space on two legs and no good between them ears… Arrogant and foolish is what you are! And wasting my time as well!"

Dee started to get tired of getting yelled at, so she jumped in when the creature took a breath, probably to continue yelling.

"Look, thank you for taking care of me, I didn't mean to intrude…" she was not able to finish her sentence before the yelling started again.

"Taking care of you?! Ha! Like I would care! Only saving myself a lot of trouble. Should you lay here and die of hunger or thirst I would only have to carry your heavy corps all the way to the ocean. Much easier to have you walk yourself. Groll not stupid you see! Oh no! Think of everything, I do! Ha! Care for a human! Almost funny, big one! Almost funny!"

The little one silenced and Dee saw her chance.

"Groll, is that your name? And are you a troll?" she was expecting another blowout from the creature.

"Yes! Groll is my name. And troll I am!" he said in the most of proud ways.

"Nice to meet you Groll. My name is Dee, and I'm a filthy human. A waste of space on two legs…" she said.

The troll laughed. A heartwarming laughter that caught Dee as well.

As their laughter silenced, neither of the two knew how to continue, so they sat there, in the dark, looking into the fire. After a long while, Dee felt sleepy again, and broke the soundless void.

"Is it long till dawn?" she asked.

"Yes! Still long to dawn…" Groll answered. His thoughts were far away.

"Would it be alright if I caught some more sleep? So you won't have to carry me tomorrow?" she asked…

Groll laughed again.

"Yes, get some sleep… I do not have to carry you!" he laughed again. She could almost see a faint smile in his face, not only on his lips, but in his eyes as well…

Dee lay down on the moss bed again, she felt warm inside. Not hungry anymore. And she felt safe. It was something about this little troll, Groll. Something about him. Or was it a she? Dee was not sure she dared to ask, she thought to herself just before fading away into a deep sleep.

**ten.**

The hawk man woke up to the sound of a familiar shriek from somewhere very close. He tried to open his eye and could swear that he opened his eyes. But everything was still black. He tried again. Closed his eyes and made sure to close them extra hard and then open them again. Still nothing, pitch black. He was laying down and started to feel with his hands around him. One of his hands touched water and the other some kind of steep mountain wall. Carefully he lifted his upper body and turned his head from left to right. Still nothing. Everything was black around him.

He heard the shriek again, a little up to the right and slightly behind him. He turned his head around, there behind him, maybe thirty feet, he saw a piece of night-sky. It was surreal in a way, like someone had sliced out a thin line of night-sky and put it on a black background. He slowly rose, turned and walked towards the slice of night-sky, walking with the water on his right side, instead of to the left when he woke up. He took small steps all the way and found himself standing on the edge of a tiny waterfall, dropping about a hundred feet down. Below he could hear the sounds of waves slowly washing over the shoreline. In front of him was a magnificent night-sky. The two moons like shiny pearls, the right blood-moon was two or three nights from being full and turning red. The left silver-moon was as clear and calm as always.

There was no evidence of the storm that was the last thing he could remember. The night seemed still and peaceful. He tried to think. The last thing he remembered was standing on the Glory, he had just sent his hawk scouting. They got attacked, he fell overboard and… no… had he drowned? Was this the afterlife? Was he facing an image of his life and behind him was the eternal darkness of nothingness? Was this it? What about an eternal life with the creator? What about seeing all that had died before him? His brother's? His grandfather? Should he wait here for someone to come and get him and show him the way? He was chilled to the bones and shivered. Uncertain if it was due to the cold night or the thoughts that rushed through him.

The familiar shriek made him come back to the present. Without thinking of what he was doing, he raised his arm for the hawk to land, and it did. As it had done thousand times before.

He whispered partly to the hawk and partly to himself:

"Are we dead, my little friend?"

But the hawk did not answer, it expected its reward, a silverfish. But the hawk-man could not provide any this time.

So, they stood there, in silence. The hawk waiting for its fish, and the hawk-man alone with his thoughts, gazing the moons over his head, and the million stars on the creator's sky.

**eleven**

Dee was sleeping uneasy. Had the strangest dreams. One time she was watching a great grass-field. She witnessed the birth of many various animals on the great field. Then there was a great war, between two human clans. One side wore a red flag, the other a blue.

Then she was deep down in the caves of a very old mountain, watching the dwarf's underground fires, melting ore from their mines, and in the river of melted ore, there was something shiny floating away.

Then she stood on the top of the great old mountain, the largest mountain in the world. From its peak she could see two battling dragons. A red and a blue. Just like the fighting humans.

Then she was in a dark cold forest. Watching an egg in its nest. A silver egg, as she bent towards it, she could see her own reflection in it, only she was not herself, she was another creature. Darker and larger. Maybe a werewolf.

Then she watched the blood moon from a small window. She was chained.

What did it all mean?

Suddenly she was standing in water up to her belly, cold water, watching a huge waterfall, she could feel the movement of the water as it pushed against her feet, almost making her lose her grip.

Another jump to a raging fire, she was standing in the middle, unable to move, around her there was a crowd. She was uncertain, hard to see, but it looked like the crowd was dancing or celebrating. Strange to go from cold water to warm and raging fire.

As the dream jumped around, she could experience every change in her body, reacting to the surrounding environment.

When Dee woke up, she felt very strange. As if the dream was not a dream, but something she lived through. Something she remembered. But it was impossible, since she had only been in the village, on the path to the harbour camp and in the harbour camp. Never anywhere else. Even if she often wished she could go on adventures or trading routes to other places, far away. But she knew it was too dangerous. A girl of sixteen winters was not an appropriate nor competent companion on such a journey.

She saw that it was already morning, and only a day had passed since she defied her father and set off by herself towards the harbour camp. But it felt like a lifetime. So much had happened since then. She literally was another person now. Without being able to explain what had change, she felt it.

She looked around but could not see Groll anywhere near. The fire was already put out and there was almost no trace of it ever being there. She looked up stream, but saw no trace of him, and as she turned downstream, she heard someone yell from far away.

"Hurry up and let's go! Filthy human! Lazy and sleepy! Move along already! No time to waste!"

Yes, there he was, there was no doubt in her mind that it was Groll who yelled at her. She felt warm inside, even if he was yelling, she remembered his laughter from the night before. He was a warmhearted individual, even if he probably would not admit to it. She was certain of that.

It did not take long for her to catch up with Groll, and when she did, she had to walk very, very slow, or else she would outrun, err, rather out walk him in no time. She was right from the night before, his full height was just above her knees, and his legs was about the length of her longest fingers. As so, his steps were tiny, and even if he kept a high pace, she still had a hard time to follow his tempo. It felt like she had to decrease her speed for each step. After a while of walking in silence she asked him if he would like to ride on her shoulder.

"Ride on your shoulder you say?! And be carried by a filthy human? Never! Not even if the blood moon itself chased me through this ravine, I would. Stupid suggestion… Do not you think I can walk? Huh? More than twenty ages I am, still young with a lot of energy in my legs."

Dee smiled.

"But it would take us to the ocean a lot faster, and you would get rid of me quicker if you did that…" she said…

Groll stopped to think for a while, he had to admit that she was right. But ride on a human…

"Ha! Yes, lift me up already! Groll getting a human horse! Incredible! Never thought the day would come…"

Dee lifted up Groll on her shoulder and started to walk in normal pace, which was considerably faster than they were going before. She could hear Groll laugh to himself and muttering in a positive way.

"Human horse. Hahaha! Who would have thought? Not Groll? Oh no, not Groll would."

After a while Dee asked Groll how much further the ocean was.

"Do not know, horse! Do not know! Have no reference to this speed, it would be two days in my own pace. But now, I do not know!" he replied, then yelled with the enthusiasm of a five-year-old:

"Silent and move along horse! Faster! Carry on! TO THE OCEAN!"

**twelve.**

The dawn had passed, the hawk-man hadn't slept anything during the night, and as the moons had faded and left the creators heavenly arena for the sun to make its daily show, he started to believe that he might not be dead after all.

With the rising light something else faded away. Hope. There was no way for him to get down from the edge of this ravine, and as far as he could see it separated land in a straight line leading from the ocean to an unknown source. Even the ravine itself was divided in two by a tiny water-stream floating in the middle.

The walls of the ravine rose almost straight up on both sides, leaving nothing to climb on. Either he followed the water down and took a leap to a certain death, or, which he felt was the better of the two alternatives, he started to walk upstream to see if he could find a way out of there.

As he started to walk with the hawk on his shoulder his lack of sleep surfaced, and on top of that, his stomach reminded him, in a most polite way, that he had not eaten anything in a long time.

What normally would be an easy walk forced him to struggle with each step.

Either it was the lack of food and sleep, or it was the relief he felt, no longer sure he was dead.

He had been lucky somehow. Could it be the hand of the creator? It could be the raging waves of the storm that just happened to lift him and leave him in the ravine, but it was unlikely, the waves hadn't been that high, and what would be the odds of his wave, among thousands of waves, rising in the right height (without rolling low over the sharp edges of the shoreline beneath) at the exact place for the ravine. A couple of feet in each direction to the left or right would have meant that the wave had crushed him against the mountain wall, and if it didn't crush him, there was no way that the wave could bring him unharmed back to the ocean, without dragging him through the sharp edges of the cliffs below.

The more he reflected on it, the surer he was, the creator had to have a say in what had happened, which made another question rise. Why? Why him? Why save him of all the people aboard the Glory? Was he destined to do something that he had not yet been able to complete?

And what would that task be?

He could not get his head around it while dragging his feet step after step away from the ocean.

An eternity later he was so tired that he sat down in the bottom of the ravine. He had walked a lifetime, or at least that is how it felt, in reality it was closer to fifty-three minutes. The entire situation, lack of sleep, lack of food, all his thoughts and probably the little weight of the hawk, still sitting on his shoulder, had drained all his powers. Literally he could not take another step. Not a single one. And he sat there, staring out in the emptiness of the ravine. No end in sight.

**Thirteen.**

Dee got bored by just walking and tried to make small talk with Groll, more or less successful.

"So, you're twenty Groll?" she asked. "I am sixteen winters myself, soon turning seventeen, so you just a tad older than me…"

"Ha! A tad older you say? Ignorant fool! But, yes, a tad older you could say. Poor little human horse!" He replied without correcting her. What Dee did not know was that there is a great difference between twenty ages and almost twenty winters. An age starts when a person is born and ends with the death of his or her grandchild. So, twenty ages were a lot more than almost twenty winters.

Dee was determined to get a conversation going with Groll and continued:

"Have you met humans before? You seem to be familiar with my kind."

Groll muttered something she could barely hear and then yelled so her right ear almost fell of:

"Yes! Sad to say I have! No good you humans! All the same! All ignorant! Thinking of nothing but yourselves and not even that."

"What do you mean, how are we all the same?" she asked.

"So hard to understand?" Groll asked. "All the same! Nothing more, nothing less, nothing hidden in those words, all clear! Mean exactly what they say, all the same!"

"But we're not the same!" Dee protested. "We are hugely different between us. We are old and young, male, and female, warm-blood and cold-blood, tall and short, thin and fat. We have different hair colors, eye colors and skin colors. We're not all the same!"

"Yes, all the same! Only yourselves that divide and categorize. But it changes nothing. You're all the same." Groll answered, a little annoyed.

Dee was almost insulted by this and did not feel to continue pursuing any more of this small talk. In fact, she almost threw Groll off her shoulder but hesitated and figured it was best to let him sit there so they could arrive faster to the ocean. The sooner the better, then she would head back for the harbour camp. She had done some thinking, and she was pretty sure she should turn left once they got out of the ravine. Follow the coastline to the north. When she fled in the forest she was most likely running south before falling down in the ravine. She thought about asking Groll for direction advice at first, but now she did not want to ask this little horrible creature anything more.

Suddenly Groll started to yell in-comprehensive again.

"A hundred summers and nothing, now two of them in two day! Why can't you just leave me alone? Stupid, filthy humans! What is next I wonder? And look, the other one is already a corpse, birds have started eating already. Might be good, then Groll will not have to drag the heavy corpse to the ocean! Why just you do not leave Groll alone? Is it too much to ask, I wonder!"

Dee wondered what Groll was yelling about, and it took her several more steps to realize that further away in the ravine, there was something lying at the bottom.

"Is it another human Groll?" she asked with a worried tone in her voice.

"Filthy humans! No good you are, raining down like leaves in the autumn! What have I done to deserve this?" Groll mumbled.

Dee walked faster, almost started to run, she wanted to come to the other person, chase away the birds Groll was talking about.

"Are you sure the person is dead?" she asked, with her breath affected by the faster pace.

"A bird is eating on it, of course it's dead! Human corpse, even more disgusting than a live one. Oh, the smell of it! You drag it all the way to the ocean, human horse!" Groll muttered.

Again, Dee felt a little insulted, but at the moment she cared less about her own pride and more about the poor human they approached.

When they only had about thirty feet left to the body, Dee saw that the bird was a hawk, but it was not eating on the body, like Groll had said, more like keeping watch over it. She saw that it was a man, and from the looks of it, he has had a rough time before ending up here in the ravine.

As they approached, she saw that the man was breathing, he was still alive!

**fourteen**

The commander of the Vampires looked at their small battlefield. One of the beasts had escaped, one was dead and the third was captured and disarmed. Of his little army of fifteen, only six was still alive. A high price it may seem, but taking into account what was at stake, nine Vampires was nothing.

The captured werewolf would be brought back for interrogation, but this time they would not use their usual tactics, they would have to be more thorough and aggressive this time. Time was running out. Time they did not have to spend. It was a long journey back and they only had a few shelters, so they all would have to use all their strength to get the beast home safely. They all had a desperate need to feed, but it was a luxury they could not afford at the moment. If they were lucky, they would find prey on the way back.

There was not time, nor energy, to salvage the silver armor from the fallen Vampires. Pity, the dwarf masters had demanded a high prize for the silver pieces, they knew it was essential to the Vampires to have them in their mission, and greedy as they are they claimed much more than they should have. At least from his point of view.

Fair enough, their armor had to be much purer and of much higher quality than the average silver the dwarves produced. But still. Lucky for the dwarf master that dwarf blood tastes so bad.

Oh, well, when this enterprise was over, the dwarves would know their place. As would the rest of the creatures of this world.

Now they had no time to waste, off to nearest shelter, get their covers on, and then head back home.

Blasted mist! It was impossible to know how high the sun stood. On the other hand, the mist helped them. The silver armor might protect them against the werewolves, but it did not protect them against the sun.

Direct sun would dry them instantly, so would long time of heat. But they could survive short periods carrying special lightweight cloth keeping the sunbeams out, and providing darkness for their entire body, even their faces if they had their hood up. The lightweight cloth also had cooling capabilities, especially when it was wet.

They had left those coverage in their last shelter, along with carrier animals of various kinds.

All of them was almost dried out, none of them had gotten a good meal in a while. Not that it would kill them in anyway, only make them weaker and more sensitive to the sun.

Then, in an instant, the mist was completely gone. It had appeared out of nowhere in the middle of their hunt, and no it vanished with the same intensity. Strange.

But it could mean one thing. His sister could be close. And if she were, he would need to leave two scouts behind to look for her. Should they capture her as well, then it would be an even greater success than only bringing a beast back.

Should they be able to capture her, then their end goal would be as good as completed. They only had to...

...yes, what did they have to do if they caught her? It was clear she would not reveal anything by free will, and it was most likely that her secrets would follow her to the grave. And it was not possible to use her brother anymore, that opportunity had passed. A shame it was.

But first, focus on the beast and get it to base. That was the current main priority.

**fifteen.**

The hawk-man did not know where he was at first, or who the girl was or what in the creator's world the little thing beside her was. The little creature muttered something that he could not hear, and the girl that stood on her knees beside him (still taller than the little creature), looked at him like she was expecting something from him.

"Where am I?" he asked the girl.

"In a ravine in the forest," she answered, "I'm Dee. Who are you and how did you get here?"

"Water!" the hawk-man said, his world was slightly spinning, probably from exhaustion.

Dee had previously been drinking water from the stream, so had Groll, so she helped the man shape his hands to scoop up water from the stream, but he only got annoyed.

"No, I come from the water." he continued.

"Impossible!" muttered Groll, "He is not of the sea-folk. I doubt he could even swim a rainy day on dry land by the looks of him!"

"The Glory" he said. Trying to explain himself.

Groll snorted.

"No underwater city with that name!"

"The Glory is a ship!" Dee exclaimed, giving Groll a razor-sharp eye wishing him to shut up. Groll however did not seem to take any notice of this.

"Do you serve on the Glory?" she asked the man.

"Yes!" he said. "I'm a hawk-man on the Glory!" then silenced. "Was…" he said.

His words struck Dee like a knife aimed straight at her heart.

"What do you mean, was…?" she asked.

"It is…" he tried to wrap his head around it, "we were caught in a storm…"

"Did she make it?" asked Dee, thinking of Rick.

The hawks-man looked for words, the only thing he knew was that he was no longer aboard the ship, he did not know the fate of the Glory.

"I do not know" he answered truthfully. "We were in a storm and was attacked by several sea monsters. Six I think." he silenced a while again. Tears started to burn behind Dee's eyes.

"It didn't look good last time I saw her. I was swept of board during an attack, and the next thing I knew, I was here. Not sure if I am dead. I walked forever in this ravine and then you woke me up."

Dee burst into tears. She would never see Rick again!

"Might as well cry, you're in the Sorrow now…" muttered Groll, and then turned to the other human again.

"Can you stand up and walk? Or should we drag you in the stream all the way to the ocean? Human scum!"

"I'm sorry, I do not think I can, the world is spinning, and we are far from the ocean!" he answered.

"Here! Eat, filthy human! So you can walk by yourself!" Groll tossed the man a piece of bread.

The hawk, who now circled above its master quickly dived to get its fair share (more than half, at least) of the bread.

Dee sat in tears on the riverbank, and the hawks-man shared his bread with the hawk that now had landed on his shoulder. Groll strolled a bit further back, still muttering.

The hawks-man leaned over to Dee and asked with a faint whisper:

"Are you his prisoner?"

Dee awoke from her tears.

"No, not at all, he is helping me and leading the way to the ocean. That is the only way out of here."

"There are no way out of the ravine by the ocean, I've been there, these walls raise high all the way there and at the end there is a small waterfall dropping much longer than it is safe to jump." the hawks-man said. "And besides, the cliffs beneath are razor-sharp graphite cliffs." he added and continued with an even lower whisper: "Should he push us down there it would be the end of us. I mean, he doesn't seem to like us much..."

**sixteen.**

The Werewolf kept running through the forest. Not with its usual speed and stamina, it was bleeding from several cuts and bruises from the fight with the Vampires.

Normally it would have stayed and fought to the end, but now they could not. Neither of them could. Now it was the only one in their scouting team. He knew there was others in the region, they could all feel it calling. Like a homing beacon that turned on an autopilot in them.

Their task was to find it and keep it safe. Hidden. Guard it.

There was a safekeeping not far from here. But they could not use it until their task was fulfilled. They needed to find it. Time was running out. It had been missing for too long now. They had searched for many ages. Now it had resurfaced again, calling them. They could not lose track of it again.

As the werewolf kept running, it felt the signal stronger and stronger.

Unaware if it was the only werewolf in pursuit or if there were others nearby that felt the same calling the werewolf continued on, and on, and on.

The source kept moving, so the signal sometimes weakened.

Strange in a way, but at the same time it was not really surprising. The power it contained could change everything, the outcome of the world as it currently was.

The werewolf was in great need of pray to regain strength, but at the same time there was no time for eating. Should the opportunity arise, the werewolf would carefully need to way the upside of spending time stopping for a meal and the energy it would take to hunt versus the lost ground in the ongoing pursuit.

The thought rushed through its mind as trees, bushes and naked rocks passed by in a speed far beyond what a human had been able to produce, even with the use of horses. And yet, far from the top speed of a werewolf.

The werewolves' sole purpose was protecting, haunting, killing. There was no other instinct. No other objective that would divide its attention.

How could the signal move so fast? It was not in its nature.

It must be carried by some kind of vessel, but any man-made vessels could not reach speeds like this, not even the sea crafts.

Was it the vampires? Was there another party involved? Had one of the wizards surfaced again?

Damned be the wizards! It was their fault that it was gone in the first place. The werewolves had played a big part in their extinction, but the main factor had been their own pride and disability to honor their own code.

The werewolves took pride in being an active part in reducing the numbers of wizard in this world. Cleanse it, of their impurity. Their way was an insult to the creators wish. The world would be better off without them. And the witches. But the witches had not been as terrible, not yet anyway. And even so if a witch crossed their path every werewolf enjoyed the kill. Then it was not only killing for food, then it was killing for food and the creation.

But now, only focusing on the signal. It was getting weaker now. The werewolf pushed itself further. Must not lose it now!

**seventeen.**

Dee turned to Groll, he was still strolling away from them going upstream, not fast since his legs was so short.

"You said there's a way out of here by the ocean" she yelled after him.

Groll stopped without turning. She caught his attention.

"What's your name?" she asked the Hawk-man before continuing.

"Tadao" he replied short, still whispering.

"Tadao came from the ocean, there is no way out of this ravine that way!" she continued towards Groll.

"Stupid humans!" Groll muttered, "There is always more than meets the eye!" he continued and started to walk away from the humans again.

Dee looked after him, not sure what to think. Since they lay eyes on Tadao, Groll seemed changed. The bitter little creature seemed angrier now and she was uncertain if her first instinct would prove her wrong. She did not know whether to trust Groll or not. Nor if she could trust Tadao. She decided to remain neutral for the time being. If Tadao was right, the two of them could leave Groll when they got to the edge of the ravine and try to find a way out themselves. Should Groll be right he would lead them out of this ravine.

She turned to Tadao again.

"Do you know if there was a Scout called Rick on the Glory? He signed aboard when she started her journey, about a year ago."

"Is he a loved one?" Tadao asked with pity in his voice, slowly regaining strength from the bread he got from Groll.

Dee nodded, but did not say anything, she only waited to see what news he could give her.

"I signed on at the start of the journey. But I do not remember any scout by the name of Rick. The first three stops of the journey were very hectic, we were few aboard and had to recruit in every harbour. As you probably know, when a ship reaches the last harbour before the northern orifice of the Red river, she is on her own until she passes the southern orifice. And when passing there we lost several scouts to the Vampire elder."

Dee looked at him and did not understand.

"What about the Vampire elder? Can it swim?"

Tadao shook his head and lowered his voice.

"It can fly…"

Dee burst out in laughter! It was ridiculous! A flying vampire. She had never heard anybody telling anything remotely like that. She welcomed the laugh, but it also raised more questions. Could she trust this Tadao? It seemed highly unlikely that he had not heard of Rick, given that they were a small crew from the beginning and losing Scouts to a flying Vampire. No. Did not seem likely at all. She did not even know if he in fact had been on the Glory. And if he had not then maybe it was not lost at sea in a storm as he claimed. That meant that there still was a good chance Rick was alive and well.

She was brought back from her thought by the return of Groll, he had gathered woods to make a fire, it was getting dark.

Neither said anything.

Groll did not even mutter, he just piled up the wood and started the fire.

It was a long evening. Tadao did not start any conversation with Dee, he felt a little insulted that she did not believe him. Groll did not speak to either of the humans because he did not have anything to say. Dee did not know who of the two she should talk to, since she did not know who of them to trust.

Just as Dee lay down to get some sleep Groll open his mouth.

"We're close to the ocean. Tomorrow I will follow you there, show you the way out, then we part, and I wish not to see any of you here ever again. Understood?"

Dee nodded, but Tadao protested.

"We are far from the ocean, I walked for a long time before I ended up here!"

"We'll see tomorrow! Stupid human!" Groll answered annoyed, and nothing more was said that night.

Eventually Dee was on the rim to fall asleep, and just before she did, she had a thought she barely could grasp: Where did Groll find the wood for the fire? They had walked a long way that day, and had not passed a single piece of wood or anything else for that matter? Only the bare walls and the tiny water stream. But she fell asleep before the thought had any impact on her.

**eighteen**

The vampire commander oversaw the handling of their captive with pride. His men were highly competent and drilled to utter most perfection.

They quickly wrapped the werewolf in the extra strong fabric with woven with a silver thread mixture and then chained it in silver chains, both around hands, feet, and neck. This prevented the werewolf from escaping and at the same time did not kill it. But from its body language it was clear that it was not a joyful treatment.

They pushed it in front of them still covered in their silver arming. They would stop at their last camp where they kept the headpiece for the beast. It was designed to keep its large and deadly mouth shut and with no possibility to open the jaws, not even to growl, and perhaps more importantly, preventing the beast from howling to call the attention of its fellow beasts.

It was a short walk to the camp, and after they had put the headpiece on, they would be able to drop the silver armor and change to their protective clothing. Even if they would travel in the forest, they still needed protection from the sun.

It was unlikely, but maybe they would find prey along the way. They were all in need of feeding.

Once they reached the camp, he would have to decide if he would leave two men behind.

If she were in the forest, it would be great to capture her. If not, they would be of little use in this sector. Maybe leave two behind and ask them to search for two days, if they do not find anything, they would head back. Then only one question remained, would the others be able to transport the beast back with only three men and himself?

This was a critical transport, loss of this beast would set them back considerably in their timetable, and the master would be furious.

On the other hand, the master would be furious if he would find out that he did not pursue the opportunity to capture her.

They had one witch in their possession. But think of all the possibilities they had if they would capture her. It would mean a whole new different approach to their end game.

He would need to gamble on this one. Yes, leaving two men behind. But then again. What could two men do compared to her?

She is most powerful, even if she is known for not using her powers excessively.

So few of them left. It could be that she is the last of her kind, no one knew for sure. The rumor said they were extinct, but the Vampire clan had known for several ages that there was some left, scattered around the known world, in hiding.

She had come from the north.

Her timing was precise, as if she knew their plan, knew their progress, as if she could feel that they were close to achieve their goal and had come to stop them.

Not even the Master was strong enough to foresee her moves or stop her if she attempted to interfere.

The more the commander thought of it, the more convinced he got. Leaving two men behind was a good cause of action.

He played with the thought of being one of the two remaining himself, but then he might jeopardize the whole mission in bringing the beast back.

He trusted his men with his life, but he did not trust them to make all tactical decisions that could be needed along the way. They were carved as fighters, damn good one too. But it is a big difference being a fighter and being strategic. No, he would remain with the beast and would let two of the others stay behind to track, and if possible, capture her. Even if it only was a very faint chance of success in doing so.

Once the beast was secure back home, he would head out with a new group of men. Come back and reinforce the two, let them head back and feed and regain strength.

He had been looking forward to being there to break the beast and learn its secrets, but if there was a remote chance to capture her, it was a much sweeter victory. The choice was easy.

He could not help it, but to speculate in her reasons. But every scenario seemed too farfetched and almost all argumentation to fragile.

As history stated, her motives were hidden to the naked eye, and he would probably not be able to get close, no matter how many scenarios he created.

**nineteen.**

The two anchormen sat silent in the dark, feeling the fresh and cold sea air, and noticed that the waves had stopped raging. Now the sea kept rocking the compartment with its still but constant movements.

Just as they were about to search for a way to open the compartment something happened. What they assumed to be (correctly I might add) a sea monster, grabbed the compartment in its mouth and started to swim fast along the shore (which they did not know). And only after a long while of high speed they stopped instantly when (again they assumed correct) a bigger monster grabbed their capturer, and going from high speed to almost full stop made them and the compartment tumble around a couple of times before resuming their slow and steady glide through the waves.

One main difference from before their little run-into-the-sea-monster escapade, they had gone from complete dark to having a neat view of the bypassing coastline.

As beautiful as it was, as frustrating it was. They had no means of steering the compartment towards the land, they could only continue to drift to wherever the creator was guiding them.

As reality started to catch up with the two, they realized just how lucky they were in this particular moment. The rest of the Glory had been swallowed by the ocean, but they had survived as of now. Even survived another encounter with a sea monster.

Just as they had decided to abandon their little vessel and swim ashore, they noticed that there was sea monsters all around them in the water, not as big as they had seen aboard the Glory, but big enough to easily make the decision to cancel their little swim session.

Through everything they had been through, the cargo lay undamaged in the middle of the compartment, exactly where they had put it when they secured it.

They found it very odd that the waters were boiling with little sea monsters, when neither of them had seen a single one of these smaller creatures for the duration of their voyages with the Glory.

And these waters were close to home and no one had ever talked about these smaller versions of the big scary things in the ocean. Not that these were any less scary.

Between them, there was a silent agreement that the rich sea life was somehow connected to the cargo. Since they brought it aboard, the frequency and number of encounters had completely gone nuts. From being rare to be a part of the daily routine. Maybe it was not strange that the Glory ended up at the bottom of the sea. But then again. What was this strange cargo they carried? Why did they have orders to secure it at any cost? What was so important that it was worth losing an entire ship along with its crew? Did the elders of the village really know what they were up to?

They bounced really hard against an underwater cliff. The impact made the former compartment cry with stress and almost fell to pieces but remained in more or less one piece. It also changed their course and gave it a new heading towards the shoreline. With a little luck they would strand shortly and complete the journey by foot. It could not be too far from the harbour camp. A day or two at the most. Then they would be richly rewarded by the elders.

There, another bump, driving them even further to land. They could almost reach out from their vessel now, but the waters still swarmed with tiny, and probably deadly, sea life.

It took longer than they expected, but they finally hit solid ground and could leave the last floating pieces of the Glory. The cargo was still secured, but they now had to carry it by hand the rest of the way.

After carefully navigating through the sharp graphite cliffs they stood by the tree-line but before they could enter the forest, they found themselves in front of another obstacle. A werewolf lured just in the tree-line. Since one of them was carrying the cargo, the other one tried to attack with a stick and his knife, but it took only one bite from the werewolf to put an end to the attack. Then there was only one. Nowhere else to go. The werewolf howled and then took a step towards the last of the two anchormen. The growl from the werewolf made him think that the beast was not interested in a chitchat nor any of the stories he had gained from his time on the Glory.

**Twenty.**

"Wake up filthy humans!" Groll screamed, "It's time to start, the sooner we get there, the sooner I can show you the way out and the sooner we part ways! Everybody happy!"

Dee looked around. She saw that Tadao was also asleep until Groll had started to yell. What a way to wake up. The fire was out and no breakfast insight. The hawk took place on Tadao's shoulder the moment he sat up.

They both took a while to get back to reality after a night's sleep. Groll shouted again, urging them in a not so polite way, to stand up on their feet and get moving already.

"Human horse," he continued his yelling, "pick me up so we get there as fast as possible!"

Groll was in his best mood since Dee had met him two days ago. Cranky as ever. She lifted him and put him on his shoulder, making the scene a bit amusing. A man with his hawk on the shoulder, walking next to a girl with a troll on her shoulder. Who would have imagined?

Groll muttered but Dee ignored him and started to talk to Tadao. Asking where he was from and so on, just making small talk. When Tadao had talked about himself nonstop for almost fifteen minutes and boring Dee with his bragging, he asked her how she ended up in the ravine.

Dee chose the short story and said that she was on her way to the harbour camp and got caught between werewolves and then escaped. Ran blind in the forest only to fall and end up in the ravine.

Groll had been silent the entire time she had been talking but then surprised with a question:

"The werewolf, how does it look?"

Dee looked at him. She was not expecting a question like that from Groll, he seemed to be familiar with everything and very urbane in the known world.

"It's a beast, twice the height of any man, almost three of me, it has a long nose and a big mouth filled with sharp teeth. It has an appetite for all living things of this world, even the dwarves! So from a dwarf perspective, it is their only natural enemy, since the vampires does not like them." she answered mixing in what she had experienced herself and stuff from legends and stories she had been told.

Groll did not ask anything more, and Dee would say that he almost looked a little pale if that was possible for a troll.

The rest of their walk towards the ocean was in silence, and a few minutes before they arrived at the ocean, they could hear the breathing of the ocean, as the waves reached the shore.

Now they could see the end of the ravine in a distance, and Tadao started to protest.

"There is no way out of there that way, only down! And that is not a way out. He is fooling us!" he said and gave Groll a sharp eye.

"More than meets the eye, always!" Groll replied, putting an end to the discussion before it even surfaced.

Tadao thought that it was strange that they had walked this distance in about an hour, given that he had struggled for much longer than that on his way in the ravine.

As they came to the edge, Dee was just about to give Tadao right, there was no way out, when Groll pointed to the right and as he had said from the start, there was a way out. They had only to walk across a small rim that barely had room for their feet. It was a small, but dangerous walk, only three or four feet, but they had to round a salient cliff, and should they slip, the fall would not be gentle on their bodies. It would be the last thing they did.

To her surprise, Groll was the first one out and yelled at them to hurry up from around the corner.

**Twenty one.**

As the wizard kept moving forward in the forest, trying to locate its bearing, it regretted the whole mist coverup. It was good in theory and had, as intended, confused both the werewolves and the Vampires, not to mention saving a little girls life. The flip side was a lost bearing, and as always it seemed, there was these unintended consequences of using the powerful magic that nature provided. Not like the witches who only used the flow of the life essence, enhancing it or slowing it, giving it a nudge here and there to steer the flow in a new direction. The magic of a wizard was way more powerful. Taming the forces of the nature, bending the rules and use the forces for new things. But, as it seemed, the more powerful the magic was, and the more astonishing things a wizard was able to achieve, the more unintended the aftermath became. Even if they always tried to predict the aftermath of each and every use of magic, it seemed they could never grasp the whole picture. Time and again, this particular wizard had sworn never to use magic again, but circumstances had forced the wizard's hand to act over and over again.

Even if it were hard, the wizard had to admit, getting lost in the mist was not to blame on the magic, it could only be credited the wizards outstanding sense of direction. And from the wizard's current perspective, nothing else had gone bad this time due the use of magic. But then again, it is very rare that the aftermath could be seen directly after. It usually took time.

Now, where was that bloody mountain?

The wizard played around in its mind to look for easy spells that only used a little magic, to identify the right direction.

It could not even use the sun in this heavy part of the forest. It was rare to get a good look of the sky, even more rare to actually see the sun. But even if there was a tiny glimpse of the sun, it was hard to say where in the sky it was located.

Of course, there was always the easy way in stop and ask for direction. But that was very much below the pride of any wizard. And the entire forest knew it, so the best course of action was just to pretend to be on the right path. Which, unfortunately, ruled out using even the smallest of spells to get the right bearing.

Stupid forest, looking the same everywhere, not even the moss could be used as guidance here, it grew all over the place, on all sides of all trees and everything else for that matter.

And the paths from the villagers did not cover this part of the forest, so they could not be used to determine the way.

No points of reference, no nothing.

If only the wizard could find something, maybe like the Sorrow, something that actually lead to the mountain itself.

Or the ocean.

At the ocean it would be easy to determine the right course, only hard to keep it once back in the forest.

Why, oh why, was there so many trees in the way, making finding one's way much harder.

Maybe swallowing the pride and ask for direction was the best course of action after all. But no, not yet! There was still the small possibility that there could be something ahead, something small that would make finding the way easy. Or maybe an obvious path.

Well, as they say, the hope is the last thing that leaves every living being, only sad that the first thing is not pride.

**twenty two.**

Dee, Groll and Tadao made the climb from the ravine up to the forest above without any incidents. Looking back, the only hard part was rounding the salient cliff. The rest of the way it was just a normal path, except from it being very steep, which most normal paths are not, at least not that steep, and not very often. Dee had no problems with the slope, but Tadao sounded like a male horse in the middle of the mating process, and of course, Groll was not affected by it at all, since he once again was riding on Dee's shoulder.

As they reached the top Dee expected Groll to return down to the ravine again, but he did not show any signs of wanting to do so. Instead she asked Groll:

"We need to cross the ravine and follow the coastline back north to the harbour camp, do you know where we can find a crossing?"

"No crossing" he said, "only way is to go back to the mountain and cross before the Sorrow begins." he continued somewhat unfocused on his own words.

"To the mountain?" Tadao asked a bit frustrated. "That would be at least a twenty day walk without food, water or protection. That is an impossible task to complete!"

"There is…" Groll started, but got interrupted by Tadao making fun of him:

"There is always more than meets the eye, stupid human! Yeah, I know! But what is there, oh you little talking and walking piece of the creator's mistake? What is here that does not meet the eye?"

"Trees…" Dee answered, almost mumbling to herself… "Trees are what does not meet the eyes at first, because there are so many of them!"

Both Groll and Tadao looked at her and did not understand what she meant. It probably showed in the expression in their faces because Dee continued:

"Either we climb a tree, taking the branches across the ravine, or we try to tumble over a tree to create a bridge over…"

"Not bad for a human…" Groll said, rather impressed.

"I know," Dee answered with a smile, "you know, there is always more than meets the eye!"

Both Groll and Dee laughed. Tadao however, did not. He felt like he was not a part of their team and sought any and all means to win over Dee to his side.

"Shouldn't you crawl back to the ravine already?" he asked Groll in a very short tone.

"Not yet" Groll answered to Dee's unexpected satisfaction. "I will follow you a while longer!".

They walked along the ravine all day, looking for a tree to climb, or possibly a tree that the three of them was able to overthrow. There was a clear tension in the group and not much was said.

Close to nightfall Groll took tone, they hadn't eaten anything the entire day and might as well set shelter in daylight.

"Take your hawk and go find some wood to make fire!" he commanded Tadao, "and Dee, would you be so kind to gather some roots for us? I'll show you where to dig." he said to Dee in a much warmer tone.

"I'll go a bit further down the ravine to see what else I can find to eat. We'll set up camp here for the night!" he said, pointing at a big rock where the moss actually hadn't taken over everything. After showing Dee how to find the roots, he continued a bit further and before Groll came back, Tadao returned with some sticks and pieces of wood. Nothing near the pieces Groll had provided when they still were at the bottom of the ravine.

It was hard to get a fire going, but after a while, they had created a small fire, and Dee had provided a great pile of various roots, not knowing what to do with them, so they lay by the fire waiting for Groll to return.

That night they had roasted roots, Groll turned out to be a real master chef! After their meal Groll constructed warm and soft beds to both Dee and Tadao, even if he planted some quite large rocks in Tadao's bed and had a good laugh when Tadao exploded when he found them.

Just before Dee fell asleep the for the third night in a row out in the wild, she thought of her dad, how worried he must be for her. She longed to get back to him. She thought of Rick, her dear brother, and that she would never see him again. And of Groll, this strange little creature. He was quite something. Exactly what, she could not say, but she had a good feeling about him, despite his grumpy side.

The night passed without any incidents.

By dawn Groll woke them with fresh pieces of bread. They tasted lovely. The best bread Dee had ever tasted.

They quickly got on their feet when Groll said that he had found a passage over, and only a ten minute walk from their camp a tree had grown in a strange way, creating a passage from one side to the other. Well on the other side they started to walk backwards towards the ocean, keeping a little to the north all the time.

Tadao was walking in front with his hawk on the shoulder, and he made a sudden stop signing to the others to follow his example. They all stood quiet, careful not to move. Dee got cold chills down her spines, was it another werewolf?

They could all hear something approach.

**twenty three**

The witch looked out the small window. The only thing visible was the blood moon. The chains were chafing on both wrists, ankles and around the neck. Standing up for an infinite amount of time had its toll on the body. Knowing the days was counted already from the start, almost no one had left captivity of the vampires with their breath still in their body. Maybe one or two black witches, but never a grey, and definitely not a white.

The benefits of being a grey witch was that you could use the entire spectra of the life essence but breaching the golden rule of never use it for your own benefit. As long as you didn't cross the line and used it against the creation, then you would be a black witch.

For ages there had only been grey witches, with a few black ones along the way, it was only in the beginning there was still white witches. Could be that the white witches needed guidance from the creator and nowadays, the creator lived on only as a belief and something that people cared for mostly by tradition. There were very few actual followers of the creator left.

"Probably what happens when you do not show!" the witch thought, longing to see the silver-moon instead of the blood moon. There was something ominous over the red moon, whilst the silver-moon gave hope.

Trying to keep sane, the witch again repeated the amount of days and nights in captivity, seventy-six days, seventy-seven night, feeling unsure if the count had been added from yesterday. Probably.

Thinking back to the night of the capture, remembering it with remorse. So many lives lost for one witch. So unnecessary. So horrible. What a feast for the vampires it had been. So sure that none would survive, the witch almost crossed the line to become a black witch, but in the end, it wouldn't have mattered, so the line was still uncrossed.

Not that it mattered anymore. Should there be an afterlife, there would most likely be a suiting punishment waiting. The last seventy-oh, what was it again, seventy-seven? The last seventy-something nights had made any possibility of a decent afterlife disappear to never return again. But enough is enough. Now there would not be any more suffering, at least not for others, the only suffering left that this witch was the cause of would be its own. No doubt! And what a suffering.

The stage had passed where the thoughts "I'm lucky if I survive another night" was expressed. Now it was more like "I'm lucky if this is my last night".

The vampire elder was not a gentle host, nor very generous. But the normal basic feelings like hunger, getting sleepy and feeling pain was since long gone.

The body was in survival state, struggling to keep the heart beating and keep the lungs inflating with fresh air. Or rather, as fresh air as there would be in a cold and misty dungeon.

The little energy that could be retrieved from the sun was effectively blocked each morning as the entire castle was sealed with sun blocking drapes, and the dirty drinking water and old pieces of bread contained just enough energy to keep the body alive, nothing more.

The witch knew that as long as the food was poor, there was still time and death did await shortly. But once the vampires started to serve food rich with energy to rebuild the body, then their feast was not long away, and death was nearby.

There was the usual noise by the dungeon door, the key clicking in the locking mechanism, the chains and the metal bars removed, the crying from the door when it was awakened from its dormant sleep, only to be closed minutes later.

What kind of meal had they prepared today? Water from the moat or from the sewer? Bread with white, green, or blue mold?

There was a plate put on the table to the left, almost out of reach, but it did not sound as empty as it used to.

Since the left eye was brutally beaten and still swollen, the witch had made an extra effort to see what was on the plate.

Oh no! Hot, steaming, roasted lamb with potatoes and sauce. A weird thing, best cooks was vampires, and they could not even enjoy the food. It was soon time. Soon the last meal. Might as well enjoy it while it lasts.

**twenty four.**

Even with restraints, it is hard to move a werewolf. It is like pushing a big rock upstream in a river. It is a good thing that the mouth is secured, otherwise they would all be a head shorter and maybe miss an arm or a leg.

They pushed the beast in front of them, aiming southeast to get closer to home and closer to the ocean at the same time.

Since it was hard to move the beast in the heavy terrain of the forest, they figured that it would be easier closer to the ocean where the trees stood more scattered. But they had to find a good compromise between scattered trees and easier to move and still having protection of the forest from the sun. But their main focus had to be getting the beast back to the castle, and the commander was fully prepared to push their own safety limits close to the edge to make that happen as fast as possible. He had ordered no rest and movement around the clock.

At daybreak after their first night in transit they reached the shoreline, but their hopes that it would be easier to move the beast turned to disappointment, since it now, without fear for its life, tried to ally with the sun and constantly tried to move in the direction of the water so its captures would be more exposed to the sun. The behavior suggested intelligence and calculated behavior, but the truth is that all werewolves, even if they had intelligence and full awareness, was beings driven primarily by instinct. As this was not clear to the commander, he tried to reason with his prisoner, which of course did not change the situation at all.

At a particularly difficult passage when all, including the werewolf, had to focus on where they put their feet down, the beast took a leap of chance and moved straight out towards the sea and after only a few steps, it was out in the open sun. The vampires were close by but could not stop it from making a full exit of the protective forest into the sunbathing cliffs. As one of the vampires took a leap after it, still covered in the protective clothing, the beast turned and got a lucky hit on the vampire with some strange waving of its front paws, causing it to lose its balance, since its hands was linked to its feet. The end result was a fallen werewolf on the ground, and a vampire with the skin exposed to direct sun. If the vampire had eaten recently, that would not have been a pleasant experience, but not lethal as it was in this case. It was very long since they all had eaten, and the sun dried the vampire in less than a second, and all that was left in the pile of the protective clothing was dust, slowly spreading in the wind.

With the beast on the ground, it was no match for the others to secure their prisoner without risking the same faith as their kinsman. The commander was glad that he in the last second decided not to leave anyone behind to search for her. Should this continue, it would be very difficult to secure the transport of the beast back to the castle.

As they had secured the beast, the commander saw something by the water. It was a creation made of wood, he had never seen anything like it. Obviously man made. It looked as if it was part of some mechanical machinery, but had gotten severed from the rest, floating free for a while before ending up here, crashing into the sharp graphite cliffs. No sign of any humans, no bodies, not a single trace. Only the wreckage.

They continued through the forest, slowly, too slow if you asked the commander. This would take forever.

## Twenty five.

The three of them (four if you count the hawk) stood still, completely quiet. Something was definitely coming towards them, it was still too early to say what it was, but by the sounds, it was either something large, or many smaller things. They could not make out the exact sounds yet, but here and there was something that sounded like a voice, and not a very friendly or pleased voice. Still most of the sound was breaking sticks and bushes protesting as something went through them with force.

Dee dared not to breath. It was almost like she was back at the path in the middle of the werewolves. Only this time her mind was not as calm. It was like she had something to lose. Which she has had then as well, but somehow this was different.

The source kept coming closer, and the closer it got, the clearer the words got. Dee tried to identify them. Was it Vampirski? No, it did not sound like that, or did it? Still hard to say, the words were polluted by all the other sounds.

The three (four) of them still hadn't moved, there was nowhere to hide, only behind a tree, but it was not a very good protection, so they collectively hoped that whatever, or whoever was the cause of these sounds would pass them and that they would stay undetected.

Obviously, that didn't happen. Before they knew it, they saw an old lady coming through a big thicket. She looked equally surprised to see others in the woods, as the three of them was to see an old lady in the forest. Alone as it seemed. Made no sense whatsoever.

The mutual surprise caused an awkward silence that no one wanted to break, so for a long while they just stood there, all of them.

The first who broke the fragile moment was Dee.

"Are you a beggar?" she asked since it was the only logical explanation to an old lady walking alone without any kind of protection. Besides, there was something familiar about her, so she could be a beggar that had passed through the village at some point and she did not carry any packing of any kind. Typical beggars.

"A beggar?" she asked, a little confused. "No, not a beggar. Only passing through, I do not mean you no harm."

"It is mutual." Tadao answered. "Are you alone?"

"Yes!" she answered short, apparently not wanting to continue the conversation.

Then Groll muttered. "Typically a human, alone in the forest!"

The woman looked at Groll as if she had not seen him at first, there on Dee's shoulder. Her whole expression and body language and face changed in an instant. Dee could not tell if it was because she was trying to process Groll's appearance or if she found his muttering offensive or if it was something completely different. She was hard to read.

"And the three of you?" she asked after a while. "Where are you heading, if I might ask?"

"First towards the ocean, then up north, to my villages harbour camp." Dee answered truthfully.

"Up north?" she said thoughtfully, as if it disturbed her plans. "Me too. You mind if I join you?"

Dee was surprised of her direct question and straightforwardness.

"You might as well" Groll answered with a big sigh and then muttered to himself "great, another one…"

The expression in the woman's face changed again, not sure if she should reply on the insult or let it pass by and pretend like it did not happen.

The four (five) started to walk again, nobody said anything.

**twenty six**

The witch expected the next meal at any moment now. And even if the past days had been filled with delicious meals, and it only pointed to one possible outcome, the meals were actually very enjoyable.

There it was, the familiar scrapes with the locking mechanism. The mere sound activated the taste buds and made them almost vibrate of expectations. The vampire chefs had thought them well.

But when the doors opened, there was not the ordinary guard bringing in the meal. There were two other guards, armed with some kind of strange sword with two blades instead of one, and the edges was black as a contrast to their ordinary weapons that always was shiny and spotless. These blades looked very dirty in a weird way, almost like they had been laying in the fire for too long.

The two guards did not pay much attention to the prisoner, nor the comfort of the prisoner, they released the chains from the hooks on the wall and attached them to small weights instead. Then pushed the prisoner in front of them as if they were trying to get sheep into a fold or a horse into a stable.

Every inch of the witches' body was aching. It had been a lot of days without being able to move more than a little bit, and now, there was a kind of tumbling march through endless corridors and stairs leading both up and down, in chains and not to mention the extra weight of them. Either the castle was much bigger than the witch expected, or they took an extra-long walk just for the fun of it.

Uncertain of how many corridors and stairs they had passed, they suddenly stopped in front of two gigantic doors, carved in darken oak with silver details. At first it only looked like a nice well-crafted door, but as they stood there waiting, the details cleared and showed various scenes.

The witch could tell that they were crafted by someone that really loved, and took great pride in, every detail of the creation. Pure passion. The levels of detail in each scene made it look almost real, even if it was tiny. Both doors were entirely covered and there were over hundred, if not two hundred scenes on each door.

The witch wished there were more time to study the details of the doors, there was something about them, like they held a key within, hidden. But the doors opened wide to a great hall.

The hall was almost empty, except from several chairs along the walls.

At the far end of the hall there was a strange silhouette, the vampire master. The patron saint of the wicked. He was said to be the first of their kind. The oldest. The black witches first experiment. But he was not created as he currently appeared. About an age ago, a black witch gave him wings. The master had captured a dwarf king, and in return for his release he had gotten a small amount of pure life essence. Using that, the black witch had crafted wings on his body, enhancing his strength, making him untouchable and an unquestioned leader of the vampire clan. He returned the favor by feasting on her, something he later regretted, but at that moment, he was completely thrilled of his newly gained powers.

There he was in his unholy appearance, in front of the witch, facing the back wall of the hall.

As the doors was shut close, the vampire elder slowly turned.

**twenty seven.**

It was not common to see, but this particular day a dwarf had surfaced. In the middle of the West Great Mountains, there was a small opening on the northern slope of a high peak.

The dwarves used openings like this to get fresh air down into the mines, and each air vent was carefully crafted to be invisible to the naked eye. So, if anyone had walked by, they would see a dark silhouette of a dwarf, hovering mid-air, in the middle of the steep slope, with no way up nor down. This dwarf in particular was keener than others to get a glimpse of the world outside of the mines. Every other month, he climbed up an air vent in hopes to catch a glimpse of a sunset, or a sunrise, or maybe even the two moons. Most other dwarves protested loudly if they had to leave the underground more than once per decade. But this dwarf took every given chance to get a glimpse of the open wide. But today it was cloudy, and impossible to see anything but the clouds. Even so, the dwarf enjoyed the view. Mountain as far as the eye could see, which in a dwarves case is not very far, their eyes had adapted to underground chambers and tunnels, so they could see very sharp and wide (not to miss anything valuable) at close distance, but not very good in longer distances. Apart from that, their eyes were very sensitive to light, so it was hard for them to be out in daylight, which was the reason that dwarves always wore helmets when being outside of the mines.

The dwarf stood in the air vent, enjoying the view of the creation, and the air, and dreamt away when he heard a voice approaching.

"Uncle Veron, Uncle Veron!" a young dwarf struggled up the small stairway, short of breath.

"Here, come Saculg!" he welcomed his nephew. "Come and join me to see the view!".

While Saculg caught his breath, his uncle made a gesture towards the magnificent view.

"Look Saculg! These are the mountains we live in. Our home. The most wonderful roof anyone could ever ask for, and most of us does not even see it…" Veron said with a sad tone in his voice.

"Uncle, you are needed in the great hall, they ask for you, it is urgent!" Saculg said without paying attention to his uncles' admiration of the land above.

Together the both of them made the steep descents climb below, back to where they came from, back to where they belonged, following various tunnels, stairways, up and down, to the left and to the right. Like all dwarves, they knew each tunnel, stair and turn by heart. Almost like the layout of their work had been coded in the blood of each individual.

It took a while to come to the great hall, the pride of the dwarf society. Here the dwarf masters had performed their greatest art, sculptures with rare stones and minerals, delicate metalwork, massive statues of solid rock, beautifully carved thrones for each and every one of the twelve elders, just to mention a small portion of all the beauty that was gathered here.

There was full activity in the great hall, compared to the usual stillness and respect that the hall inclined.

Veron quickly realized that this was an extraordinary event, probably caused as a reaction to some even bigger thing. But he could not figure out what it could be. Given the state in the hall, he guessed it would not be long before he knew.

"Veron, there you are! What took you so long? Have you heard?" a dwarf with long beard that swelled over his even bigger stomach approached him.

"No, what is going on?" Veron asked.

"You have been selected to carry our flag in the delegation to our province in the north." the big bellied dwarf said. "It is a great honor for our clan, and it also mean that you will be the first to greet king Thidas."

"Why are we sending a delegation to the northern province?" Veron asked, a bit troubled. "Have we gotten word from them, or have we found something of importance?"

The big belly wobbled as the dwarf it was attached to snorted and stopped abruptly. "Found something of importance? When was the last time we found something, we do not already have found?" The question was more rhetorical than intended to be answered. "Ages ago! I doubt there is something new that we can discover. And as for hearing something from the northern province, that would be the day! The most likely scenario would be if they dug a tunnel from the north that interconnected with one of our own. But they are too lazy to do that. Shame of our kinsmen they are!"

"Then why are we sending a delegation there?" Veron asked again, really not expecting a straight answer.

"Yes, why are we?" the belly-wobbling dwarf asked, again more rhetorically. "Waste of time and resources it is, mark my words, but you, my lad" he patted Veron hard on the back, "you get to greet king Thidas. And that my friend. That is a true honor, even if he is not worthy of it."

Veron sighed, how hard could it be to get a straight answer on this place?

**Twenty eight.**

The vampire master stood silent a long while, studying the prisoner. Then he cleared his throat addressing the witch directly.

"So…. you've been with us for a while now…" silent again. "How do you like…." the vampire master was looking for words on the human language, "our…" another long silence, "hospitality?" The last word was followed by a grim laughter.

"I've had better!" the witch replied short and dry.

"I see…" the vampire master started to walk around with his hands behind his back, just beneath the wings. He was a truly hideous creature.

"We've tried to get your cooperation in a number of ways. And as you probably have concluded yourself, my patience is wearing thin."

The witch stood silent.

"I've decided to make one last try to gain your cooperation. You know what's at stake, I do not have to explain the details to you." the vampire's eye studied the prisoners face carefully for each word, as if to measure the impact the words had, calculating the next move.

"I will bring in ten innocent little girls, that we have captured for you." the vampires' eye was almost glowing with pride, this plan was the best ever to set in motion.

"I know you will need four or five to do what I ask of you, maybe six. The rest will be yours to do as you please. Maybe satisfy your human lust. Or set free. So they can return home to their families." the vampire watched as the words reached the prisoner and was absorbed by the entire being of the witch.

"All you have to do is to comply. Then they can go home." A small silence again. "You can be a hero, saving yourself and a few of these girls. You'll get to leave this castle unharmed by vampire hand."

The witch still stood silent, with a boiling rage inside.

"Should you choose not to comply, I will feast tonight, and then the night after that, and the next, and the next, until there are no more of the delicious little girls left to feast on… then I will unleash my guards on you. They have not eaten anything in a while. So there will be many that will enjoy the things you can offer." The vampire smiled a big wide grin. "I almost hope that you will not comply, but then again, if you do…." There was a hidden longing in the vampire master's voice, hard to say if it was for the little girls or if it could smell the completion of their end game.

To give the witch the choice to sacrifice a few to save a few, and not to have to die by the hands of the vampires, but of course, the survival means crossing the great plains and pass the hordes of the undead undetected, which was not very likely. But the vampire master had no intention of playing with open cards. Besides, he hated to lose.

He snapped his fingers and from a side door, ten girls, roughly between the ages of nine to fifteen, was brought in. All unharmed, but scared and pale, obviously not given enough to eat or drink, nor enough sunlight or sleep.

The witch hesitated.

"I expect to hear your answer within the hour!" the vampire master said, snapping his fingers again, and the prisoner was brought back to the cell where another delicious meal was waiting.

But it didn't taste good. It was spiced with defeat and abomination.

Time moved slowly and it might as well have been a full night that had passed from when the witch was locked in again until they came back to open the door.

It was a long hour to be alone with the agony.

**twenty nine.**

The four (five) had walked all day, mostly under silence, and as the sun set, they set up another temporary camp to spend the night.

The fire was warming and Groll had, still unknown how, produced one of his wonderful breads again. They all sat around the fire, strangely calm, neither worried about the dangers that the forest hosted.

Dee could not stand the unknown any longer, she had to ask.

"So, what's your name? And what are you doing here alone in the forest?" she asked, directed the question to the old lady.

"My name is Leola, and as for being here in the forest..." she paused... "the short version would be that I am looking for my brother."

"Did you travel together, and he got lost?" Tadao asked.

"No, haven't seen him in a long while. But he needs me now, and... I kind of need him as well..." Leola answered truthfully, even if it was very cryptic to the rest of them.

"What about you then?" Leola directed the question to all the others, surrounding their little campfire.

Dee was the first to answer.

"I was on my way to our harbour camp to greet my brother...." she silenced, and tears filled her eyes.

Tadao continued.

"I was on the Glory, she wrecked after she was attacked by sea monsters. I am lucky to be alive, I was swept aboard and ended up meeting these two. Her brother used to be a member of the Glory crew. I didn't know him."

Leola then looked at Groll, he looked back at her for a long while, neither of them spoke. The only thing that anybody could her was sobs from Dee and the sparkling from the fire.

Then Groll broke the silence.

"I'm with her." he nodded towards Dee. "For now."

Nothing else was said that night.

Despite her sobbing, Dee had heard everything that was being said and felt strangely revealed to hear Groll say he was with her. And in a strange way, she felt that the four of them was more connected to each other, now when they had started to talk a little.

As she was about to turn in, she thought that it was strange that they had not reached the harbour camp nor the village yet and had not seen any trace of any of the paths she knew surrounded the village. How far and how long had she been running?

Probably not that long, besides, it was a tricky terrain to maneuver, and they would probably reach the harbour camp tomorrow.

**thirty**

Roy Hicks stood at the edge of the great plains. He knew that whatever he did, he should never pass through the great plains. Not if he wanted to continue living. And he had no urge to die. Not yet anyway. The only way to pass the great plains was to go around them. Following the edge. Even so, it was a dangerous escapade, there could be undead in the outskirts of the great plains as well. The safest thing he could do was to head back to the main trading routes and head either north or south. But he knew he was not welcome there anymore. Not ever.

He thought of what he should do next. Maybe look for a way to the Mountain Village. But the thought of living there for the rest of his life was unbearable. A horrible way of living, those Mountain Villagers. No, maybe he should try to do something that he never had heard anyone do, seek out the dwarves. Maybe they could teach him to mine and work with metal. Or maybe be their spokesperson in contact with the humans. But then again, they also had contact with the vampires. Or at least that was what the rumors said. And how would the warm blood react if the dwarves had a cold blood as their spokesperson? It would probably not be a very good scenario. Maybe go see the ocean? He had always heard about the ocean, never seen it. Yeah, the more he thought about it, the more he wanted to go see the ocean.

He turned around by old habit, to grab his few belonging in the bag, only to remember, he did not have any belongings anymore. None. Not even clothes on his back. So he started to walk towards the ocean.

Even if he wanted to, he chose not to cross the great plains, instead he chose to take the northern way around it, in cover by the forest. A decision he later both would regret, and then be very grateful for. Had he, at that time, known that the northern way around the great plains was the longer, he would have selected the southern route instead, because as many already knew, Roy Hicks was rather lazy by nature.

Now Roy Hicks had no idea that the southern route was the shortest, so he turned his nose to the north and started walking.

He had never thought of it before but walking naked was a very satisfying thing to do. He could feel every single change in the air, from the smallest breeze to the hot spot when passing a rock that had spent the largest part of the day sunbathing.

Of course, this new sensation of naked well-being did not last very long. The first thing he noticed was that clothing stopped many of the small insects that was always around. Now they could freely land on his skin, taking a bite or just walk around to create an itch.

The second thing Roy Hicks learned about walking naked was just before it starts to rain, the air gets much cooler. In fact, it gets so much cooler that you start to freeze before you get wet and start to freeze even more.

The now cold Roy Hicks started to run a little, trying to find shelter faster, and hopefully to get a little warmer at the same time.

Now, for those who knew Roy Hicks, seeing him run would be such a rare occasion that most of them would lose a high stake bet on Roy Hicks not running for a month, or for the summer, or for an entire year for that matter.

The only time Roy Hicks would run, and this was common knowledge, was when the traders came back from their trade routes to the south, to see if they had brought back any barrels of Gizzy. It was rare, and they were expensive, but somehow Roy Hicks always had money to pay for a barrel of Gizzy, when just moments before, he wouldn't have a single coin to his name when people asked him to pay his debts.

Even so, he was actually running, Roy Hicks, believe it or not. But as you probably already have figured out, a person who runs is not very likely to spot what he might be looking for, so it took Roy Hick almost an hour of running in the rain, before he found shelter beneath a large tree that had fallen on another tree. There was even soft moss on the ground. Still dry. A good shelter.

**thirty one.**

Those who claim vampires does not have feelings should have been with the vampire commander after the long struggle of bringing the beast back to their castle. What a relief, no more men down, and on top of that, the pride of accomplishing the mission.

First thing to take care of was making sure the beast was secured in the dungeon. Next item on the list was making sure that all the men got something to eat, and some rest to regain their full strength, and before he would enjoy those things himself, he would report to the master.

He expected high praise for his accomplishment, and at the same time, it felt like they still had a long way to go, especially since they had no more witch. Either they had to recruit one, or capture. But nowadays it was hard to recruit, they needed a gray witch. The black was simply not powerful enough, and a white witch would never do it. And besides, nobody had heard about a white witch in ages.

The commander made all the right turns, passing each doorway, going up and down in the stairs. The vampires remade the entire castle as they took over it, reforming it to be as sheltering as possible. Sure, there was still windows here and there, all covered with protective cloth, but despite what people believed, the vampires still needed some light. Their eyesight was good in the dark, but not that good. Not that any vampire ever admitted it.

He passed the magnificent door to the main hall and went straight into the commander on duties office. Stated his reasons and demanded help with the beast and a meal and rest for his men. The commander on duty was quick and more than willing to help. The orders were given at once and he promised to personally oversee the transferring of the werewolf to the dungeons.

Now when all that was settled, the commander turned around and walked back to the main hall doors. He stated his intention and wished an audience with the master. It didn't take long before he got his audition granted and the doors opened.

Inside there was empty as always, except the presence of the great master himself.

The commander bowed and waited to speak until spoken to.

Then he summarized his mission in a full mission report. At the end he added a personal thought.

"It's a shame we do not have the witch with us still…"

"But we do!" the master replied.

"But wasn't…"

"There is a time and place for everything, the death of the witch will come, either by our hands or in another way. I saved the witch for one purpose alone, now we have two."

The commander was well acquainted with the ways of the master and understood better than to question him.

Just as he had left for his mission, he heard one of the other captains get the order to kill the witch and since that obviously did not happen, he had a feeling that there was one captain less by the officers banquet. A shame in a way, but also one less mouth to feed.

Speaking of which, the commander waited to be sent away so he himself could enjoy a fine meal. He wondered what options there would be on the menu this time. In particular, the commander enjoyed young people, preferably not over ten years of age. Their blood still had a fresh sourish taste, the older the humans got, the more mellow they tasted.

**Thirty two.**

When Dee woke up, Leola was gone. Tadao was still sleeping (snoring) and Groll sat by the fire, poking in it and giving it more fuel. As the flames grew, it almost sounded like Groll was humming.

"Where is Leola?" Dee asked.

"You mean the filthy wizard?" Groll replied, with his usual grumpy tone.

"Huh?" Dee replied. "No, I mean Leola, the old woman we met yesterday."

"Claims she is a wizard." Groll stated, ending the discussion before it even begun.

Dee let his word sink in. A wizard. Sounded like an awfully strange thing to claim. For several reasons. Wizards are old men. And extinct, as in no longer alive, at least not that many left, and they were in hiding. It would be illogical to walk around in the open claiming to be a wizard.

Then it hit Dee, she did not get an answer as to her whereabouts, only that she had claimed to be a wizard.

"You didn't say where she is." Dee pointed out to Groll.

"Oh." he thought for a while. "She is around. Should be back in a while. Breakfast is ready soon."

Dee looked towards Tadao, still no signs of waking up. And the hawk guarded him as always.

"What did you mean yesterday when you said you're with me? And what made you change your mind to join instead of going back?" Dee asked Groll.

"I have my reasons. Let us just say that I need to accompany you, and make sure you have a safe return to your village, then I have business of my own to attend to." Groll replied.

His words went straight to Dee's heart. He did care for her, this little grumpy creature.

It did not take long before Tadao woke up, and shortly thereafter Leola returned.

At breakfast Dee asked Leola how it was that a Wizard was walking alone in the forest.

Tadao reacted quickly before she had time to answer, her only reaction before Tadao started to talk was a hard stare on Groll.

"A Wizard? You can't be a Wizard. Everybody knows that Wizards are great and powerful men. Not many left, and the ones that are left are living in exile or hiding." Tadao said with his rapid tongue.

"Bah! Do not give me that prejudice crap that you've been fed along with your mother's milk." Leola replied.

Tadao laughed, "and I suppose you are about to tell us that there are male witches as well, right?" he looked at Leola trying to read her reaction.

"Of course there are male witches. My brother is one!" she said. "Wizards or Witches has nothing with the sex of the person practicing the magic, it is the description of how they use their magic and what kind of forces they use."

Before Tadao sent his tongue loose on another sharp dance, Groll took Leola in defense.

"Right you are, my child!" he said.

Tadao was surprised by Groll's comment and silenced at once, and again, Groll's words seemed to put an end to a dialogue before it even started.

After breakfast, the four of them continued to make their way back to the harbour camp of Dee's village and just as the day before, they did not meet anything dangerous and their journey was rather uneventful.

After a few hours through rough terrain, they could see the pier of the harbour camp, and it could not be more than an hour away. But something looked different, Dee thought. Could be that she was approaching from the south, rather than from the north as she was used to.

**Thirty three.**

Veron took his place among the rest of the clan, still unaware what had caused all this.

Everybody around him was very engaged in the delegation and opinions lay thick in the otherwise sound polluted air. Veron had hard to focus on what was going on in the center.

The heads of all clans were gathered, discussing something very loudly and giving each word extra weight by supporting it with big gestures.

Come to think about it, it looked rather much like some sort of advanced, choreographed dance show without music. Veron tried to make out what they said to see if he could get some idea of what was going on.

Indeed, carrying the flag was a great honor, it meant that the delegation was his responsibility, and he was also the first that was expected to greet king Thidas when they arrived, and thus, bring forth whatever news or message they carried.

So far all he could understand was something about the order of the clans, if there was one clan that was of a greater value than the other, or something like that.

All the heads tried to explain why their clan was of the most value to the entire dwarf society, and what they could provide that no one else could. Some of them bragged about all the treasures their clan possessed, making them far more valuable than all the others. Some of them tried to bring forth the diplomatic skills or trading skills or their influence in the vampire castle.

It all seemed to be some sort of power demonstration, as if…

The Grand Master! Where was the Grand Master? Veron could not see him anywhere, not on his throne, nor among the heads of clans. Had something happened to the Grand Master? Sure, he was older than most, almost three ages, but every healthy dwarf was expected to live for about five ages.

Was there anything else that held him occupied? Something so important that he could not be here now, something that directed his attention elsewhere.

But then again, why all this talk about who of the heads of the clans that was the most important? And again, even if the Grand Master was needed elsewhere, why send a delegation to the northern province?

He turned to the dwarf closest to him.

"What is all the buzz about?"

"Do not know for sure, but I think it is something about the election of a new Grand Master…"

"Where is our Grand Master now?" Veron asked, trying to get a cleared picture.

"Some said he died, some say he just walked out of here to the great plains, saying he should not return…"

That was an unexpected answer. But the election of a new Grand Master was reason enough to send a delegation to king Thidas. For several reasons, both because he was the head of the northern province, and he also was the brother of Grand Master Phidas, so from a respect perspective, king Thidas had the right to know.

Dead? Not very likely, but plausible. Walked out of here to the great plains, not very likely, but then again, crazy enough to be true. Grand Master Phidas was known for being spiritual ever since he found the life essence. And Veron had over the years gotten the feeling that he regretted his alliance with the vampire master.

But the internal politics of the clans and the outside world alliances had never interested Veron. Maybe he should have paid more attention to it.

Veron tried to focus his attention on the heads of the clans again. Still only discussing who was the most suited for the position as the new Grand Master, no focus on when to send the delegation or what message to send to king Thidas.

**Thirty four.**

The doors opened to the prisoner's cell and the vampire master entered majestically. He watched the witch who was caught in the middle of a bite of a big chunk of lamb, roasted to perfection with different kinds of herbs and vegetables.

"So… Grime, old friend! Have you made your decision yet? Will you save your own life and the life of four or five little innocent girls?"

Grime looked up at the vampire master, still chewing on the lamb. He figured that even if he pretended, he would obey, he would not get this kind of food anymore. If he declined the offer, he would most likely be a special on today's menu.

"What kind of guarantees do I have?" he asked the vampire master.

"Non-other than my word." the vampire answered.

"And the girls? What about the ones I do not need, if it comes to it? Grime asked.

"Yours to do as you please..." the vampire answered.

"And if I refuse... say you kill me and kill the girls... what then?" Grime demanded to know.

"I only loose time, and I'll find someone else who can do it...." the vampire smiled.

"Who?" Grime asked, in a way already knowing he would not like the answer.

"Your sister…." the vampire answered.

His words felt like a hard punch in the stomach. No, that could not be true. She would never do that!

"You are lying" he yelled to the vampire, but the vampire only laughed.

"Maybe I am, but then again, maybe I'm not. My word is all you got, I will let you go, and the girls that are not needed for this procedure. You may take it and trust me, but then again, you never know if I will keep it."

With those words, the vampire master exited the cell and commanded one of the guards to go back in the cell and chain the prisoner.

If agony had tormented Grime before, it had grown tenfold now. Would his own sister be in alliance with the vampires? It could not be! If she was, then why go through all trouble? Why not come directly and speak with him?

It was a trick, it had to be! The vampires are not to be trusted; Grime already knew that. And he would not proceed with the extraction of the life essence. He could not trust that the others or himself was going to be set free.

He had to work out some kind of plan. An escape plan. He probably needed help from the outside and the only person he could think of was his sister. But what if that part was actually true? What if his sister was indeed in collaboration with the vampire overlord?

Then his attempt would fail, nevertheless.

If not…

A thought was born in Grime's mind, a thought he kept well hidden, just in case there was someone powerful enough to know mind-reading or mind-control. He had to be very careful with each step. It just might work. Maybe. Yes, it was plausible he could pull it off.

First step of course was to stay alive. And healthy. He needed time. How could he negotiate for more time?

First piece of the puzzle. This would be a complex thing to pull off. And the more he thought about it, the more likely it was that he would succeed. If he was not deceived by his own hope.

That was also a factor to calculate.

But maybe, just maybe. He would have to sacrifice one or two of the girls.

May the creator greet them well in the afterlife.

**thirty five**


Roy Hicks stayed under the trees the rest of the day, looking out at the rain and felt kind of sorry for himself.

In a way, he fully understood why they had taken everything from him and left him out here, but on the other hand, he was still a young man, and like everybody else he made mistakes and tried to learn from them. Sure, he had cheated his way through life on many occasions, but he still thought his punishment was undeserved.

But she was worth it. Every single second, and every questionable action that lead up to that point. Now he could live on those few precious moments for the rest of his life.

Chills went down his spine as he thought about it, and his body reacted with arousal as he thought about it.

Even if he easily could say, and mean it, stealing from others is always wrong. Never the less, the thrill he felt when he took the mayor's key, and the power he felt when using it, unlocking all the places other people could only dream about visiting, seeing things no one would believe if he spoke about it.

When he took the key, he was not aware of her, not at all. He passed many secret passages, doors and rooms. Opened some of them, peeked at the hidden wealth and treasures of the city.

In one room, he saw the jaws of a dragon, still filled with teeth. To Roy this meant that the legends of the dragons became history, not legends.

In another room, there was a most beautiful crystal forest in miniature. Complete trees, rocks, moss, leaves, sticks, all made of delicate and colorful, perfectly mimicked, crystals. Below the creation there seemed to flow a glowing river of something he did not know what it was, that gave the entire forest illumination. In the crystal forest, he could see tiny creatures, both animals and what seemed to be people, all alive. The room was large, and the forest would easily cover twice the space of the central city square.

Another room was filled with so much gold, silver and gemstones that the mighty dwarf masters would be filled with envy for the rest of their long lives, and no matter how much they plundered the mountains of its treasures, they would ever be able to gather even half the riches of this chamber.

Roy Hicks spent almost two full days and nights in the gigantic underground city exploring before he found the room with her.

A more beautiful creature had never existed in the creator's good world.

Her skin was light green, almost shimmering, and her eyes was large and deep blue. Her red hair stood wild from her head and swirled down her shoulders in a lively dance.

She had not a single piece of clothes on her body and oh, the goodness of the creator, she needed none.

Roy Hicks did not know what to do, maybe for the first time in his life (but not the last), so he just stood there, quietly staring for a very long time and it was not until she laughed (this perfect, pearling, giggling laugh) and waved at him to come into the room that he could do anything else than just stand there.

As he thought about it, the time he spent in that room was the happiest twenty hours of his life.

They didn't talk much, in fact, he remembered every single word they exchanged.

First, he said:

"Uh… hmm… ehr… I… ehh.."

Then she laughed at him again, and the next time he opened his mouth it was to say:

"I… eh…. who…. I mean…. like…. uhm…"

Then she just looked at him with her big blue eyes and he felt like he drowned in an eternity.

There was nothing sexual about her, even if she was completely naked, there was only this feeling of complete happiness, perfect harmony, inner peace, stillness and joy.

She enjoyed his company, somehow, he knew that, and come to think of it, the actually never talked… strange… it felt like they talked, they exchanged so much… but what was it? Not words, more like…. feelings… yes, that's it, they exchanged feelings…

And the last thing he said to her, just before being dragged out of the room by the guards was:

"I… think…. I…. love…" then he was hit in the head by one of the guards and did not remember anything else until he found himself in front of the mayor.

**thirty six.**

Veron put on his finest clothes, then slowly, with the respect it demanded, applied the thin but strong silver-plated armor. Last, but certainly not least, he took his helmet on. The other dwarves in the delegation would be protected by the shield bearers, but as the flag bearer he would go in front of them all, unprotected. Solely dependent on his own skills as a fighter, which Veron knew was limited, no, rephrase that to very limited. Should they get attacked by either humans, vampires or werewolves he would most likely be the first to fall victim of the other parties aggressivity. He was also the one who had the responsibility to negotiate if the need for it arose. Veron was not overly enthusiastic about his duties, but more than overly thrilled to be able to go to the surface, to walk up there, see all the beauty it offered. Even if he was a dwarf and belonged beneath the surface, he had a constant longing for the world above. The fresh air. The sunlight. The colors. The softness. The beauty. So even if he himself thought he was insane for accepting this mission, he thought it worth the risks to get the chance to be up there, at least for the duration of the delegation. Should all go well he would return here. Maybe advance a degree or two for completing this mission, but he would still be stuck down here. Below the mountain.

As he exited his chamber Saculg joined him as he walked towards the great hall. Saculg was very excited, he wanted to join the delegation, but he knew he was to young and too inexperienced. He bombarded Veron with a thousand questions, questions Veron would not know how to answer until he had returned and completed the task.

So mostly he opened his mouth to capture some air to try and give a reply or ask Saculg to ask him again when he returned, but he never got a chance to say anything before a new question had been raised.

As they reached the great hall Saculg was lost in the throng of the lively preparations.

Veron reported ready and got his orders, his negotiation tables (which is the amounts he should offer in the given situations and how much he could offer to raise the payment if he was asked to do it) and the rules of engagement. As always, the negotiation table was getting as much as possible for as little as possible and the rules of engagement was: none. Do not engage with any other species until absolutely necessary. Take the long way around if possible. No ransom would be paid for their release, it was cheaper to send a new delegation.

Veron sighed. Even if dwarves are known to be greedy and cheap, it was hard to hear that the value for his life was almost nothing to the others. They would probably grieve more over the loss of the silver flag stand and the beautiful flag, than over the lost life of the dwarf that was carrying it. Veron wondered if the greed was a trait of their kind, or a product of their way of life. Living isolated underground must have its toll when it comes to interacting with others and not only among themselves.

Well, Veron hoped that he should not need to use the rules of engagement nor his limited negotiation table. He played with the thoughts of putting in his personal treasures, if it could possibly save their lives, but he knew that it would mean political suicide and most likely he would be excluded from the clan and be forced to move to the abandoned parts of the mines, along with the other non-worthy dwarves. A dwarf that cared so little for richness and wealth was a danger to the whole dwarf society, he knew that, but at the same time… wasn't it worth more to be alive?

The horn sounded. Time to get going. Helmet on. Gear secured. Flag stand ready. Flag attached. Now the climb towards the outside and the sunlight.

## thirty seven

It was truly a sight for sore eyes, this little man, with long beard and wild hair sticking out beneath the helmet. The man was not taller than a human child at the age of five or so, but the whole appearance gave a different impression. The determined look on his face, his strong arms and legs that looked like they had done their fair share of hard physical work. One underarm alone was almost as wide as a grown man's fist, and the hands seemed too big compared to the rest of the body, but they looked strong and could probably easy break a bone or two in your own hand, if you were to shake his hand while saying something that would deeply offend him.

He was dressed in the finest fabrics and in some lights, it seemed that the fabric itself was shimmering.

It was easy to see that this little man was not used to move in the forest at all. Studying his movements with only that as a reference, you could see that he was working hard to get his body moving, and the effort could easily translate to a great speed in whatever terrain. But looking at the environment around him, it seemed that the effort for three steps only took him one forward. More will and power than agility it seemed.

This was typical for dwarves in general, and it was no difference for Grand Master Phidas. Or former Grand Master Phidas. Now he was only Master Phidas, or no, scratch that, only Phidas, and from the dwarf community hardly worth his dwarf name.

But as strange as it may seem, this dwarf was more at peace with himself than he had been for many, many years now, almost an age, but who was counting?

In fact, for each step he put behind him, Phidas felt his burden ease.

He was not sure what he could do, one dwarf (not that any dwarf ever should be underestimated, they are a resourceful race) do against the entire vampire clan? As if the odds were not uneven from the start, the life essence he traded years ago had most likely been used to enhance them in some way. Or giving one a greater power. Either way, he had the element of surprise on his side. He only had to make it to the great fields, cross them without getting consumed by the undead, find his way through the eastern forest and locate their stronghold and then attack somehow. With something. One dwarf. Against several vampires. In their home base.

"Madness!" he muttered to himself as he walked on, breathing heavily.

"Utterly, pure madness!"

He did not have any clue as to what he was supposed to do once he got there. He just knew that he had to go. Not for the dwarves. No, at this stage he had stopped caring what was best for the dwarves. Now he thought of what was best for the entire world. All beings. And at himself. This was his chance to repay for the benefits he had given the vampires. Repay for all the help he had given them. Even if it would cost him his precious life in the process. It most likely would. Hopefully not too soon though. He hoped he would reach his destination, no, rephrase that, his destiny, and make some serious damage before his last breath.

Damned be the softness of the ground! He longed to feel the hard rock beneath his feet again. But he had to pass this, overcome it. Rise above it somehow.

**thirty eight.**


With Groll still sitting on her shoulder, Dee approached what had once been the harbour camp of her village. Tadao and Leola waited a bit behind for an unclear reason.

Whatever had happened here must have happened quick and swift. The fence that used to run around the camp lay useless and scattered on the ground. All buildings and huts had signs of heavy violence. Everywhere there were arrows, both silver headed, iron headed, and stone headed. Looked like they had used all they got to defend themselves. Did not look like they made it through.

There were no bodies in the entire camp, or rather, what was left of the camp. Whatever that meant Dee could only imagine. She knew that there was both werewolves and vampires nearby.

Neither Dee nor Groll said anything. Groll did not even mutter. They both understood that whatever had taken place here had been quick and without mercy. Even so, the lack of bodies, both human and from the attackers, puzzled Dee.

They did not spend more than ten or fifteen minutes in what was once the harbour camp. There was simply no point.

The four continued in silence. Dee was worried. If the harbour camp looked like this, how did her village look? Had they made it?

It was easy to follow the path now, and after a short while they came to the point where Dee left the path to rescue herself just a few days ago. Yet it felt like a lifetime ago.

It's odd how a person can change in a short timeframe when exposed to different circumstances and environments. She was still sixteen, but she felt like she had aged and matured a lot. The foolish decision to run away without permission felt wrong, yet it was the single most important decision to the huge changes she had gone through the last days.

Meeting Groll, Tadao and his bird, learning that Rick was gone, meeting Leola. Learning that things might not always be as she has been thought.

Being on her own for the first time in her life, without her father or Rick. Spending time outside in this horrible world, that just did not seem so horrible, and yet even more horrible than she ever had imagined before.

She had been close to the evil forces of this world, but not yet seen exactly how evil they were, she could only imagine from what she had seen now.

About halfway between the harbour camp there started to be traces of battle again. First alone, stray arrows. The closer they got, the more signs there were. Damages on trees, large areas where the ground was a total mess, moss ripped off by the roots, revealing bare dirt and roots from the surrounding trees and rocks that had not seen daylight in ages. Large chunks of bushes were ripped apart and the familiar surroundings of the path had turned to a horrid wasteland. Completely unrecognizable. Yet the path itself seemed fairly untouched.

Dee knew that just in just a little while they would reach the buffer tower, the same she had been sneaking around just a few days ago, to stay undetected.

The buffer tower was a manned tower and acted as an early alarm system if there should ever come an attack from the ocean.

The tower reported with horns back to the village. Should the horn sound the guards in the village had about ten minutes to prepare for a rapid attack, maybe fifteen if the front did not advance quicker than walking pace.

In the evening, the horns were replaced by a fire, and one guard had the task to constantly observe it. In case of an attack the tower would put the fire out by throwing it down on the hay bales that were spread around like a low wall. This way the tower would see the attackers better and the village would know when something was wrong.

But the hay bales were still intact, or rather, no one had tried to light them up, but they looked like a mess. It was almost like a horde had ran over it, leaving hay all over the place, and the once so tidy hay bales beaten beyond recognition.

It was hard for Dee to see; she knew that this meant that there had been an attack on the village itself as well. That also meant that anything could have happened to her father. She dared not think of all the things that might have happened, she just hurried down the path towards the village. She could not stand the thought of having lost her father as well. That pain would be unbearable. The others had a hard time of keeping up with Dee. Only Groll made her company in the front, and for once, he was completely quiet, as if he understood the agony inside her, and let her be alone with her thoughts, without intervening.

**Thirty nine.**

Veron enjoyed this, the outdoors. At first, or rather still, it was hard for the eyes to adapt to the sunlight. Too bright, and Veron was grateful for the tiny openings in his helmet. He figured that this applied to all the members of the delegation.

Being used to work with various heavy tools to conquer the mountain and reveal its secrets, carrying the silver flag stand was a physical relief. Like an ant that normally carried sticks back to the hive that suddenly got hold of a tiny leaf. Or a straw. Come to think of it, more like a straw.

And all this fresh air… If the creator ever created an afterlife for the dwarves, the air in the mines of the afterlife was like this. Fresh. With a nice breeze. And all kinds of strange and exotic fragrances. It was almost like being reborn.

From what Veron could hear from the rest of the tightly shielded delegation members, they did not share his enthusiasm of being on the ground instead of under it.

He sighed, he was definitely born in the wrong body, or in the wrong era. Maybe in the future it would be accepted for dwarves to walk the world as an equal to man. But if he would do it now, he would be an outcast to both mankind and the entire dwarf society. Even among the outcasts of the dwarves. There was simply no place for a dwarf somewhere else, except in the mines.

Someone from the back yelled at him to slow down, but Veron just continued. As long as he held the flag, they had to follow him, he led the way, he set the pace, he decided when to rest, when to walk, talk, eat and sleep. And the responsibility was his alone.

The first night Veron had them camp in the middle of the forest, close to a rill. And as they sat by the campfire that night, one of the delegation members started to hum. Now, the dwarves were widely known for their creativity and their skill with rocks and metal. They were not especially famous for their singing capabilities. Nevertheless, they had a traditional tune, The Hymn of the Dwarves, and it was something every dwarf knew by heart and once every now and then, one of them started to sing it. In fact, this was their only tune for singing. That is why everybody knew it. Veron hardly slept that night. He was too thrilled to be on the surface.

The next morning, they took off again. It must be a pretty impressive sight to see the delegation pass. One silver flag in the front, then a squad of five silver shields long and three silver shields wide. On top, they were only shielded by their helmets. For now. Should they need, the dwarves in the middle could add additional shielding on top, but they now carried them on their backs to save their strength to when they might need it. IF they would need it.

Most other flag-bearers would lead the delegation by night, and rest in hiding by day, so the sun would not blind their eyes. But Veron liked the daylight and would enjoy it as much as he could, no matter what the others thought. Even though he knew that it put them in greater risk in running into others, except maybe vampires, but that was not the greatest of his concerns.

This journey was expected to take at least twenty days. And the visit in the northern province at least two, and then the return trip. This meant that Veron had a total of 42 days in freedom from the mines. And he was going to make each of those 42 days' worth while.

He had studied the maps of the known world, so he knew a little about what to expect and where to expect it. He had memorized all possible camps, good places to rest where they could find water and prepare their meals. Where they could stop for provisioning. He had planned a route for them that would take them through as varied environment as possible.

In all honesty, this was probably not the safest route, but it was the route that would enrich Veron as much as possible. He wished to see the different types of forests, see all kinds of landscapes, follow free, running water, watch it float still and steady, see cliff formations and pass by other mountains. Yes, he was still a dwarf, and he loved the mountains, no doubt about that.

Even if the biggest part of him wished for an eventless journey, a small part of him wished for an adventure. Something that he would remember for the rest of his life. Something that would redefine him as a person, maybe even earn him some respect among the other species. Or change the way the others looked at dwarves entirely.

In a way, both parts of him would be right. This journey to the northern province was rather uneventful.

**forty.**

The vampire master entered the room, swinging the door so hard that it almost broke against the wall. Grime almost crapped his pants as he was far from reality in his daydreams that he invoked to get time going in this terrible chamber.

From the grin on the vampire masters face, Grime could tell that his rapid entrance had the desired effect on the prisoner.

"Well, Grime…" the vampire master looked at the prisoner with an expression that was hard to read, either it was concealed hope or masked abomination, or something completely different that Grime could not interpret.

"Have you made your decision yet? Do you want to stay alive, save some of the girls and get out of here in one piece, or have you chosen the high road, trying to serve some divine idea in a misguided attempt to try and save this world and keep it as it is?" Grime felt the impatience in the master's voice. Maybe he could use it somehow.

"Well, first I want to know exactly what it is that you ask of me, even if I have my suspicions. And then I will need time to plan how I should proceed to reach optimal result, maybe even gather some things that cannot be found here. Only then I can present what solution I can provide. Should you accept it, even if it does not meet your requirements completely, we can reach an agreement, but I need to have some insurance and will not act in good faith alone."

Grime hoped that this answer would provoke the master and in doing so, maybe reveal more than he intended in the first place.

"Let's be clear on one point, Grime, I will not ever give you any insurance, this is not negotiable whatsoever, either you do what I ask you to do, or you will die, simple as that."

"What is it, exactly, that you ask of me?" Grime asked, pretending to be a bit scared, this just might work.

"I want to be able to reproduce. Our numbers decrease in a concerning rate. Should this continue, we as a species will not survive." the vampire master answered, swallowing the bait, as Grime had hoped. That was just the piece of information he needed.

"Reproduce? You mean mating and having children? That is something beyond me! I am not nearly that powerful, I do not think anyone are!" Grime answered, pretending to be terrified.

"But I have something different in mind." the vampire master replied, falling for Grime's theatrical performance.

"When humans mate, they share a small piece of the life essence from the mother and the father, merging it into one inside the mother's wound. There it matures, collecting energy from everywhere. Balance is kept." Now the vampire master smiled confident, "should we mate the same way, our lack of blood would keep the baby from growing and gathering energy, so there would be no new life." Triumphant he continued. "Now, what I have in mind would not only shorten the time to create new life, but it would also mean that we would be able to reproduce exponentially. But before I say more, I need you to prove yourself to me. You can do so in one of two ways, or both if you prefer. Either you rape one of the girls that I have chosen from you, or you kill her. Either way you will cause her pain."

Now Grime did not act, he was terrified for real. The color left his face and in no time, he was almost as pale as the vampire master himself.

"I.... eh... is it really necessary? What if I need all ten girls to perform what you ask of me?" he heard himself say.

"In that case, I will capture some more. Bring her in! Let the prisoner loose!" he ordered and a guard immediately freed Grime and another brought in one of the girls. She looked young, maybe twelve or so…

Grimes stomach reacted and emptied itself right there and then. He felt awful.

The vampires left and locked the door. Grime was left alone with this scared little girl, still hearing the harsh laughter of the vampire master as he walked down the hallway outside the door.

## forty one

As they approached the outer fence of the village Dee could tell that there was something out of the ordinary.

There were a lot fewer guards patrolling the fence, but even so, the village looked unharmed from here. Could be that the elders had sent out everybody that could fight outside of the fences, after all, they had walked through a battlefield on their way here.

She tried to get one of the guard's attention, but he just walked away in the other direction, so their only option was to circle around to the main entrance to the village.

On their way around Dee got more and more anxious, the village did not look anything near the one she left a few days ago. She barely recognizes it.

At the gates, she asked for her father. She had a bad feeling, did not recognize any of the guards.

As one of the guards went inside to check with the active commander, she asked the remaining guard what had happened.

He looked at her as if he did not understand the question.

"What happened here? We passed what seems to be the remainder of a battlefield on our way here. And the harbour camp is wiped out." Dee tried again.

The guard looked strangely at her again.

"Yes, we took the harbour camp when we got here, then we took this vil…" he muted abruptly as his commanding officer came out of the booth. The commander had a distinct look on his face, and Dee did not like it.

"This man you ask for… your father…." the commander said.

"He died in the attacks… There is nothing for you here… I suggest you leave right away… We have no use for a little girl, an old woman, a…. whatever that thing is… However…" the commander turned to Tadao:

"We could make use of you, if you are willing to work hard, we can provide you food and shelter… It's a harsh world here… I doubt the lot of you will survive more than a few days…"

Tadao hesitated… Dee hated him for even consider this offer…

"I think it is time for us to continue our journey…" Tadao said, talking to Dee, Groll and Leola.

"There is nothing for us here, and I would prefer to get as far away from this village as possible, before the nightfall…"

With those words the four of them continued to walk inland.

Dees thoughts ran all over the place. Who were those men, what had happened to her father? A part of her knew that her father was still alive, but she was afraid that it was wishful thinking, rather than intuition. And on the other hand, what had happened with all the people in the village? Sure, it was a fairly large village, but she recognized just about everyone by their looks, even if she did not know their name or had ever talked to them. All those men were new to her, they had a strange accent when they talked, and the guard had said when they came, they took the harbour camp. Could it be an invasion of the cold bloods to get a stronghold or a province here in the northern parts? No matter how hard she tried to bring order to her thoughts, something just did not add up. There was a piece of the puzzle missing. And her father, he was certainly missing.

Where was he? A string of bad conscious hit her hard inside. If she only had obeyed him. Or at least said goodbye somehow. Now she did not know if she ever could say that she loved him again. Or hug him. Tears filled her eyes as they walked away from her home village, heading inland.

**forty two (the answer without question)**

The horns echoed in the chambers of the northern dwarf province as Veron approached King Thidas throne room.

This was a rare occasion indeed. Only once before, as far as Veron could recall, had there been a delegation of this magnitude, and that was six or seven ages ago, when the old king Midas had died, leaving his split kingdom to his two sons. He had lived a long life, even for a dwarf, and during his rule the dwarf kingdom had expanded further than any king before him had been able to do. To start a province in the northern mountains had proven very fortunate, and the taxes that the province paid every year compensated well for the ever-decreasing findings in the main mountain. True, the expansion to the west was necessary and very sound in terms of profit, but everybody knew (even if no one ever mentioned it) that the dwarf society was very depending of all the rich findings in the northern province.

Come to think of it, the only delegations lately had been quarrels over how much tax that should be paid, and Thidas had done a very good job of lowering the tax burden for the northern province. This was one of the reasons for his great support back home, and probably the main reason why he was most likely to take over as king of the entire dwarf domains now when Grand Master Phidas was no longer in service, wherever he was…

"Who may I welcome to my domain?" King Thidas voice broke the silence after the horns had stopped echoing.

"Veron of the Ingm clan, from the great dwarf mines in the west. I come bearing news!"

"What news would that be, messenger from Ingm clan?" King Thidas demanded to know.

"First, I want to apologize for not bringing any official gift. The heads of our clans could not come to terms and find a fitting gift, for reasons I will come to later…" Veron paused and put his hand inside his armor and reached deep under it and pulled out something wrapped in a piece of cloth.

"…I hope you can accept this humble gift from my personal collection instead." he unwrapped the cloth and handed over a large crystal, clear but with a tiny stream of white smoke in the center.

"The Heaven Stone!" King Thidas whispered with great anticipation in his voice.

"Rumor states that you are currently in possession of three of the legendary stones and wish to collect them all. The Heaven Stone has been in my family since the Great King decided to divide the Legendary stones." Venom continued, but King Thidas did not pay much attention to what he was saying, since he had his eyes fixed on The Heaven Stone.

Venom waited for the traditional request from King Thidas where he was supposed to ask for the message, but since the King seemed to have forgotten all about Dwarf traditions now, Veron choose to continue:

"I bear news from the West. Your brother, Grand Master Phidas, is no longer with us. We request that you oversee the election of a new leader or appoint one at your discretion."

King Thidas did not respond.

Veron got tired of keeping to protocol, so he walked over to King Thidas and handed him The Heaven Stone.

"Here is the fourth of the Legendary Stones, my king, only three to go!"

King Thidas looked with great eyes on the latest addition to his great treasures, but still did not say anything. Veron thought it best to return to his position in front of the throne and wait until spoken to.

**forty three.**

Roy had spent the night shivering in a bush under a large tree. At least it was not raining, but the nights in the valley was really cold. As he stretched his long and skinny body, slowly rising from the cover of the bush, he felt a cold morning breeze running all over his naked skin. It was dawn, and a bit misty, and even if he still shivered, he could truly see the beauty of the landscape. In front of him was a large open grass field. Fortunate enough it was not part of the Great Plains, so the chance of running into undead was minimal, even if the risk is always there outside the protection of the villages or cities.

As he stood there and watched the first beams of the rising sun touching the ground a rather large house appeared out of thin air in front of him. Seconds passed, and suddenly the only door he could see on the house was opened with great force, and a large man walked out. The man looked worn and had an almost hysteric exit from the building. As he walked out his entire appearance changed to a mix of relief and happiness. He stopped suddenly, just steps away from the door, lay down on the ground and kissed it and hugged it as best as he could.

Roy could not really tell if this was really happening, or if this was a weird part of dream, and as he watched the scene, he expected to wake up any time. But the scene kept playing in front of him, and equally sudden the house disappeared into thin air, leaving the man still laying on the ground. Then like nothing was out of the ordinary, he rose, brushed of the remains of the grass and dirt that covered his strange clothing, and like that, he vanished as well.

This was indeed the strangest thing Roy Hicks had ever seen, and little did he expect that this was only the beginning of his adventures to come.

As he stood there expecting to wake up from this weird dream, he saw another thing that convinced him that this truly was a dream.

Out of the forest came a dwarf, long beard, helmet and all. Any other day, this would have been an extraordinary sight, but now it felt completely natural, and Roy expected the dwarf to vanish as well. But to his surprise, the little dwarf did not vanish, but he was not surprised when the dwarf stopped just in front of him and spoke.

"It's none of my business, but I am curious, I have never seen a man standing naked outside in the middle of nowhere, looking cold like you."

Roy laughed.

"Well, even if I am naked in this dream of mine, I am sad to say that I will be naked when I wake up."

The dwarf muttered.

"You will be disappointed then. This is no dream, and I suggest you get going as soon as you can, both to keep you warm and to avoid what is coming."

"What do you mean 'what is coming'?" Roy asked, not sure he believed the little strange dwarf.

"Been walking all night, thought I heard some werewolves close by. For me, that does not really matter, they do not like the taste of me, but you… that is a different matter altogether."

When the dwarf mentioned werewolves, Roy did not hesitate much. Whether this was a dream or not, werewolves were not a pleasant meeting, so he hurried out from the bushes, as much as he could, without scratching himself on the branches or anything else. The last thing he wanted was an open wound when werewolves was nearby.

"So, Master Dwarf, where might you be heading, and would you be in need of the services of this poor soul, in exchange for food and clothing?"

"Clothing I can arrange, just because I pity you, but I know better than trust a naked human in the middle of nowhere, seems to me your word is no good and your honor even worse." Phidas said, not looking at the naked man, nor slowing down or changing his heading.

"Well, I can't blame you for that, Master Dwarf, but I would be truly grateful if you could help me with clothing and whatever else you can spare." Roy answered with renewed hope in his voice. This just might be a good day after all.

**Forty four.**

Grime tried to grasp the full situation. He needed to come up with something solid. He had no time to do it, and the girl's sobbing did not help.

He had to do something. If he knew the Vampire Master, there was eyes and ears watching, to see if he could be trusted.

"Undress" he whispered to the girl. "Take off all your clothes."

The girl did not move a muscle, but her sobbing escalated heavily.

"Do not force my hand… I need you to take off all your clothes…"

The girl looked at him and her red eyes begged him for mercy.

"Are you going to kill me?" she asked with a faint voice.

"Not unless I have to…" he heard himself answer.

She started to undress as she understood that there was no mercy from this man. Even if there was a possibility there was good in him, she heard what the Vampire Master said. Rape her or kill her, or it would be the end of it.

As she undressed and stood completely naked in front of him, she felt his eyes wandering over her young and untouched body. This was not how she had imagined her first experience with a man.

"If you kill me, can you please get word out to my mother and father, and my brothers and sisters, and my cousins…"

Grime looked at her. Had he not been a prisoner between cold stone walls, the view of this naked young girl would have been tempting, too tempting he had to admit to himself. She was not yet of age to be married or to be with a man, and these stone walls and the entire situation made the thought of being with her even more impossible.

One side of him was grateful for that, another side thought it was a pity.

"How many sisters do you have?" he said, with his thoughts in a distance.

"Two, and four brothers" she answered, feeling inconvenient and tried to cover herself using her arms and hands.

Something came over Grime and he snapped back to presence in the cell.

"Your mother, does she have any sisters?" he looked at her with renewed eyes, and she could not tell if it was lust or something else that drove him.

"I have two aunts… My mother is the youngest of the three…" she said, not knowing where this was going.

"…and your sisters, are they older than you?"

"Yes, and my brothers as well… I am the youngest..."

Grime took a few steps forward. Touched her gently on her stomach.

"Have you ever been with a man before?"

She embraced herself mentally, this was really happening, this was it…

"No…"

To her surprise, the prisoner rushed to the door and started to pound it with both fists.

"Get me your Master, right away! It's important..." he yelled.

She stood there waiting, the man did not look at her anymore, he avoided her. He did not yell or pound. He just stood there, with his head leaning on the cold stone wall.

She could not tell for how long, but she did not dare to move. Still trying to cover herself as best as she could, still waiting and preparing for the worst. Why did he not look at her, why didn't he kill her or touch her?

It felt like forever, and then the door opened, and the Vampire Master reentered.

Grime had learned from experience not to start to talk before he was spoken to. The Vampire Master walked into the room, looked at Grime, looked at the naked girl.

"She is still standing, untouched, alive… Why?" he said with his low, almost growling voice.

"She is pure, the third daughter of a third daughter. I'll gladly kill her right here, but she is pure, and it would be a terrible waste. I could make good use of her, but I need her untouched and pure…"

The Vampire Master did not answer…

"If you want me to prove myself, that I am loyal to my word, give me one of the other girls, preferably one of the oldest you have. It is a better chance that she bleeds, and if so, she will not be as pure as this one. And I doubt that you are so lucky that you will have two girls that are the third daughter of the third daughter..."

The Vampire Master walked around the cell for a while. Looked at Grime, looked at the naked girl.

"Very well…" he said as he left…

A few minutes later, a guard came and ordered the girl to get dressed, brought her out of the room and put the chains back on Grime.

**forty five.**

The visit in the Northern province was over for the time being. Veron had a bad feeling about it. King Midas had not spoken to either one of them and there had been no dialog whatsoever. After the first audience in King Midas chamber the whole of the delegation had been shown to a remote room near the entrance to the mines. They had been instructed to stay there and wait for further instructions. After two days Achim had come to introduce himself. Achim was the second in command after King Midas, and he had asked Veron to lead him back to the mines, the safest and quickest route as possible, the rest of the delegation was ordered to stay behind for the time being.

Veron felt that it was very awkward since they all longed back to familiar caves and rocks.

But they could not defy their new orders.

Two legion squads protected Achim and in front of them all Veron walked alone with the flag proudly waving in the wind. This time Veron figured that he could as well take the large routs and skip all caution and try to stay hidden. Two legion squads could not easily hide anywhere, except below ground, but here in the open, pointless to try. Achim did not seem too pleased with the route, and constantly sent runners asking if they could take a more suited route for passage in discretion. Veron gave the same answer every time.

"Where can more than thousand dwarfs hide on the surface?"

Even so, Achim kept sending runners with the same request, and what could have been an eventless and calm return trip turned out to be an annoying and far from eventless journey, even if nothing dangerous occurred. Veron thought to himself that the only danger on this journey was of him losing his mind from the nagging question of a childish and scared second in command.

It was a true relief when they arrived back home again, but when Veron saw all the soldiers that kept flowing through the entrance he realized that this was nothing but an invasion, peaceful, but still an invasion. Nothing good could come out of this.

Achim summoned the head of the clans as soon as he had taken his first breath of real air, not the humid and frisky air of the surface, but the still and rocky air of the mines.

He did not have much to say, but his word troubled them all, realizing that this was a new and darker era in the dwarf history.

"All you who are guardians of one of the legendary stones, come forth and bring your stone. King hereby overrules the old decision to keep them apart. Should I not have all stones by nightfall I will give my legions orders to search the mines and authorize any means to find them. We have been tracking the whereabouts of the stones a long time and have a good idea where to start looking. So, you are all wise to show your loyalty to King Thidas by bringing them forth without the use of force. These terms are not negotiable."

Veron had never heard a silence this deep in the great hall. This was indeed an invasion and life as they knew it had ended. This new era would be led by greed and violence. Veron made a very easy decision. It was time to leave. Most likely Achim would like to go back, or at least send someone or something back to King Thidas shortly. That journey would give Veron the possibility he needed to leave.

He looked at all the faces around him. Some of them looked at him to seek answers on where their loved ones were, some of them looked at him wondering why he brought this madness back to them, all realizing that he could not control the events only follow as the rest of them. But yes, it was time to leave the dwarf society for good. He figured he had a few days to make all the necessary arrangements. Saculg would get to take his place and his living quarters, after all, he was too old to live by his parents anyway.

Before Veron was about to make a silent exit from the great hall he heard Achim request the hundred best diggers and miners to report to him for a special mission.

**forty six.**

No other girl was taken to Grime and he was not chained again. Odd, but on the other hand, the Vampire Master was not one that acted predictable.

Grime wandered around in his cold cell, counting the stones of the walls, trying to figure out what he would do next. Time passed slowly and if not the time, it had to be Grime's thoughts. Counting the stones of the wall became counting the times he had counted the stones, and it transformed in trying to calculate the steps he had taken for each turn he completed in this terrible chamber. This dark and evil place that took advantage and used the worst sides of him. Pride and hope were far from Grime at this moment. His selfish desire to survive, somehow escape, maybe even be released, made his creativity visit and use the darkest corners of his soul, of his entire being. A place where he could find much inspiration, very needed inspiration. He needed to sacrifice some of the girls, at least one, to prepare something that the Vampire Master would buy as loyalty. He could not see any other way. He had to do it. He prepared to do it. Once set in motion, there was no turning back. He would need to give the dark Master what he wanted.

With part of a plan, some ideas and guts almost worked up he sent message that he wished an audience, the sooner the better.

To his surprise, he was taken from his cell right away, taken a different route through the old castle, this time to a different location, probably below ground level.

Along the sides there was torches, at least a dozen on each side. In the middle there was five empty wooden tables, each measuring at least six-man lengths.

In the far end of the room there was a cage, inside it the girls.

Grime was expecting the master to hide in the dark somewhere, but to his surprise he was not present in the room at first.

As Grime waited, he got closer to the cage to get a look at the girls. A decision had to be made, at least one of them would not make it out. Sacrifice one and maybe be able to save the others.

No, that would be too obvious. He needed to do something more. But did he really need to kill? He understood that it all had to be done by his hands.

No, only kill one. But what more?

At least three of the girls was a little older. With any luck they would be bleeders.

He could use that, both for his own pleasure and to save them. But it would require much time. Could he convince the dark master of the necessity of this?

It could work. It was the best he had to go on, and buying time was much needed. A part of a plan and some ideas was not going to let him escape nor alive, so yes, getting more time was essential.

As he stood there, watching the girls, he was startled by the sudden appearance of the Vampire Master right in front of him, between him and the cage.

Grime knew he was not supposed to talk first, even so he could not wait, he needed to act confident if this would have a chance of succeeding.

"I am ready, let me know what you have in mind. I have a few ideas of my own, but I am curious to hear what you have in mind."

"Before I tell you, let me know what you are thinking…" the Vampire Master was cautious.

"I was thinking two things, and depending on what I can get from that, I can get clues on what the most suitable next step will be. First, I need to see how you feed, both when you actually feed on a person, then compare what happens when you drink blood, without feeding. I would like to use one of the girls, preferably a pure, but not the one I met earlier. Then I am thinking that I could us unborn babies, different stages, to see if I can harvest some of the merged life essence from them. From what I can tell there are at least three of the girls that are bleeders, and if so, I would like to make sure they get pregnant myself, this way I can follow all the stages and see when harvesting are the most suitable for the different stages. Of course, all of this with your approval, Master..."

The master did not speak at first, and for each passing breath Grime thought that his own death was closing in faster and faster.

"You may proceed with your plans, keep me informed of the progress. As for my plan, I suspect your thoughts may be in the same direction. I believe feeding is the key to use to procreate. Enhanced feeding could be what we could use instead of breeding. It would be more efficient."

Safe, for now, Grime thought, not trying to reveal any of his relief. A bit ashamed of his scam, but the darkest parts of him was looking very much forward to these new events.

**forty seven**

Dee kept looking back and Groll kept mumbling to her to keep looking forward, but there was something that Dee just could not let go. A strange feeling that she could not resist.

Tadao was certainly in a hurry and advanced as quickly as he could, leading this motley crew. But not as the alpha male of a wolf pack, rather like a frightened rabbit, fleeing a predator.

He did not even stop when Dee burst into tears and cried, sobbing something incoherent about home sweet home and fell down on her knees. Groll almost crash-landed on the ground next to her and Leola stopped and tried to bring Dee back on her feet again.

Leola shouted to Tadao to come and help her, or stop or at least slow down, but he just continued, did not even look back.

"Humans..." Groll muttered as he saw Tadao disappear among the trees in front of them. "...had hope I did, but not for you, only her..." he turned his focus to Dee again only to get distracted by two things simultaneously.

The first thing was that they got company, a few men had followed them from the village and the second thing was a desperate cry echoing from the direction where he last saw Tadao stampeded. The cry sounded like a mixture of human agony and bird shriek. And the hawk left the scene in a straight uprising motion, only to be penetrated by one of the attacker's arrow and drop dead to the ground. Perhaps it would serve as evening supper for the attackers.

Leola only seemed to notice the cry and turned her attention forward away from Dee and away from their followers.

"I'm not sure we can help him." Leola said to Groll with her eyes fixed at an unclear point among the trees ahead.

"...and he cannot help us..." Groll answered with a subtle nod towards the village.

Leola turned around and saw their entourage rapidly closing in on their position. They were all armed with something, cudgel, bow, knife, sword and various other objects that easily could cause them seriously harm if their bearer intended so... and they did not exactly look like they were about to ask them to join them for a cup of bale-root tea and some cookies.

Dee was still in her own despair, unaware of the situation that was about to develop around them.

The three of them surrounded from all directions, trapped like the pray in the middle of the wolf-pack.

Leola considered the use of magic, but something held her back. She was not sure if it were Groll or if it could be one of their attackers. Either way, it was an uncertain situation, magic could backfire if it were not planned or performed carefully, this situation had too much pressure. And besides, if she used magic now, it would be in the open, but if she saved it for a later situation, she would have the element of surprise.

Leola could hear the heavy breathing from some of the closest members of the wolf-pack. By the looks in their face, she had little hope for a friendly and peaceful resolution. The outcome looked at best painful and captivating.

**Forty eight.**

Grime did not have to return to his chains, he was moved to a much bigger room in close proximity to the hall where the girls were held captive.

The room was almost empty, except for a small wooden table, an empty cupboard and what some would refer to as a pile of wood and straw, but it was a much more comfortable bed than lead on by its looks. Not only a suitable place for sleep, but also the place for wonders, he thought to himself.

Grime, filled with hopes that his plan would actually work, called for a guard who entered the room almost before his words had cleared his mouth and throat.

"I will need supplies. Scrolls, ink, coal, feathers to write with... and books, I need a full volume of the Herbal notes, the Stars and Moons of the night sky, the Dwarf mining and minerals for starters. And take me to the girls..." the last few words he spoke with an inner trembling, either of anticipation, sorrow or disgust, or maybe a little of everything...

To his surprise his guardian bloodsucker did not leave the room, but somehow managed to communicate with his kin since more of his kind came along with the requested items, one by one, and he could only conclude that the Master was already in possession of far more things than he would be able to grasp. And at the same time, the insight was a bit comforting, for he could keep requesting things, and maybe even find a sport in requesting things that the Master did not already have.

Well, first things first. Now an inspection of the entire stack of girls. He needed to subside his manners, his questionable sense of right and wrong, now he needed to make a selection to convince the Master of his authenticity, commitment and ability. And at the same time a selection that would satisfy his own lusts. His entire body started to react to his thoughts, and he started to feel greedy, what if he would modify his original plan, not only one, maybe all of them? What would be the harm in that? What if it would be their way to pay him for actually trying to rescue them? Yes, certainly a small price for them to pay. His pleasure for their life, or at least for most of them. A few probably needed to be left behind. Sacrificed for the rest of them, for him. To stage the scene to his Master's approval. His Master... oh no, had he already come to obedience, that easily?

He did not notice that he wandered this new chamber. Nor the activity of his capturers. Then all of a sudden, he stopped, he thought of her. What would she say? Would she approve? He was disgusted with himself and his thoughts in an instant. Trying to convince himself there was no other options. There certainly were no other options! Or was there? No, there was no other way. This was a necessary evil. A necessary sacrifice. A necessary pleasure... A necessary pleasure indeed...

Now he longed to let his eyes inspect the girls, no, not only eyes, his eyes and hands… both mind and body trembled, eyes and hands and...

**Forty nine.**

As the two unlikely traveling companions kept walking, Grand Master Phidas and Roy Hicks started talking and sharing, moving from complete strangers to acquaintances and slowly arriving at being friends, well shallow friends at least.

Roy being who he is just had to satisfy his curiosity and kept bombarding Phidas with questions as to what he, a master dwarf, was doing so far from the mountain and out in the open. Roy had never heard, little less seen, a dwarf wandering around alone in the open without the usual security company and trading goods and carriers.

At first, Roy was a bit uncomfortable about being naked, but after the first day with his new companion, he did not think about it anymore. That was probably why, on their second day of joint walking, he was surprised by the reactions of the traveling trading party they ran into.

At first, they just stared, from Roy to Phidas, from Phidas to Roy, and when Roy greeted them with the usual travelers greeting, the did not reply at first.

Phidas who was unaccustomed to this strange social ritual did not speak, nor had he any intention in getting involved in whatever was going on.

However, Roy found himself quickly in the situation and made up a story of being robbed of all his possessions, before meeting this traveling dwarf master, that promised to help him with clothing.

The oldest of the traders avoided to speak to Roy and turned directly to the dwarf master.

"Is it true, will you provide him with clothes and pay for a strangers bad luck and stupidity?"

Phidas only muttered something but nodded.

The trader stopped his wagon and called back to one of the others to unload some clothes.

So it was, Phidas a gemstone shorter (which value was far above the value of the ragged clothes that now sheltered Roy) and a trading party who laughed and thanked the creator for this unfortunate fool that lead to this magnificent trading-opportunity.

Phidas did not seem to mind that they had gotten the poorer part of the deal, which in itself was unheard of for a dwarf.

Roy was filled with gratefulness and also a little guilt, since he had the feeling that Phidas did not like the fact that he did not tell the truth about how he ended up naked and alone in the middle of nowhere.

Even so, Phidas and Roy continued their unlikely journey, Roy still unaware of their destination.

In a silent part of their joint walking escapade Roy found his thoughts running freely. He did not know where Phidas were headed. Nor did he know where he himself were headed. For the first time in his life Roy had no place to call home, no possessions that needed caring, no family, no friends. He was an outlaw and condemned to walk this world as a beggar, something that he knew very well that he would not manage for long.

He did not feel like a beggar (only those who could survive the wilderness and evil of this world would last), nor saw himself in that wicked state between a poor excluded person and fighting survival legend.

Phidas on his end also drifted in thoughts.

He was so focused on his goal and destination that he had not paid a single thought on what to do or how to do it, to complete his little one-man mission. He considered asking Roy to help him, but he could not ask an innocent (how innocent this man really was could be questioned) man to assist in this mission of redemption.

Maybe a little longer ahead, when he knew more of where Roy was heading and planning to do now. But for the time being, he chose to keep it to himself.

**Fifty.**

Everybody except Groll had traces in various degrees of brutality of their captivators. Fortunately, Dee was still untouched by men, which no one would take for granted in situations like this, nor did anyone dare to utter anything but the faintest hope that she would stay untouched.

Tadao had been beaten the worst and drifted in and out of consciousness as their cage rocked back and forth on the uneven and bumpy road.

Their cage was mounted on an old carrier that was pulled by two horses. The weight from the iron impacted the poor creatures heavy as they struggled forward, whipped by the men of this slave caravan.

Dee thought to herself that if these slavers had captured anybody from the village, they would most likely be in this caravan as well, but as far as she could tell, the four of them was the only slaves of this caravan.

The slavers were not very talkative amongst themselves, but what they did say and how they acted, Dee concluded that they must be cold bloods from down south.

Leola tended Tadao as best she could during the circumstances. She had asked for water and some cloth to tend his wounds and clean of the dried blood all over his body.

She had given them a hard time about beating him so bad, since she expected that they would not get as much for him now that he was incapable of working and probably needed a great deal of time to recover. Bad for their business she yelled at them.

And indeed, their commander had given Tadao's capturers a hard time and had treated the lot of them better since Leola made her point.

Leola hoped that this strategy would give them three things. First and foremost, that they did not take Dee for their own pleasure, or at least not in a while. Second that they would be treated a little better than slaves would be treated otherwise, and third, that they would be given a little time to design an escape plan.

Groll had said nothing since they were liberated from their freedom. Not even to Dee. The slavers had treated him as if he carried a deadly decease and had barley laid hands on him.

Not that he cared about the insult of this behavior, but he could not believe how low the humans had fallen.

He remembered a time when he had lived side by side with the humans. A happy time. When he was not lonely. When he still believed in the good. When there was still love. Still hope. Now. Different story all together.

As Tadao drifted, he did not know his whereabouts, and time and again, he believed he was back on the Glory. Like the past few days had been erased from his conscious mind. He sometimes mistook Leola's caring and believed it was his mother, which he could not understand, she had been dead since before he left on the Glory.

As Leola struggled and bended her mind around the current situation, trying to get a glimpse of the upcoming events, trying to find an escape, but no matter how hard she tried, she could not see a bright future nor see a happy ending to their captivity. One thing she felt rather sure of. Tadao, he was not going to make it. To badly beaten. Should he beat the odds, there was no telling of what his physical and mental scars would be, but she doubted that he would ever come back to the old Tadao she had gotten to know a bit.

**fifty one**

Grime looked up from his books. He had been deep down in every possible book he had requested looking for clues on what he might be able to use to complete this impossible task.

The more he read the more convinced he was that he would be able to complete his masters request, make good of his escape plan including saving some of the girls, but most important, gain a great deal himself in the process.

Initially he had gained physical pleasure, and oh what a pleasure. From his calculations, at least three of the four girls were now carrying, but he did not want to take any chances, so he still had routing daily impregnation rituals. By now, they had gotten used to the procedure and all of them mentally fled the moment, leaving Grime to do as he pleased. Which suited Grime perfectly. This was only satisfying his physical manly needs, while his mind benefitted from the physical reward of the intercourse and contributed positively to his mental challenge.

It had not been hard selecting four of the girls. He inspected them all, naked of course, made sure to closely examine them all using all his senses, touching them, smelling them, tasting them, seeing and hearing their reactions to his various actions.

He knew he had passed the line for all decency, but to himself he justified his questionable actions with having no choice.

Even so, it nagged his mind, like an unwelcome bird tweeting outside the window, day and night, interfering with sleep, focus, daily tasks and most of all, the pureness of his soul.

He knew he polluted it, but this was only the beginning. The constant reminder that the creator intended as an inner sign that you are on the wrong way was transformed into a force of good. Grime was using this moral compass, and the more it told him he was on the wrong way, the more he continued with open eyes and renewed energy. Fully aware that this poison was addictive, fully aware that this would change him entirely, which in fact was part of his plan.

His latest book was covering almost everything there was to know about herbs. And now he was sure that he needed a great deal of herbs to be able to complete the enhancements. Both enhancements.

One thing troubled him. From what he could read and understand from the books, he was pretty sure that he would need to use the roots of a truth flower. And his sister had always warned him about the truth flower, its roots in particular. The flower itself was commonly used to persuade people to tell the truth when one might suspect that they would try to hide it. Its roots, different story all together. While the beautiful and fragile flower gently affected the energy flow to and from the brain and the eyes, the roots affected the heart and the blood flow.

His sources also alerted caution when using the roots, there were several documented experiments involving the root where the subject had bled dry from the tiniest hole in the skin and tissue.

Maybe his sister knew about this and issued the warnings out of concern for his wellbeing. Wellbeing… Grime looked at the time-candle in the end of his long table. Time for the next pleasure round. He definitely could get used to this. No rush in completing the mission too soon…

**fifty two.**

Phidas had gotten used to walking the ground instead of the solid mountain floor he was used to. Roy could notice the increase in pace day by day, not by much, but still noticeable.

After a few days on the road together, they had covered a serious distance, but had not even started walking a little east, which meant that they still had not reached the northern rim of the great plains.

At night, they camped under a tree, making a small fire with what they could find, eating what the nature could provide them with. In the morning they started of early, trying to walk out the cold of their stiff limbs and get the blood flowing in their veins again.

One morning, Roy woke up by Phidas hand poking him really hard, and before he grasped for air, Phidas covered his mouth and nose with his big, strong hand.

This made Roy rapidly leave his sleep and he became wide awake in an instant. He did not for one split second think that Phidas would do him any harm, even if he currently were choking him pretty good and Roy had to struggle to get air.

Phidas pointed a bit further east, about a stone away, an undead was walking mindless in random directions, changing at any given noise.

This was a very rare sight, and Roy almost forgot he had to breath. The undead almost always wandered around in crowds. To see a single individual on its own has practically unheard of.

They both knew that they would have to keep absolutely still and quiet if they wished to stay undetected. And they also knew that if they wanted to get out of this unharmed, it was a good idea to get moving.

It is said that sometimes, seconds can feel like minutes, minutes like hours and hours like days. This was not one of those moments. Now every second passed in ever slow pace and Roy could swear that each second felt like a week, at least. So, after a few years of waiting, yes, Roy was an expert on over exaggerating, the undead finally wandered off lead by new sounds in directions away from Phidas and Roy.

This was not an alarming situation in any way, but the fact that there was one undead wandering alone raised the unfortunate odds of there being more of them nearby.

Phidas and Roy did not stick around long to find out if there indeed was a horde waiting for them, they changed direction straight into the woods, away from the great plain. Away from whatever destination they were heading to in the first place.

This lowered Phidas mood but strengthened his determination to reach his goal. There were too many terrible things in this world and settling his score with the vampires was perhaps the best way Phidas could help the world become a better place.

Roy on the other hand did not mind moving away from the great plains, he knew that a day's walk or two into the forest would most likely mean that they would stumble on one of the bigger trade routes and quite possible even a town or at least a village of some sort.

But the more he thought about it, the more unsure he was if he was looking forward to joining the rest of humanity again, after all, he was a nobody now. Nothing to his name, discredited for everything he had done in the past, both good and bad.

His only possibility was probably to fake a name and a background story, which he would not mind doing, but he really liked being himself, so for now, that was not an option.

Better stick with Phidas, whatever he was up to and see where that took him. Could be interesting to see, who knew what possibilities lay ahead on this journey. And besides, how many can say that they had walked for days with a dwarf? And not only any dwarf, Grand Master Phidas himself!

**Fifty three.**

Veron had made quick and precise preparations, mostly with a bunch of letters, addressed to different members of their clan. And of course, one to Saculg, stating that his intentions are to leave everything to him to do as he pleased. All neatly placed at his main table, carefully addressed to the right person.

Veron had planned to just walk out of the main gates and disappear. The route was planned, to the south, towards the ocean, away from dwarf territory, away from dwarf society, or what would be left of the dwarf society in this upcoming madness.

But it had not gone according to plan.

The first failing step was answering a knock on the door, where he hastily was summoned by a messenger from Achim. His presence was needed in the great hall.

Second failing step was requesting to be relieved of his honor in leading a delegation back to King Thidas. Achim was not pleased with this request and appointed Veron to the official flag bearer for all delegations between the main mine and the northern province.

Third failing step was to loudly sigh after this unfortunate decision, fueling Achim's rage even further, and was immediately ordered a personal security detail day and night. No exceptions.

This is how Veron yet again was on his way to the northern province, and yet again filled his lungs with the fresh surface air. His only worry now was that someone (most likely Saculg) would enter his chambers and find the letters, which now already had become obsolete, since he no longer had the possibility to escape.

This time there was only a few soldiers in the delegation. The greater part of the invasion force had remained along with Achim in the great hall. Veron could only suspect what they were up to and thanked the creator that his father had a talent for forgery and was very, very good at it.

As they continued their mission, Veron thought that this would be another uneventful march, but he could not be more wrong. The same night, when setting up camp, there came a lonely undead heading straight at them. Veron was lucky to be accompanied with trained and armed soldiers. It took all of them for a very long time before they had turned the undead to very dead. The only way to kill them is to pierce their heart and stab them multiple times all over their body and bleed them dry. All this while the undead constantly, and very stubborn, is trying to physically overman everybody and rip everybody into pieces.

After the long fight they did not take any chances, two guards by the dead undead body, in case there still was some life left in it, and four guards around the camp to keep watch for more.

At first shift end, one of the relieving guards could not find anyone to relieve and sounded the alarm as loud as he dared, to avoid attract more undead.

The entire pack of dwarves, armed with torches gathered at the missing guard's station, only to find marks and traces that could come from a werewolf.

Needless to say, they did not stick around any longer, one missing dwarf was better than a whole group of dead dwarves. Veron got orders to take them away from here, as quick as possible, and on direct route to the northern province, without running into more of whatever creatures was out there.

Veron pushed their party to walk day and night for a few eventless days, then, all of a sudden, to everybody's surprise, out of nowhere they stumbled into another group. Slavers from the look of them, but with only one cage of slaves. A pitiful sight if you asked Veron. An old lady, a young girl, a man half beaten to death and a horrid small creature that Veron had never seen before. Or heard of for that matter.

By that time, they were all exhausted and when the slavers offered to share night camp the dwarves were not hard to convince, even if they kept a bit to themselves.

**Fifty four.**


Phidas was beginning to enjoy both the open air and his somewhat odd traveling companion. And just as he was preparing to reveal his goal and intentions, the both of them was taken by surprise.

Walking through the forest, away from the great plains a most unexpected sound reached them from behind:

"ROY!"

As they both turned around the saw a complete stranger coming towards them from behind. A woman. Her hair black as raven feather, wild as rampant thicket and eyes clearer and truer than Roy had ever seen in another human (not counting the love of his life beneath the city).

"I'm sorry, do I know you" Roy shouted back, as the woman approached.

"No, let me apologize, I was mistaken…" she replied with a shrug.

"But how do you know my name?" Roy wondered…

"I didn't" she replied, "but now I do…" she was close now but did not intend to stop walking.

"What's your name, and where are you heading, if I may ask" Roy hurried to ask, before she had passed them.

"Home" she replied shortly, "and my name is Yena if you must know…" She continued to walk, and without turning around she said out loud, probably addressed to the two gentlemen she had just passed:

"You are welcome to join me if you like… soon dinnertime, and we'll have you for dinner if you're interested…."

"Have us for dinner?" Roy and Phidas exchanged confused eyes, not sure what they should do. Roy was the first to break their joint confusion, and without a word he started to walk after Yena. Turned quickly to Phidas, encouraging him to come along.

Phidas hurried and came alongside Roy.

"Should we trust this woman and follow her blindly? We do not know her or her intentions…"

Phidas whispered so quiet that Roy had hard to hear what he said.

"I have a good feeling about this!" Roy replied, ending the discussion before it had a chance to begin.

None of the three said anything, and Yena walked here and there, turned seemingly at random, no path in sight, as if she decided direction for each step, following the rapid flight of a butterfly or happy bounces of a rabbit coming out of the rabbit hole from a winters sleep.

Both Phidas and Roy was actually surprised when their hostess randomly leads them to a house that she seemed very familiar with.

Just as she laid hand on the door handle, she hesitated, turned around with a real serious expression in her face.

"I'd better tell my husband that we expect company," her eyes wandered from one to the other, "wait here, and do not enter until one of us calls for you."

Then she turned and entered the house.

Phidas looked at Roy, and mimed voiceless, formed the words: "Are you sure about this?"

Roy could only shrug his shoulders as reply.

Then they waited in front of the door, forever it seemed. Then they heard a man's voice. Commanding rather than friendly.

"Enter!"

They looked at each other, Roy reached for the handle, opened the door, and they both entered.

**Fifty five.**

Even if all the chosen girls had become pregnant, all but one who Grime was uncertain, he still satisfied his lusts daily.

The first girl had now carried her child almost six weeks, the second almost as long, and the third only four weeks.

Even if he hated it, he would need to perform the first ritual. He could not be weakened by this, he had to stand fast and continue this dark path he had chosen.

So, after dinner, and a relieving pleasure round whit the girl who maybe not had been impregnated yet (combining work and pleasure is not always bad, Grime thought to himself), he started to prepare for the ritual.

First, he made a mixture of herbs and boiled it together, then he took another set of herbs and grinded to a powder, added a small amount of water and stirred it to a green, thick cream.

"Guard! Bring me the dark-haired girl, number three." he yelled to the vampire on duty.

When she was brought to him, a few minutes later, Grime forced her to drink the boiled herbal mixture, and not long after that she fell in some kind of delirious sleep.

Grime hesitated, only for a second. Then he pulled her dress over her head and lay her naked on a table. Then he spread the herbal cream on her stomach where he intended to open her up to extract the baby.

This was a risky procedure for the mother-to-be, and for the child, but this child was bread with only one purpose, which it now would fulfill.

An unborn child of four weeks had barely developed a heart but had started to convert its life essence and integrating it with the body itself.

Grime needed to see how this looked like and figure out if this mechanism could be duplicated and used for his greater goal.

Unfortunately, Grime did not know a great deal about the human body, so he had to dig around a bit to find what he was looking for, and when he was finished, he realized that he had lost the girl, so there was no need to patch her up again.

"Guard, she is all yours now, as your master requested if one should not make the procedure…"

Grime stood there with his hands all bloody and passively watched as other guards entered the room and removed the body.

One of them stayed behind and as soon as the others had left the room he rushed to Grime, brought him down on a table with great force, kept pushing him hard against the wooden surface and with great tenderness and care, licking the girls blood of his hands and fingers.

It was a strange feeling, Grime thought. Almost like feeding a wild animal while in its captivating claws.

**fifty six**

Leola tried to find any weakness in their cage, but it seemed solid. The slavers were busy at the moment, they had invited a big party of dwarves, all dressed up on some big parade-thing. All dwarves looked exhausted, almost like a big pack of tiny undead.

As she systematically inspected all parts of their cage, she saw one of the dwarves approach the leader of the slavers.

She could not hear exactly what they talked about, but from what little she heard there was some kind of bargaining.

The head of the slavers burst out in a huge laugh, then the dwarf held out his hand and the slaver took something from it and examined it closely. Then an agreement.

Leola had heard enough from the conversation that she could conclude that they had just been sold to a bunch of dwarves. And not very cheap either, from what she could understand.

This seemed very unlikely and was very unexpected. Leola had never heard of dwarves trading with slaves, nor using them for any purpose. So, this was truly unexpected and could very possibly change her entire escape plan.

She knew, or at lease had a pretty good idea of what drove the slavers and what their weak spots were. But the dwarves, not a clue. Uncharted territory for Leola, and this scared her very much.

She played with the idea of telling the others, but could not see any beneficial reason to why, so for now she kept it to herself.

She turned her attention to Tadao. He spoke in-comprehensive, and Leola considered using magic to get him well again, but this could not be done unnoticeable, but it was risky not doing anything, they could lose him any moment.

Groll had been watching Leola a while, and without a word he moved over, took the closest of Tadao's loose hands and held it in one of his, and put his other hand on Tadao's stomach. Then he closed his eyes and lowered his head as if concentrating very hard.

Leola looked at the whole thing admiring the procedure. Dee did not see it; she was almost asleep and unaware of the things around her. Drifting away in a dream. Far away. A waterfall, and something that looked as a little valley surrounded by mountains. A boy, or possibly a man. Looked alone and miserable. Even scared. Very skinny. He was guarded, there was several guards. No not guards. A familiar shape. Werewolves. Dee woke up choking on her scream, it got stuck in her throat.

 Wide awake.

It did not feel like a dream. Those werewolves felt real. She could almost smell them. She feared them. As she woke up, her body was back on the path in the mist.

It took a while for her to realize she was still in the cage.

But something was different.

Tadao, Groll and Leola all sat smiling, looking at her.

Tadao! Awake! And looking really well!

Dee could not help herself and exclaimed "…how…?!" and then reached over and hugged Tadao.

**fifty seven.**

In all the mess that had followed since the last delegation left for the northern province, Saculg missed his uncle very much. He was scared and had nowhere to hide.

Achim acted like a tyrant. No, correction, he was a tyrant in the flesh. Only one of the Legendary stones had been surrendered to Achim, one dwarf had already died in the search for the remaining two. Achim and his men had tortured the poor soul. Either the brave dwarf knew something and chose to protect the secret with his life, or he simply did not know anything, as he claimed to his last breath.

After stating this example another stone surfaced, by itself it seemed, it was found by Achim on Grand Master Phidas throne as he was about to take his seat after another inspection round.

The hundred best diggers had not returned since they were sent away. Nobody knew where they were, and the general population had got moving restrictions and Achim's men had set up guard posts along the main tunnels to prevent unauthorized movement.

Saculg wandered restless without any goal along the allowed corridors and halls. He felt uneasy. If only uncle Veron was here. Then he at least would have someone to talk to. Veron always took time to talk to him. Explaining in a way he understood. Not as the other adults, who would just get mad if he did not understand.

Without really deciding it, Saculg's feet lead him in a straight (not literally, the Dwarves rarely built straight tunnels) to Veron's home.

He knew all the twists and tweaks on the door to open it, and as he walked into the empty home, he felt a strange loneliness coming over him. The usual friendliness and calmness were gone. Nothing remained, not a single trace.

He walked around in the different rooms, ending up by the fireplace and sat down in Veron's favorite chair. Even if it was a few weeks since Veron left, his living quarter had not gone cold. Even if Veron was still of the old way and had not installed modern lava heating in the walls, enough of his neighbors had done it, so the mountain in this part of the main dwarf society did never get cold or damp anymore. Besides, Veron always talked about how much he enjoyed sitting in front of a coal fire listening to the breath of the fire, looking at its dancing, violent consuming everything around it. Everything except the mountain itself.

As Saculg sat there he imagined what it would be like if this was his living quarters. And what it would feel like if the vault were his own. The treasures in there was more than most dwarves would see in their lifetime, yet Veron never spoke of them, nor did he brag about his wealth, like most other.

Saculg rose from the chair and slowly walked around in his own fantasy world. Until he came to the main table. There he noticed a big bunch of letters, and the first was addressed to him.

**fifty eight**

Roy and Phidas opened the first door only to find themselves in a small compartment where Phidas noticed a clever mechanical construction where the first door had to be closed before the second could be opened. And after the second door, they stood in a huge dark room. Only lit by a few candles. Phidas turned around and looked at the door they just came through, no door handle on this side, so they could not get out if they needed to.

Roy was still unaware of this, and Phidas had no way of telling him, except to tell him, but he chose not to, since he did not want to offend Yena and her husband.

What they both noticed, which neither of them had noticed when standing outside, was the absence of windows. The room was completely windowless, which helped in the entire "make-the-room-dark" theme that obviously was important to the habitants of this house.

"What business have a man and a dwarf in my house?" the voice from the man they could not yet see demanded to know.

Phidas answered rapidly, since he knew Roy had no business at the moment.

"I have left the dwarf society to complete a life mission, which is of personal nature, and while traveling, this gentleman was kind enough to accompany me, without knowing my mission or goal."

Roy continued:

"We are grateful for your hospitality! We were invited by Yena and she was kind enough to offer us dinner. My name is Roy Hicks, and the dwarf by my side is none other than Grand Master Phidas of the main dwarf kingdom." Roy almost bowed when he presented Phidas.

"Not a bad introduction" the voice replied, without any admiration in its tone, "you have entered the house of Vladir, and you have already met my wife Yena."

They saw movement in a dark corner of the room. Both Roy and Phidas grasped their breath as their host reveled himself, a vampire.

Phidas' mind tried to grasp the situation, no handle on the door. No escape. And Yena's words came back to mock him: "We'll have you for dinner" she said…

**Fifty nine.**

Grime looked over his shoulder. The guard was still following him, but the feeling to be outside in the open air was wonderful. No matter how hard he tried to remember, he could not remember the last time he was out. He could not even remember which season it was when he was captured.

He looked up at the moons. So still, so powerful, so beautiful, so mysterious. He had often thought about the moons as a child, what was the meaning and purpose with one silver moon and one blood moon? How did they get that way?

And tonight, he felt the same wonder as he did as a child, looking up in the night sky, moons and stars and all. Trees standing tall, the entire forest surrounded him, the trees standing tall, reaching for the stars. The cold, clear and fresh air filled his nose and lungs.

When asking the vampire master for herbs, he never expected to be allowed to gather them himself. This was a great token of trust. Well, there was the guard of course, but still. Grime was confident he had proven himself and he constantly made progress that the master could see and follow. Soon it would be time to start the treatments on the master, and himself as well.

This was indeed a great night. He had found most of the herbs he expected to find in these parts, and the rest had to be gathered elsewhere, but most of them was not urgent, since they were for later stages in the process.

He did not rush when he was ready, but the guard seemed anxious to get back. Grime took many chances to stop and examine yet another bush or plant or mushroom along the way back. Stretching time outside the old castle as much as possible. But regardless of how many stops he did, the inevitable walls got closer and closer, and before he knew it, the main gates closed behind him again.

The darkness inside these walls was very different compared to the darkness in the forest. As Grime was guided along corridors and passages his mood shifted and dulled. Then he heard something that he probably was not meant to hear, not yet anyway, but you never know with the vampire master.

Between these stonewalls a strong howl echoed, miserable and alone. Almost heart breaking. And the howl followed by intense activity from what seemed like a legion of guards, running to an unclear destination ahead.

"Do you have a werewolf here in the caste?!" Grime turned to his supervisor for the night.

The stone-faced the guard only continued to lead Grime back towards his quarters.

"This is important! You must not harm the creature! It is most valuable to both me and your master!"

Still no reaction.

"Let me see it!" Grime demanded with rising frustration. "Take me to it immediately!"

"If it is the only one you have, you MUST, and I cannot stress that matter strongly enough, inform your master! And I need to examine it as soon as possible!"

The stone-faced guard did not pay any attention. Damn vampires! Grime knew they were not mindless creatures, but they dared not defy their master. He had indeed gained a lot of strength, but now he was more a tyrant than a leader. And Grime was helping him to gain even more strength and power. Question was if the other vampires like what Grime was doing or if they hated him for doing it. Either way, they could not harm him, he was under the questionable protection of their master…

…nevertheless, could there be somebody he could use as ally? A new dimension to Grime's plan. But was it useful? How could he possibly identify anybody who might go against their master?

**sixty.**

Veron woke up to singing birds and bright sunlight straight in his eyes. To most dwarves this would be the worst possible way of waking up. But to Veron it was better than all his treasures in the vault. Which for most dwarves was the sole purpose of being alive. But Veron had already figured out that he was not like most dwarves, not even close. And despite the gloomy thoughts of being close to escape the dwarf society, but instead appointed this dreadful task, for life as it seemed, Veron was determined to do the best he could of any moment of any journey.

When they were ready to depart, Veron could at first not understand why, in the creator's name, they had to drag along the cage with the humans. But pretty soon he understood that they were now part of the delegation. A gift to King Thidas upon the return from the main mines. Indeed, a new darker era in the history of the dwarves. Slaves. Had it really come to this low mark?

Veron did not know how, but he was determined to not let this happen, not on his watch.

What he did not know, was that he very soon would be given an opportunity to make a choice. And regardless of what choice he was going to make, he would set things in motion, darker things than he could ever imagine.

From his point of view, it would be a choice between right and wrong. Between dignity and disgrace. Not only for himself, but for the dwarf society at large, and, as destiny had lined up, three humans and a troll.

But in the greater perspective, it would be doing something unthinkable and turning his back on all the dwarves, turning his back on everyone he knew, his entire life and risk it all for some strangers. Or accept the unfortunate events and swallow his pride, his sense of right and wrong, go against his own being, polluting his own soul, letting the darkness in.

Looking back at this moment years from now (because this much is certain, Veron would influence the future for many beings in this world, and live to see it) he would see this choice as a defining moment, without ever questioning it, since he at that moment was unaware of the consequences. Had he known what two evil things he chose from; he might have second guessed himself. But even if he later learned one of the consequences of his action, he still did not regret it, even if it caused death to many of his kinsmen and others along the road. None of which was Veron's fault or blame.

Now Veron only observed the party, led it along path that started to be familiar to him. Calculating the journey onward, both to make it as long as possible, and as hard for transporting the cage as possible.

Fueled by the mutters and dislike of the other delegation members, he continued forward. Pleased with himself to make the road difficult for the others. Balancing keeping them on course, but continually adjusting course to "safer" terrain. Safe was something the others knew and respected, even valued, and since there was no other with as much time outside the mines, they did not dare questioning his decisions.

He knew that there was a ravine up ahead, leading the wrong way, but maybe he could use that somehow. After all, he needed an escape route leading away from the others. Hopefully, they would not be anxious to follow him.

Now, the only thing he needed was to come up with some kind of diversion. And as it turns out, you should always be careful what you wish for, it just might come true…

**Sixty one.**

Saculg slowly reached out his hand and took the letter. It was undoubtedly uncle Veron's handwriting. He opened the envelope and folded out the letter.

*My dear Saculg,*

*It is with great sorrow in my heart that I leave you this letter. For it means that we probably never will see each other again. I have decided to leave the mines, the mountain, everything that is our way of life. I will go out in the world and live in it, see it, learn it. I know what you and everybody might think. Veron you fool, the outside world is no place for a dwarf. It is harsh, unfriendly and dangerous. Yes, it most likely is, but I also believe it is a wonderful place, full of possibilities. Full of light and color. Full of life.*

*I do not ask you to understand my decision, but I ask of you to accept it and respect it. You might be the only one that I can ask this of. To everybody else I will be a fool, and they will tell you that, trying to convince you that your uncle Veron is indeed a fool and that you are wise to forget everything about me. But remember me, dear Saculg, remember the things we have done together, the times we have climbed the ventilation shafts to see the sky, night and day. See the stars and the moons. See the sun. Feel the fresh air. See the heaven. It is very important that you remember this. The heaven. Given time, you might understand just how important it is that you remember to go see the heaven, as I did with my father, your grandfather.*

*I know the others do not treat you as they should. They are mean to you. But know this, my dear Saculg, you are special, and I am very proud of you in many ways. Always keep asking when you do not understand the ways of old. When the others do things you find strange. You have a great mind and while others think of you as stupid, I see that you have unique point of view and if it where up to me, you would be the one to take over after Grand Master Phidas when he retires.*

*You have a good heart, and your soul is uninfected by the ways of old. Your mind is open. You are just, you know right from wrong! Which is more than you can say of most of our kin. Greed does not pollute you. You will be a great dwarf! And I am sorry that I will not be around to see it for myself.*

*Always be yourself, even if it means that the others keep treating you bad. It is because they do not understand better, and not because there is something wrong with you. Always remember that, there is nothing wrong with you!*

*Keep asking when you do not understand, keep questioning things that do not add up to you, keep your point of view. Always. It is unique, and my hope, and guess, is that your point of view is needed in the future. Seeing Achim and his men enter our mine, I fear that this future is closer than I first anticipated. This is also the reason why I choose to leave at this moment. Hopefully unnoticed, before things heat up in here. So, this is my goodbye to you.*

*Give the letters to the others, every envelope is named and sealed. Give all of them to your father, and he will distribute them at appropriate time. Keep this letter to yourself, no need to let the others know. It is our little secret!*

*Speaking of secrets, I almost forgot a most important thing. I trust you still remember how to open my vault. Your grandfather designed this vault, and we both know that there was none greater at rock mechanics, so if you do not remember it, it is not much to do. But either way, it is all yours! And my home is now your home, with everything in it! It is time you get your own quarters and leave your parents place anyway!*

*When you go through the vault, you will find things you never thought possible, and I trust your judgement, keep some things to yourself. The rest – it is yours to do with as you please.*

*If you want to play the dwarf game and do it the dwarf way, I would advise you to place a huge amount in external trading, I believe this might be the future for us, rather than the inflated internal market or developing new refined ways to extract the wealth from our beloved mountain.*

*But that is just my thinking. You have enough in the vault to keep you settled for life if you keep your calm and do not spend everything at once. But your grandfather told me before he left for the war – he regretted not spending more and living life more. His wealth did not serve him in death, and he regretted not living more. I guess that advice is part of the reason I choose to leave now. And I have realized that the treasures are nothing that enriches my life. It only provides the necessary material things to ensure a decent life in the limited material world of dwarves. A fine world, indeed, but also a closed, conservative and possible corrupt world. Limited by the walls we have created. Imprisoning ourselves, limiting us.*

*Sorry, Saculg, now I am rambling to you, I guess it is hard for me to end this letter, since I do not want to say goodbye to you. But even so, it is what I am doing.*

*Enjoy everything around you. It is yours! All yours! In the pile of letters, you will find all the necessary paperwork. Legally binding.*

*I will miss you, I will miss our talks, our walks, our heavenly adventures.*

*Take care, dear Saculg!*

*May your days be many, your mining profitable, your beard long and your treasures infinitely growing.*

*Yours,*

*Uncle Veron.*

Saculg read the letter twice. He could not believe it. Veron had been appointed official duty as flag-bearer. He was on his way to King Thidas, he had not disappeared. Had he planned on leaving, but was hindered by the orders from Achim? Saculg did not know what to make of this.

He stood paralyzed a long while, then, as if waking up, he put down the letter, turned around and left Veron's quarters.

**Sixty two.**


"Well, well, two travelers joining just in time for dinner" Vladir said, looking at Roy and Phidas.

"I have never had a dwarf for dinner before!" he continued, almost amused.

"Just to be clear on one thing" Roy said, a bit in panic, "…is it Phidas and me that is your dinner, or are you and Yena inviting Phidas and me to join you at the table for a mutual meal – without us being the main course?"

Vladir burst out in heavy laughter, so did Yena, who had magically appeared and joined them, with a most pleasant sight for both Phidas and Roy. She carried plates, three to be exact. On them three beautifully carved wooden spoons.

"We welcome you as old friends…" Vladir said barley hearable, halfway choking with laughter…

Roy found it rather contagious, and joined in the laughter, but Phidas was not very amused, which was very clear just by looking at him.

As Yena set the plates by the table, still with a smile on her face, she asked Phidas in particular to join her at the table:

"It is a true honor having you, Grand Master Phidas, to join us at our table! We have heard so much about you that we feel like we already know you. Please come sit here in the master's chair." She made a gesture towards the huge, beautifully carved chair by the short end of the table.

Phidas looked around as he approached the chair, everything in this house was wooden, and beautifully carved, almost as beautiful as the best dwarf craftsmen, he had to admit. Climbing up in the chair, it was clear to him that this human chair was much bigger than the throne he was used to back home.

He sat down, feet dangling halfway down to the floor. Roy had a hard time to conceal his big smile. Yena looked away, trying to hide hers, Vladir was he only one who laughed out loud.

"It brings joy to my heart, Grand Master Phidas, seeing you sit in my beautiful chair. Believe it or not, I have carved it just for you!".

Phidas could believe it, but not understand it. The chair was covered with the finest dwarf art and symbols, but the rest of the wooden work was vampire related, with a few exceptions, which Phidas guessed was made to or on request of Yena.

"I must ask," Phidas started, "how come you know so much about me, and how do you know so much about dwarf art and symbols?"

Vladir shrug his shoulders and answered while turning his attention to Roy:

"Stories from an old friend. So, Roy, what's new?"

Roy did not expect the change in focus and was trying to figure out how they would get out, since he now had noticed the lack of handles on the inside of the door they came through, and at the same time wondered how Yena could appear out of nowhere, as it seemed.

"Uhm, what's new? I do not even know what's old…" he seemed a bit uncomfortable with the question, since it was usually asked among friends, "I guess what's new is that I am officially homeless, and have joined a dwarf on an unknown quest with an unknown goal."

"That my friend, is something we can help you shed some light on, can't we, Phidas?" Vladir made a sudden shift in focus again.

Phidas was quiet, looking down on his empty plate. Surrounded by this horrid silence. Could he really tell a vampire that he was going after their master? Or was this a good time to make up a lie? Since Roy had not asked any direct questions regarding the mission or the goal, there had been no need to lie. But now?

"I…. eh, I do not know…." he started and paused again. "Maybe this is not the time to…"

"Aw, come on, Grand Master! Who knows, there might be more who do not like vampires" Vladir challenged him.

Phidas met Vladir's eyes. And for what seemed to be an eternity, the sat quiet looking at each-other. Then Phidas cleared his throat and started talking.

**sixty three**

Dee was a bit amused by their new owners. There was one who always lead the others, carrying a white flag with golden symbols that she did not know the meaning of. The others did not seem to like him very much, when settling for the night, they sent him away to keep the first night watch. He did not seem very amused by this. In fact, he tried to talk his way out of it, arguing he needed the sleep, in order to find the best and safest path's, but the others did not agree and sent him away in the dark.

Living her life in a cage was not something Dee had ever imagined, her father had mentioned once or twice that Slavers existed, but she had never fully understood what that meant. Or how anybody could accept or tolerate that slaves even existed.

And another strange thing, she had never questioned her value as a human being before, but now, caged, treated like a second-class human, she did not feel like she used to, she felt less valuable than others. With her head, she could think straight, and know that nothing had changed, but in her heart, she had become a filthy human, but not like Groll called her, no, a true filthy human without a value, that others could, and rightfully, command to fulfill their wishes.

This feeling was most unwelcome and unpleasant, but it had consumed her over the past days. Which is probably why she caught interest in the flag-bearer, he too seemed to be treated with less respect than the others treated each other. Even if Dee saw there was some sort of hierarchy amongst the dwarves, the flag-bearer seemed to be outside, a type of outcast, like she was.

The others whispered that they all would escape, at the right moment. Tadao was back to his old self, full of strength and energy, Groll was his old muttering self, and Leola, well, she was a bit quieter than she had been earlier, almost frustrated. The cage had a totally different effect on her than on Dee. While it broke Dee down to a shadow of her former self, Leola turned the frustration inward, as if she was saving up energy for a great burst…

Dee snapped out of her thoughts, something in the dark caught her attention. A noise she was unfamiliar with, but instinctively knew could only mean one thing, the undead. Not just one, a whole bunch of them. It was the quiet choir of many numb, quivering voices, heavy breathing and dragging steps. The tiny hairs on her entire body stood straight up as a chill trembled through her body. The others heard it as well. Tadao and Leola started to rattle the bars of the cage, hoping one of the bars would give in, creating a small opening through which they could escape. Tadao even tried to get the attention from one of the sleeping dwarves nearby, hoping he could release them. But by the time the dwarf woke up, the entire dwarf-pack had caught attention to the immediate threat. No one payed any attention to the cage or the motley gathering of slaves in it.

The dwarves mounted an improvised defense, but it did not take long before it was scattered, the undead were simply too many. Dee and the others could barely see the slaughter around them, but the sounds revealed far more than they needed to get a clear picture of what was going on.

Leola casted a fire-spell on one side of the cage, but that did not help much, the only effect it had was literally lighting them up like a beacon buoy in the dark, for all to see, dwarves and undead. Besides, neither of the slaves was fireproof, so they were all a bit burned from the tremendous heat from the magical fire.

For a split second, Dee figured that it might be better to die from the flames of a fire, locked in a cage, than torn to pieces by the hands and teeth of the undead. She covered her face with her hands trying to get some protection from the heat from the fire. A futile attempt. As the fire rose in intensity as it slowly spread, accompanied by the screams of the falling dwarves, the fighting attempts of those who still had hope and kept fighting, and the slowly moving mass of the undead, the back of the cage suddenly opened. They were all free, safe from the fire.

As they stumbled out, Dee saw the flag-bearer, he threw away the keys to the cage, signing at them to come along, and started running away from the horde of undead, away from the fallen night camp.

As they ran for their lives from the inferno, Dee could not help but to turn around. She saw an undead walking through the fire, struggling with the bars of the cage, getting through and continuing towards them, all lit up like a torch in the night. It did not seem to be affected by the fire, but as it consumed the flesh of the body, the undead weakened, and the last Dee saw of the undead was a rolling head from an attack by a dwarf armed with an extended axe, then she was pulled away by Tadao, who had lifted Groll and carried him in his arms, almost like a child. They all turned away from the madness and chaos and escaped in the dark.

**Sixty four.**


"You have to tell me… it is very important!" Grime tried to convince the vampire master that he had to get permission to examine the werewolf.

"Preferably a while ago, if it could be arranged."

"Why?" The vampire Master examined Grime closely.

"Why?! I do not know where to start… Because it is possible that it has turned into a mother…"

"What do you mean?"

"There is no way of explaining this in a short way, and we might be running out of time…"

"Try, from my perspective we have all the time we need."

Grime started to explain.

"You already know some of this, but it is important that I give you the full picture. As you know, when the Black Witches started to experiment, they took two humans, let a Wizard wipe their memories, took the life essence from one, the blood from the other. To compensate the drained blood, they replaced with the life essence. To compensate the lost life essence, they replaced it with blood. They created a vampire who lived without blood in its body, always craving for the blood of others. They created an undead who lived without life essence, always taunted by their loss, seeking it in others without ever being able to fill their emptiness…"

"Yes, all of this I already know, what is your point?"

"I am getting there… The first two that was created was also destroyed, but the knowledge lived on, and over the years more of your kind and the undead was created by Black Witches all over.

Some who had learned to wipe the memories of their subjects, some who hadn't…"

The vampire master was starting to get impatient.

"Both new races started to grow in numbers. At first, only a few here and there, then more, and more. It came to the point where both your races became a threat to humanity itself. This is all common knowledge, and now we get to the roomer parts. This is a puzzle that I have gathered pieces to over a very long time. And I cannot guarantee that it is entirely true, but over time I have found evidences to support parts here and there. This has been an obsession for me and my sister since before I can remember."

Grime got a small nod, encouraging him to continue.

"There are no written scours', only stories, roomers, paintings and reliefs. But I believe that the creators, and I believe there were two of them, saw what happened and in secret visited each and every human, extracted as much life essence as possible for the humans to survive and reproduce, but not enough for the Black Witches to find and extract from the human body. After they did this, they erased the memory of the procedure so that no one would know or remember the existence of the creators. And they vanished, never to be seen again. But this is just the popular version of the roomers among today's wizards and witches. And I have not come to the best part. I have found parts of an old painting, that shows the creators with a silver egg, heading for an opening in a mountain. And there is a sarcophagus in stone, probably created by the dwarves, that shows an egg surrounded by werewolves. We also know that werewolves were unheard of for a long time in history, then suddenly, they appeared. We know they are hurt by silver. Most believe that the reason for this is to give the rest of us a chance against the werewolves. I believe they were created by the creators to protect, but not be able to touch, a silver egg. And I believe this silver egg is the concentrated life essence that was extracted by the creators. I also believe that they were sealed in a cave in a mountain, in great numbers, surrounding the egg, protecting it. Protecting is their main function, and as so, they are created in a special way. When alone, I believe they change, turning into mothers. Then their bite will turn the bitten to one of them. If there are more than one of them, their bite is just lethal."

**Sixty five.**


Saculg followed his father to the great hall. Nobody knew why they were summoned. Saculg still wrestled with the information in the letter from Veron. He had not yet decided if or when it was a good time to break the news to the others.

There was a silent mumble in the great halls, and everybody looked worried, and when Achim rose from his throne everybody silenced and waited for him to speak.

"Now we can let everybody know three wonderful news. First of all, we have secured the last of the legendary stones. All is now in the ownership of King Thidas, even if he has not yet got the pleasure to see them joined. That is why the second thing should please you all. The miners that you have assigned to aid King Thidas are working around the clock, building a tunnel through the mountains, joining our two great societies. As we speak, there are good dwarves working from the other end, and given time, they should meet up. And last, but certainly not least, dear dwarves, I have the honor of informing you all that we are no longer a divided society, as of today, we are a united kingdom again. Lead by our own magnificent King Thidas, who will once again make the dwarf society flourish. The tunnel that connects our two cities will also act as a route for expansion, building an even greater kingdom."

Achim paused looking out over his new subjects.

"It is your honor to contribute to this new, united, stronger and more powerful dwarf society. Frist, you are being taxed for all your treasures, you are required to give every tenth to King Thidas, then, as your personal treasures grow with the new society, you will pay every fifth to King Thidas on every new finding or earning."

Nobody in the crowed dared say a thing, most did not even dare to continue looking up at Achim, but the silence was speaking very strongly for them all.

"My men will set up a registry division, from now, you are all confined to your living quarters until you have been registered and given your new papers. Tax collection will be made, and then you will be full-fledged members of the New Greater Dwarf Kingdom."

Achim looked out over the new subjects with a disappointed look.

"I was expecting cheers and applauds, but clearly your joy paralyzes you all. Anybody who does not comply will be banished from the New Kingdom. And as so, all who is not part of the New Kingdom will be forced out of the mines and out of the mountain, they are no longer welcome, and there are no room for any who cannot, or will not, contribute to the Kingdom."

This part caused mumbles among the audience, but Achim continued without paying any attention to it.

"As of now, all clans are relieved of responsability, and new ministers will be selected as we start to build this new city."

This started heavy protests in the crowed, but those who spoke up was quickly removed with force by Achim's men.

"Now, all of you, go to your living quarters, stay there until you are asked differently. Patrols will walk through each and every passage, and anyone who does not obey will be dealt with accordingly."

This made it very easy for Saculg, better to go to Veron's, no, his own quarters and claim it now, than risk losing more to the greedy King at a later point where it might be looked at as earnings and be taxed every fifth.

**Sixty six.**


Phidas felt uneasy, all eyes were on him. A strange feeling that three pair of eyes scared him, when he was used to the several thousand pair of eyes of the habitats in the great mines. But he felt that this was his chance. Roy had earned his trust, the other two, well, what could be the harm.

"A long time ago I was caught by the dwarf greed. As leader of the great mines a special finding was brought to me, several ages ago. A small piece of life essence. A silver stone, not bigger than a baby dwarf tooth. This was given to me, as a gift to the leader. A big treasure. But word spread of the Stone of Life. And I was approached by many with wishes to buy this precious gem. I always declined, no matter how much I was offered. But as they kept coming back, offering more and more, my greed started to grow. And when I was offered almost twice of my personal treasure, including peace and trading relations with the Vampires, I could no longer resist."

Phidas spoke with low voice, and by now his voice was clouded by tears that nearly breached his eyes.

"I sold the Life Stone, along with my soul, to the Vampire, knowing in my heart that this was a wrongdoing, but ignoring it for my own personal wealth. I already had more than any other dwarf dared dreaming of, yet, I longed for more…"

Phidas looked down in the table, ashamed of his wrongdoing.

"Later I learned that the Vampire Master had allied with a great wizard and some black witches to use the Life Stone to enhance him in some way. Shortly after that, I got reports that the Vampire Master could fly. Nothing good could possibly come out of that. And since then I have longed to try and repair the damage, I have caused this world. The Vampire itself is a curse, and a flying one does not make it better."

Phidas looked up to meet the eyes of his host.

"No offense, but my goal and mission are to destroy the Vampire Master, and as many Vampires as possible in the castle of theirs."

Vladir looked directly at Phidas, with a strange neutral expression, as if he did not know what to make of Phidas honest confession. And before he could answer anything Phidas continued:

"So, now you know, and it is nothing personal, kill me if you must, or let us dine together tonight and set our differences aside, if we have any. Tomorrow I will continue my journey, with Roy, if you still wish to accompany me, now when you know the destination and goal of my mission."

Roy tried to get eye contact with Phidas, but he continued to look down in the table, at an undefined spot. And before he could get through to Phidas, Vladir took to word.

"So, Phidas. You come as a guest, to my table, the table of the finest woodcrafts-man there is to find among the vampire kind, and you tell me that you want to start a war against the vampire race?"

The silence in the room was very uncomfortable to both Roy and Phidas but was broken like scattered glass when Yena's laugh bubbled over, and tiny pearly drops of laughter bounced through the room slowly filling it. Soon Vladir joined in, and Roy could not help but to join in, letting the laughter relieve the tension he just felt. Only Phidas sat in silence, with a most puzzled look on his face.

"Phidas, dear friend, I am sorry, I could not help myself, it was just too tempting!" Vladir explained, nearly choking on his own laughter.

It took a while, Phidas still with his puzzled look, before Vladir could gather himself to continue.

"You are among friends, Phidas. In fact, we have been waiting for you. For this day to come. And for you Roy, old friend. And we have been preparing a long time. We are ready to set things in motion. But you, Phidas, are the one who will start it all. We will help, and hopefully reach both your and our goal!"

**sixty seven**

Veron is constantly slipping behind, short of breath, unable to keep up with the others even if he almost runs beside them. Tadao is in the lead, carrying Groll, Dee and Leola shortly behind. All tired from being on the move the entire night and way past daybreak. It was almost noon, and they were all in desperate need of rest. Most of all Veron. He shouted ahead towards Tadao that he needed to stop, slow down, and stop. Dee was still terrified, and was not very reluctant to stop, but she too would need to stay and rest soon enough.

Tadao, in cooperation with Groll, found a little place just next to tiny stream, providing them with cool and fresh water, and some shade from the sun.

They all sat down, almost on top of each other, and for a long while all that could be heard was heavy breathing. Tadao was the first to break the silence.

"Well, thank you master dwarf! I believe you have just saved our lives! My name is Tadao, former Hawks-man on the Glory, this is Groll, our most appreciated traveling companion, Dee who ran away from home and got lost, and Leola."

Veron was still heavy on the breathing but still managed to speak, somewhat coherent.

"Yes, my name is Veron… Flag-bearer… no, former… posted as guard… saw them coming… did not warn the others… horrible, just horrible… nobody should be slave…"

Dee let the words from the dwarf sink in a moment, before she opened her mouth…

"Why did you not warn the others? You must have realized that the undead would…" she could not continue, the horror of what she had witnessed, she just couldn't make herself say it.

"Yes… invasion force from King Thidas… would keep you… force you to work the mines… you would be gift to King Thidas… Something not right… not the way of the Dwarves…"

Groll had studied the dwarf a while, trying to make heads and tales of what he had done, trying to understand his actions and put it in perspective to what had just happened.

"So, in short, betrayed your own kind to save a few strangers, sacrificed your kin, saved yourself and us. That is certainly not the way of the dwarf. Must tell us more, master dwarf!"

"Veron… please say Veron… my name…"

They were all on guard, reacting to every sound around them, but they remained still and silent until they all had caught their breath. Dee was the first to stand.

"Drink what you need, we must keep going, they could still be after us."

They all took her advice and drank what they needed and then continued.

"You are a mystery, Veron, but still we are grateful for what you have done for us. I wish to learn more and understand the decision you made to save us. And what is going on in the dwarf domains."

Leola looked down at Veron as she walked next to him, now in a slower pace than they had kept for the duration of the night.

Groll had moved back to Dee's shoulder and held a hand around her neck, in an attempt to calm her and renew her strength.

They had not walked far when the silence around them was broken by an unfamiliar loud voice.

"Hey, wait! Stop! You are in danger! They are coming this way!"

They all looked around but could not identify who the voice belonged to or where it came from.

**sixty eight**.


"My hope is that the werewolf you have in custody has turned into a mother, and if so, I hope to harvest its ability to transfer and transform through its bite. And see if its strength can be used to something."

Grime looked at the Vampire Master to see if he had any chance of getting to lay his hands on the werewolf.

"Before we continue, I would like to set some points straight, since you seem to care about what you just told me." The Vampire Master slowly turned and gathered his thoughts, and seemingly weighing his words on a golden scale.

"Overall, I am impressed to hear what you have found out, and what pieces of a lost puzzle you have uncovered. My kind has tried to get rid of all traces of our connection with both Witches, Wizards and most of all the undead. Now I know we have failed on that part. The only remaining artifact that we knew to hold the truth is the doors to this very hall. The other objects I will send for to get destroyed at once. Thank you for sharing that information. As for some minor details, the first Vampires, and far from all, did get their memory wiped. Those of us who didn't, at least most of us, have chosen to suppress the memories of our past lives, which seems to get easier as time is passing by and our memories fade."

For a brief moment, the Vampire Master seemed far away in his thoughts.

"And as for the first vampire and the first undead. Yes, they are both dead, but not as you think. I personally killed them both. And not at once, we were kept locked up at first, but we managed to escape. And it was not two, it was four of us. My brother and I became the first vampires, our sister and our mother the first undead. Neither had our memories erased. When we escaped, my brother pleaded to me to kill him, he could not stand to live as what he had become. And he could not stand seeing our sister and mother as mindless, wandering creatures. So I took their lives, my sister and my mother, and last, my brother."

He was quiet for a while before he continued.

"And last, the silver egg. I too have heard the rumors, and as one time I interrogated a person that claimed to be a member of a clan that had sworn to protect the silver egg, once it had been found in a deserted cave. There were no werewolves surrounding it or guarding it, according to my source. But I too believe that they were created and bred to protect the silver egg, longing for it, but unable to touch it…. A relatively fresh rumor says that the silver egg will be moved shortly. Up north. Either by ship or by land caravan. A safe harbour has been established, possibly with the dwarf King in their northern province. But I have not been able to confirm any of these rumors yet."

He slowly walked around Grime, whilst talking, and Grime paid undivided attention to it all, and let word by word sink in, memorizing them carefully.

"And as for your initial request. Yes, proceed with caution. Many sacrifices have been made to get it here, and I do not wish to waste it. But I will find another if it comes to it, and if so, we will negotiate a reasonable compensation from your part, if something is to happen to it."

**sixty nine.**

Saculg sat in the master's chair by the fire when the delegation knocked on his door. He had gone through all the papers, planned to give them to the delegation and let them handle the official delivery since he counted on being confined to his quarters a while longer. He had not yet opened the vault, for safety reasons only, he wanted to be able to go through it alone and without pressure. If he did not look in it, he could truthfully answer any questions regarding it with "I do not know…"

A last deep breath before he opened the door.

"Master Veron?"

"No, I am afraid not, and I regret I have to give you a piece of bad news. This is, or was, Veron's quarters, but before he left as flag-bearer with the delegation to our Great King Phidas, he wrote a letter and a lot of paperwork for me to find here. He states that he will leave the dwarf society and therefore I believe that I bring bad news. It is possible he is leaving the delegation unprotected before reaching our Great King."

"Well who are you and where are the paperwork's?"

"I am Veron's nephew Saculg. And all papers except the letter to me is over there on the table. The letter I prefer to keep private, since it was written to me personally. As for the rest of the letters, they are still unopened, but you can see that all paperwork is in order. My father can vouch for the authenticity once you have showed them to him."

"Saculg, yes, you were missing from your father's house, and they expressed that they did not know where you were. Glad to have found you son. Let us look at the papers, shall we?"

The delegation member with the pack of books and scrolls entered, while the five guards stayed outside.

"Have you access to the vault, son?"

"Yes, I believe I have, it is my grandfather who built it, but I have not opened it yet, unsure if you wanted to accompany me in doing so." Saculg lied, he felt awful for doing so, but strangely it felt like the right thing to do!

"Good thinking, boy, we'll get to that later, now, let me examine the paperwork and the letters."

The delegation member sat down at the table and started to cross-reference details in his books and scrolls, constantly making new notes, crossing over old, scratching his beard, adjust his glasses, turning pages, fiddling with his feather pen, humming to himself, nodding, all with the precision of someone with many, many years of routine in bookkeeping and administration.

"Well, my lad, everything seems to be in order, I will process these letters and make sure they are delivered to the right persons. Meanwhile, it is best you stay here, and we'll come back for the tax inventory later."

Saculg felt relieved to an extent that it had to show on him, but he was taken down on rock ground very quickly.

"Let's just open up the vault for a quick look, and then I will post one of the guards outside, to make sure everything stays the way I leave it…"

Saculg dared not defy him, and started the complex process of opening the vault, that was hidden behind a great piece of Dwarf art, covered with symbols and scenes from their proud history. Lots of small details to twist and press in certain orders, to unlock the next part of the combination lock. To buy time, Saculg made small talk with the delegation member, without even planning it, just acting along.

"As you probably understand, I have never been in here, so I look as much forward to seeing what is in here as you do."

The last of the combinations was successfully entered, and the vault door opened, revealing an astonishing treasure.

"May I suggest, as a token of my appreciation to our new King, that you select one of the finest and most valuable items in here, as a gift for the King, unregistered, and we cover everything else in the paperwork for taxation later."

Saculg was terrified that the delegation member would find some of Veron's secrets and thought it best to try and direct his attention towards something unlikely to be one of the secrets.

"Most generous of you, young boy, most generous…" the eyes of the old dwarf glittered as he looked around, most likely looking for the most valuable object of all. And again, most likely, NOT give to king Thidas, but keep to himself.

**Seventy.**

Yena passed the steaming bowl of soup to Phidas again.

"Eat, gather your strength, I know it is not what you are used to, but this soup contains a lot of necessary energy, even for dwarfs."

Phidas had never been so full in his whole life, even if he was used to both hosting and attending great feasts with unlimited food. There was indeed something with this soup.

Roy cut in.

"So, how did you two end up together, and how come you haven't eaten us or Yena yet?" he directed his question with a smile towards Vladir.

Vladir laughed again, his warm and friendly laughed that slowly grew on Roy, he liked this man, for some unknown reason.

"Well, it is a long story, the short version is that along with a few others, I escaped from the vampire collective, only to become outcasts. Without protection of the vampire unity, without any shelter, without food. Wherever we went, people were terrified of us, drove us away, even if we tried to be friendly and get help. We had vouched to each other not take lives, but as we grew weaker, we knew we had to do something to get food. I carved some wooden pieces, tried to exchange them for blood, or an animal that we could try to feed of. That is how we encountered Yena's family. Since then, they have been our protectors, for ages."

Vladir gave Yena a loving eye.

"But it was not until I came along that you fell in love!"

Vladir reached for Yena's hand and bent down to kiss it.

"True, my love and joy! You not only keep me alive; you fill it with joy and purpose."

"What do you mean keep alive?" Roy cut in…

"I feed him my blood. As my family have done for ages, we are the protectors of three vampires, and there are other families like ours, we coexist, for mutual benefits. What we know we are the first to become a couple. It has its challenges, but we make it work… besides, Vampires are excellent workers, and if they do not do what we tell them, they will starve…"

Vladir burst out in a new volley laughter…

"…and when we starve, we get cranky and take what we need… Balance restored my love…"

It was hard to tell what was actually true, given their jargon, but Roy figured that most of it was legit, and that there indeed was a coexistence.

"But can you feed one vampire alone? And how does it work? I mean the feeding part?"

"Each of us needs four humans that volunteers to donate a small amount of blood every five days. We drink directly from their veins by the wrist…"

Yena showed both her wrists, revealing two tiny bite-marks on each wrist.

"The fifth day we drink the blood of a chicken. Awful, but necessary to keep the symbioses and to give enough time for the wounds to heal without causing any harm."

"To ease the healing, we have gather herbs and moss to make salve, and these fellows like when we spice it up with certain things, like this fellow," Yena took her hand and ran it through Vladir's hair, leaving it in a mess, "he likes when we add fennel. Says the skin tastes better, making it more pleasant to eat…"

"…we all have our favorites…" Vladir added.

"Speaking of… you need to rest, a few hours, while I prepare the others and let them know you are here, we have a lot to do before sunrise…"

Vladir left the table. Nodded to both Phidas and Roy before he hurried out in the back of the room.

"I'll show you where you can rest, leave everything on the table, I'll take care of it later…"

Yena stood up, gesturing with her arms, encouraging them both to follow her.

## seventy one

It took a while for Dee to locate the origin of the voice. It came from a man high above ground in some wooden construction in a tree. The tree was connected to other trees with small bridges, built by wood and rope. But not like small boys would build to their wooden houses, no, these bridges were robust, built to last. And by the looks of them, they had been there a while, but still in great shape.

"Hurry, they are closing in, run towards the huge tree over there…" He pointed towards a tree much bigger than the others nearby, "I will throw down a ladder for you!"

No time to lose, they all ran, as fast as they could, towards the tree, and as promised, a rope ladder was lowered so they could climb up. Strangely, the ladder steps even fit Veron's short legs, and for the others, they could take two steps at the time. Only Groll needed assistance, and held on tight to Tadao, as he climbed up the ladder as quick as he could.

Once safe on the wooden platform they could all truly relax. And shortly after the ladder was safely pulled up again, they heard the first few undead pass beneath them. Close call, too close!

"Thank you, stranger! You saved us from these foul creatures! This is the second time we have been saved from them, first time was from this dwarf, Master Veron. I am Tadao, this is Dee, Leola and our friend Groll. Whom may we thank for our lives this time?"

"Wow, you talk a lot, do not you, Tadao? I am Devoras and am the caretaker of this outpost on the Sky road to Freedom. You are safe from the undead up here."

"Sky road to Freedom?" Tadao put words to the question all had, by the looks of their faces anyway.

"Yeah, Sky road to Freedom! This is it! Come along now, you look like you need rest and perhaps something to eat."

Devoras walked away along one of the bridges as if he were walking solid ground. The others did not walk that easily, not even Tadao, who still had his sea legs to lean on.

Beneath them the horde of undead flow like water along the ground, rounding the trees, almost swallowing them, but the trees kept standing tall, unaffected. The undead did not seem to notice them at all. And as if Devoras had read their mind from up ahead, he shouted back:

"Do not worry, they cannot get up here, and even if they can hear us, they keep looking at ground level, as if they are unable to comprehend anything that isn't straight in front of them. Only once one of them has tried to climb a ladder that someone had forgotten to retract, but it has been unheard of since. Besides, the biggest reason to retract the ladders are to keep others out of our Sky road, and ourselves safe from the undead."

Devoras was still ahead of them, but kept waiting on them, like a sheepherder checking on his sheep.

Dee was amazed by the Sky road. The simplicity of it, yet its brilliance. It seemed to go on forever, she could not see the end of it. Mostly because it was cleverly built into the crowns of each tree, with minimal risk of being detected from below. With each new crown, there came a new section of the Sky road on the other side.

None of them knew for how long they had walked, before they reached a platform bigger than the others, carrying some sort of shelter.

**seventy two.**

Grime moved his hand slowly. The beast was chained, but still very aggressive. Even with twelve strong vampires holding it down, it was still fighting strong and made sudden moves. Not very optimal when you are trying to move slow with precise movements to avoid the sharp teeth.

Grime carefully moved his needle and pincers to position where he thought the gland for the toxic venom was located. The trick was to get a small bottle to gather each precious drop from the beast's infamous jaws. All this while the vampire guards fettered both the beast itself, and its terrible mouth.

Grime moved all his tools to position, best he could. Before he started, he gave the signal to the guards, so that they would be ready when he started the procedure. Then, in a smooth motion, he used the needle and pincers exactly where he intended. Drops of venom was squeezed out, they all were gathered in the little bottle. The beast cried in pain, and every muscle in its body tensioned, and just as Grime was about to retract the bottle slowly from the mouth, one rope snapped and the heavy Jaws closed around Grime's little finger and ring finger. Both lost to the great beast. Blood was floating from his hand, and one of the guards lost focus, letting one of the beasts massive paws loose, and before anyone had reacted, the beast had gotten loose enough to attack two of the guards, who both fell dead to the ground.

More guards came quickly to replace the fallen, and more silver ropes was thrown to tie up the beast again.

There was no mourning, just efficient work, and there was also attention on Grime and the precious bottle he was holding.

Grime fainted from the chock and pain and was not aware that he was caught by gentle vampire arms, nor that other hands quickly took the bottle too keep it safe.

When he woke up again, Grime was put in a soft bed, his wound tended and cared for, with almost no pain. He looked at his hand and moved the thumb and the remaining two fingers. His motor skills were heavily affected, but he could still use what was left of his hand. Something positive to be happy about, and probably having a hand at all. It started to sink in, it could have ended in a whole different way. This was indeed an outcome to be grateful about. If he had got the venom. He looked around to see if he could see the little bottle, but it was nowhere to be found. Did he get it? He tried to rise, but then the room started to spin. Blood loss. Seemed reasonable. He could not help but to wonder if his blood were spilled or if one of the guards greedily licked the floor to get what could be salvaged.

This was an unwanted outcome. He did not have time to stay in bed, he had to get to work with the venom at once. There was no telling what happened to it outside the body. It could be quickly degrading while he was in the confined to the bed.

"Guard! Get in here! I know you can hear me! I need to know what happened! Time is yet again critical."

A guard entered shortly, by now he had seen so many vampires that it was hard to tell them apart. They all seemed to look alike.

"What happened in there with the beast? Did you manage to save the bottle? Where is it now? I need to examine it right away. Take me to my room so I can get back to work!"

The guard left at once. The feeling of being in power felt good, it grew on Grime. He could feel that he was changing. A good feeling. As if he grew to his true self. He longed to take one of the girls. He needed to show his new power, use it… Yes, he would take the youngest one, she was to be his price today. And comfort. She would pay to him as he had paid to the werewolf. Today she would also bleed.

**seventy three.**

"What?!" King Thidas was furious.

"We were surprised by a horde undead, only a few of us survived…"

"I heard what you said, I am not stupid nor deaf. How could this happen?"

"The horde came like a wave and crushed us, sir, we had placed watch posts as instructed, but somehow they got thru… So much death…"

The dwarf that kneeled before King Thidas silenced and tried to hold back his tears.

"Unacceptable! I hold you responsible! How could you let this happen? Where are all the bodies of our lost comrades? Did you bring them back?"

"But sir, there were too many, and only a few of us survived, and I could not affect what happened, we followed protocol, had guards posted everywhere in all directions…"

"Excuses, I do not want to hear more of them! Execute this man for insubordination! Bring me his head and put it on a stick next to the entrance as an example to others…"

The unfortunate minion was immediately removed to be prosecuted and handled. His sobbing and cries echoed through the great throne room before the doors was closed and silence yet again filled the great chamber.

The fury of King Thidas was unmistakable.

None dared questioning his decisions, no voice protested when their great leader spoke, even when they did not agree with him. Even when it was wrong. Even when it was totally wrong. They all feared him, his mood, his power.

They all knew the reputation; he was gathering the legendary stones to gain even more power. Some believed that he had already started to tame some of the power in the stones, others thought he needed to gather all of them to unlock their powers.

When the great King ruled, sorry, rephrase that, the former King, no, the old King things were different, Thidas was different. Then he died. Thidas claimed the northern province to be his kingdom. Grand Master Phidas was not strong enough to keep control of the main society and the Northern province, so he let his brother play his own little game and forced him to pay taxes.

When Thidas came to power, he banned all books and written documents. He collected everything and locked it away in his royal library. Knowledge did no linger belong to the common dwarf, only to a selected few.

At first no one predicted the extent of their new Kings actions, but over time, most saw that he was as cleaver as he was hungry for power. Some said it was a desire to prove that he was better than his bigger brother, some said he was affected by a black witch or a wizard. Rumors flourished and the more King Thidas restricted and controlled the life of the common dwarf, the more the rumors grew, widened, now they had become legends. Even truths.

By now, no one dared to speak against him, and his actions had been the leading standard behavior. The right and wrong of old was gathering dust in the older dwarves' minds, while the younger generations only had this new right and wrong as guidance.

Even so, despite everything they all had been through with King Thidas' ruling, a death penalty had never been issued before. And to most it actually seemed wrong killing this innocent survivor.

Almost better they all had died by the hands and teeth of the undead.

King Thidas was furious and walked back and forth in front of his throne. He was deeply troubled, subordination of this severity. Unacceptable! Someone needed to pay, and someone needed to put things right again. Useless subjects! Was it really only up to him to make things great again? To rebuild the dwarf society to what it once was. How could the others not see what he did? How could the others not understand and follow him blindly? They should all be grateful they had him to make the though decisions, to lead those who did not know better.

"How many soldiers do we have left here? How many do we need to keep securing this place and how many can we send off to war?" King Thidas yelled out in the hall, creating febrile activity around him.

**seventy four.**

When the delegation member had left, Saculg opened the vault again. He stood there in the opening looking into the wealth, more than he had ever seen before. How would Saculg find secrets in here, how could he tell the difference? What could be so valuable that no one else could know about it?

He moved slowly, examined everything he could lay his eyes on, slowly letting his hands hang loosely along the sides, randomly running his fingers against larger objects, through gatherings of smaller, like bowls of different gems.

He did this several times, just walking randomly around the vault. He sat down in the opening. What was out of order here, was there something that did not belong? Something that did not fit in? Artwork in pressures materials? Gemstones of various sorts and sizes? Cups in pure metals covered with the creators most precious gifts? Saculg had never seen riches' like this. And somewhere among all this there was something…

He rose, started to walk around again… if only he could put his finger on it… while thinking this he literally put down his finger on something. Nothing of significance, a small wooden box. Sure, beautifully carved, but nothing compared to everything else. Dwarf did not particularly fancy wood. Dwarfs liked metal, rock, gems, stuff like that, not wood.

He walked around some more, trying to put his finger down again. Golden plate. Very nicely done, lots of symbols, but nothing out of the ordinary. Cup. Loades with gems. Nothing out of the ordinary. A staff, way too long for a dwarf, but still very common, the more precious material something needed, the richer you needed to be, so, nothing out of the ordinary here either.

This little escapade continued for a long time. Saculg looked at dozens and dozens of objects, one more valuable than the other.

But his hunt for secrets was in vain. He found nothing.

He left the vault, closed the door, walked around his living quarters, trying to figure out what Veron meant.

He read through Veron's letter again for any clues. Go see the heaven, the moon and the sun. First thing to do when he could get out of here. No, too late. When the delegation member retuned, they would take a tenth as tax, and he did not wish to risk letting a secret be lost. He had to act now.

He closed his eyes, what would he find up a ventilation shaft, he would walk up the stairs, tired. He would sit down, look out over the mountain. If it were cloudy, he would not see anything, if it were night, he would have to raise his head to see the moons and the stars. If it were day, he would need to raise his head to see the sun.

Veron and his own grandfather used to go there. What did they do there? Just look out? Breath the outside air? Why? Was it part of the secret? Why was it important to go up the ventilation shaft? And was it only one shaft or all the shafts?

Saculg tried to remember the times he and Veron had gone up together. Had it always been a particular ventilation shaft? Yes. Veron liked the view from there he said. Had he been up any other? Yes, at least two, and by comparison, those two had no view at all, they did just exit the mountain next to another mountain wall.

His Grandfather was involved in this secret to somehow. What did Veron and grandpa share?

The frustration rose as time fled. He did not have any clue when the delegation member would return, nor was he any closer to understanding the secret Veron had left behind.

As he started to open the vault, there was that familiar knock on the door. Time's up!

**seventy five**.


Roy and Phidas had slept well in real, soft beds, and woke up well rested when Yena knocked on their door.

"Good evening gentlemen! Time to wake up! Night is still young, time to eat supper before we continue."

Supper? How long had they slept? Roy hasted out of bed while Phidas took his time. Prerogative of the old he thought to himself.

Roy walked ahead to the main room where they had dined, but the room was empty, and nothing was set up on the table. A little confused he walked back to Phidas and waited for him to get ready, then they walked together back to the main room, only to once again find it empty. Just as Roy was about to call for Yena or Vladir, Yena called for the two of them.

"Here, upstairs… come and join us! Look in the back of the room!"

It took a while, but they managed to find a ladder in the back of the room, and as they both climbed up, Roy reflected on the fact that even Phidas could easily walk up the ladder, despite his significantly shorter legs. While Roy took two steps at the time, Phidas could easily tag along only taking one, but almost twice as fast.

Arriving where the addict usually would be, they still found no place for supper, but a large woodshop where they guessed Vladir would do much of his work. In the far side, they saw light coming down from above, and another ladder.

Climbing up the hatch that lead to the roof they followed the ladder straight up to a large wooden platform right above the house. None of them had ever seen anything like it. It was like a floor of a very large room, without walls or ceiling. Only a wooden fence kept the persons on the platform from falling. Above them was the crown of the large tree and it felt magnificent being out in the open air yet protected from both sun and wind. From the platform itself, there were bridges connecting this platform with other smaller ones in the trees nearby.

Vladir saw the expression on their faces and smiled towards them and while opening his arms in a wide gesture he said:

"Welcome to the Sky road of freedom, gentlemen! Built by the finest craftsmen available, yours to use if you choose to…"

"Incredible, where does it lead?" Roy looked to his left and to his right. As far as he could see on both sides the trees were connected with each other by the Sky road.

"From the ocean in the east and the mountains to the west." A new voice belonging to a tall human with hair as wild as a bird's nest.

"Impressive, isn't it?" Vladir said. "May I introduce you to Oaks. His mother named him Oakstar since he was born beneath an oak a starry night, but we call him Oaks for short."

"Pleased to finally meet you Phidas!" Oaks shook Phidas hands and then turned to Roy. "You are serious, aren't you?" He looked with an examining eye. "We all knew this day would come, I just can't believe it is finally here. But good to see you to!" Oaks reached over and hugged Roy, who was taken by surprise, but somehow managed to stiffly hug back.

Roy did not understand, and before he managed to ask, Vladir continued, turned to Phidas.

"It just so happens that our Sky road will take you safely to, and from, the Vampire castle. We have managed to build it close to the stronghold, before it was occupied by the Vampires, and they have not detected it yet, even if we think it is just a matter of time…"

**Seventy six.**

"We have seventy-six of these bigger platforms along the Sky road, each manned with two or three of us." Devoras explained to Dee. "And in the middle, we have our base of operations, where everything is coordinated from."

"What do you coordinate?" Dee asked.

"Mostly movements of the undead. And so far, we have only been practicing, but one day, probably soon, it will be the real deal…"

"What do you mean by movements of the undead?"

"Well, our goal is to gather every horde we have in our control, and create the biggest horde known in history. And lead it to meet the other armies when they are deployed."

"What other armies?"

"The one's we know of is the Dwarf army and the Vampire army. But we suspect there could be more… but I'm really not supposed to talk about this, so you need to keep this to yourself!" Devoras looked at the others by the table near the center of the platform. "Come, we need to join the others, it is soon time four our daily rest. We sleep during the days and work during the nights. Mostly to avoid being detected, but also because some of us can't stand the sun."

Dee and Devoras walked over to the table where Tadao, Leola, Groll and Veron sat.

"We have discussed what to do and where to go from here…" Leola said, as Dee and Devoras joined them at the table.

"I want to continue the search for my brother" she continued.

"And I would like to get back to a city on the main trading rout to try and get back home." Tadao explained.

Dee looked at Groll, and as if he knew what she was thinking he said:

"I'll stay with you, filthy human!" as blunt as only Groll could, but Dee felt the warmth in his words, and smiled back at him.

They all looked at Veron.

"Well, yes, I have no idea where to head, so Dee, if you do not mind, I'll stick with you for now… I could use the company, and a friend…" Veron look a little insecure as he uttered those last words…

"I cannot speak for everybody, but I believe you are sitting among friends, this very moment…" Dee smiled back to Veron, and Veron thought to himself, there is something special with this girl, he could not put his finger on it, but he surely felt it.

The others nodded and concurred, indeed among friends.

And out of nowhere, Tadao took word again.

"On second thought, I can always find my way back at a later point, I'll gladly follow you to where ever you want to go" he turned to Dee, "in good company of friends…" he included everybody and turned to Leola.

"Can we persuade you to join us a little longer?

"Well, I…" Leola paused and hesitated, fumbling for words, took several breaths as if to continue, without getting the right words out… "I suppose…" she finally formed, "that I could tag along a while longer… If you want me to… among friends…"

"Then let's go find your brother first, then my father, and along the way, we'll figure out the rest, among friends…" Dee settled.

**seventy seven**

Grime stood with the little bottle in his hand, the venom, he could still not believe he had done it. And as he had asked for, ten bottles of the beast's blood, still warm from its veins.

An herbal tincture boiled over the fire, among other things, plenty of roots form the truth flower, which also meant there was a big bunch of truth flowers at the table. Grime had not yet decided what to do with the flowers, he could try and make a truth serum for later usage, but it seemed like a waste of time, given the situation.

Since his hand was already mutilated, he had the perfect place to test his theory. Slowly he opened one of the bottles with the beast's blood, added a few drops of his tincture and removed the bandage on his hand. With the edge of a sharp stone he cut open the wound, and with great pain he inserted a small tube made from a hollow straw and guts from a goat. He then put the other end of the loose gut-end over the opened bottle and turned it upside down.

As the first drops of blood mixture entered his own blood system a burning sensation spread through his arm, up to his chest, and then pain, tremendous pain, then cramps in his entire body. He had to focus all his willpower to remain standing and letting the blood flow and fill his body. Perfecting him.

What felt like moments later, but could be much more than that, Grime woke up, face down in the big pile of truth flowers.

First thing that came to his mind was her, his own sister, how could she? All these years, all just a big lie! Fury, oh the rage. He took the empty bottle and threw it against the wall. It scattered into a million pieces, as small as sand.

Then in the middle of the rage, joy, a sudden shift in mood, tremendous joy, had he really done it, did it work? He took a chair that stood next to him. Lifting it with no effort, crushing the wood into sticks with his bare hands. Yes, it had worked. He filled his lungs with air. Perfection. He could feel it in his body. The new strength. The rush of power. He was unstoppable, invincible. Incredible. He had successfully harvested the power of the werewolf and forged a tincture that helped his body to accept the new strength and incorporate it into his own.

In the middle of his euphoric sense he heard two lonely hands clapping. The vampire master.

"Well done, Grime! Well done! Now it is my turn I suppose?"

Grime turned and stared directly into his master's eyes.

"Yes, master, now it is your turn. With one difference. Your mixture will also contain the venom. If I have done my reading correctly, this will mean that as your body accepts the new blood and the herbs make your body accept it as part of your own system, the venom that would have transferred you into one of them will now be a part of you…"

He walked over to the nine remaining bottles.

"But I dare not do it all at once, since I am afraid that too much of the venom might start the transformation process. And I do not believe your body, even a strong body like yours, would be able to cope with that."

"Begin!"

**seventy eight.**

"Begin!" King Thidas yelled.

"Right now! At once! I demand it!"

The poor minister in front of the King was trembling.

"Sir, I report that we have…"

"Yes, what do we have?"

"Sir, we have completed our estimations of…"

"Estimations?! I need rock hard facts, not estimations!"

"Sir, we have not had time to properly run the numbers and make the calculations…"

"Then what have you had time to do? Enough with the excuses! Tell me what I need to know!"

"Well, sir, we believe that we'll manage with a thousand men here, given your clever design of the entrance, sir…"

"And that gives me what size of army to send?!"

"It'll give you roughly twenty thousand men, all included, no able left behind, sir…" the minister swallowed hard, "but that is just a rough estimate…"

"Twenty thousand you say?" King Thidas rose from his throne, walked around in his own thoughts. The others in the chamber did not dare to disturb him. Even if he was explicitly greedy, horribly cruel, almost evil, none would ever question his intelligence, he had the capacity to plan, calculate the unforeseen, and cleverly plan complex schemas of events that could possibly unfold, and as so plan how to counteract any and all possible threats, and mis-happenings to get as much profit out of minimal risk.

"Twenty thousand you say?" King Thidas turned to the minister. "That includes everybody, every able fighting soul among us? Leaving only a thousand soldiers behind defending our ground?"

"Yes, I, err, we believe so, sir, not taking any ground staff into calculation."

"Why? No ground staff? Explain yourself!"

"Well, sir, we believe that we easily can schedule a heavy rotation duty on two hundred with another two hundred standing by. That leaves six hundred that can rest and take turn in ground duties, sir, this way we think we can send more out to fight the war, sir!"

The minister feared for his life.

"And you, where would you be? Remaining here to defend us, or out there fighting for our cause?"

"Me, sir? I do not understand…"

"I mean, minister, you lazy coward, that your calculations are flawed. Every minister, every council, every official could, theoretically, join the army, and we would get what? Another thousand able fighters?"

Before the pale minister could answer King Thidas continued.

"…either that or we could kill you all right here and right now, both alternatives would ease the burden on the six hundred resting men that we depend on defending our strong hold…"

"Well, Saculg…" the delegation member was back in his vault. "…your generosity… towards our King, is not forgotten… Yet the complexity in your situation is difficult to navigate…" His eyes wandered from one valuable object to the other… "Had Veron opened the door, there would be no question, he would be taxed a tenth. Now you opened the door, as the new owner of these living quarters and the new rightful owner of this vault. All paperwork is legit, and this is truly all yours, given to you before our generous King decided to collect the tax… or rather, informed you of the tax. So, it comes down to the decision of a humble servant. Should this be taxed a tenth as yours, or a fifth as a new earning…"

Saculg tried to make heads or tails of everything and his brain was almost overheating with all the thoughts running through it… Got to protect the secret, whatever it is, got to please this greedy delegation member, got to try and look after his own treasure and keep as much as possible.

Wait, what was that, greedy delegation member… That is it, one key to the situation…

"Perhaps, if I may…" Saculg looked at the old delegation member, who turned and nodded back at him to continue. "If I am not out of my place in suggesting that there might be a way to make this situation beneficial for us all?"

"Elaborate!"

"Was thinking that if you decide to tax me a fifth of everything, I will lose the most, but our Great King would gain the most, and you would gain nothing. And if you tax me a tenth, I will lose the least, but our Great King would not gain as much, and nor would you…"

The delegation member followed Saculg with great interest as Saculg moved around in the vault trying to figure out what secrets could be hiding in there… What did his Grandfather or Uncle leave behind, hidden in here? How did they decide how to hide it?

"Say you tax me a tenth. That would mean our great king lose a tenth, and I gain a tenth. If we divide that tenth in two piles, our Great King and I gain equally much, and lose equally much, but you, dear delegation member, would have gained nothing for your trouble. Say we instead divided that tenth in three equal piles, one for our Great King, one for me, and one for you, dear delegation member, that would mean that our Great King and I lose equally much, gain equally much, and you would also gain equally much for your trouble in settling this matter…"

Saculg laid his eyes on the wooden box again… of course… hide it where no one would fancy to look! In plain sight, yet hidden from every pair of greedy dwarf eyes… It had to be there… It just had to!

"So, what you are trying to say, is that if I am, should we say, flexible, with the paperwork, it would benefit us all, and our Great King would have as much to lose on it as you… and I would have something to lose if the paperwork did not match up at the accountants…" the delegation member started to wander around, picking up random objects, weighing them, evaluating them.

Saculg did not say anything, just let the old dwarf keep wandering around. Even if he tried, he could not help but staring at the object he now believed held the secret. And just as if it were a bad dream, the delegation member picked up the wooden box, studying its beautiful carvings. Almost instinctively, Saculg reacted.

"I could even consider another gift, just to make it worth your while." Saculg approached the delegation member, took the box from him, and put it down as if he did not care about it and with his arm around the delegation member he walked further into the vault, to where the bigger and more valuable treasures were kept.

"I mean, it is not unheard of that the registers at the accountants are not entirely correct… There have been many records of individuals who wished to hide their positions, but also those who have stated false possessions to gain higher status amongst us…" Saculg was ashamed that he smeared Veron's name like this.

"…and from another perspective there is also a large black market trade where things unofficially trade places…" the delegation member filled in… not paying any attention to the beautiful wooden box that Saculg noticed had its lid open from when he carelessly put it down… revealing its secrets, at least five heaven stones by a quick glance, maybe more… Which was truly impossible… Saculg knew that the legendary stones were unique and one of a kind. Only one.

**feb 80.**

"Hurry up! We haven't got all day" Oaks turned to Roy and Phidas looking back at them struggling with a long rope passage between two trees.

"This passage is the only one of its kind. Nobody except the man who designed the entire Sky road knows why this section is designed like this. We have asked but have only gotten the answer 'You'll see one day'… And do you want to know a weird thing? It's called Dwarf Saver's passage…"

Roy and Phidas tried to keep their balance and tried to pay attention to what their guide was telling them along the route towards the vampire stronghold.

They had been told that their journey would take about three days for those who was used to tread the Sky road, so they should expect four or five days, since they were new-comers… and also because Phidas' legs wasn't too long.

When they heard that, they both thought that it was over exaggerated to take an extra two days in to account, but after walking a full night (daytime was prohibited to travel) they could easily accept that they were expected to take longer than for those who was used to the Sky road.

Phidas, who could compare solid rock and ground could add a third way of using the body to move forward to his experience bank. Roy, who only had walked the ground added his second. And Roy figured that someone with sea legs might find this easier than he did.

"The sections are calculated for your pace, which will give us a night's walk between the larger platforms. I myself am used to take one and a half or two stops in one night. So, I have spent several days in smaller trees without platforms to get the necessary daily rest."

As they had passed the Dwarf Saver's Passage both Phidas and Roy needed to stand on solid wood for a quick rest, before they could continue on the wooden bridges that followed. Compared to the rope construction they just passed, the wooden bridges seemed very stable under their feet.

"I know you might not believe me, but in some parts of the Sky road, it is impossible to say how long it takes to pass, sometimes it takes less than a night, and sometimes it takes several nights. Nobody knows why, it is just the way it is."

"I have never met anyone who talks as much as me, Oaks!" Roy tried to keep up. "But I believe you beat me…"

"I know, you've said that to me before!"

Roy was again taken with his guard down. "No, I have not, we only met last evening, and I have known you for less than a night. And even if I cannot claim to remember everything, I can clearly remember this past night, and I know I have not said this earlier!"

Oaks just shrugged his shoulders. "I suppose you are right." And just continued to walk. "We are soon at our next stop. Here we will rest for the day, get something to eat and sleep as much as you can. It'll probably be hard for you given all the light, but you get used to it after a while."

They walked on in silence for a while, then Oaks broke it again.

"Oh, Grand Master Phidas, I've been meaning to ask you. Can you teach me about dwarf economics? Once the Sky road has fulfilled its purpose, I am thinking about starting trade routes with the dwarf community."

**Eighty one.**


"Devoras – I come bearing news!"

A young boy came running on one of the bridges in the west.

"Timboy, we have discussed this a thousand times already! No shouting or screaming on the Sky road, it will get us detected!" Devoras rose from the table where they all sat, sharing a simple meal. He walked over to greet the newcomer.

"Have a seat, we are just eating our last meal before we before we start our way back to the base. What news do you carry, young friend?"

"We have seen something really strange a while ago, and a few days ago we were reached by some strange rumors." Timboy joined the others at the table, really enthusiastic. He grabbed a plate and took some food before he continued.

"A while back, we got strange reports from the seaside that a single man was accompanied by a werewolf while carrying some kind of silver stone. The werewolf did not attack him, rather guarded him or lead him." The others around the table was paying their undivided attention as he continued. This was truly unheard of, a werewolf that did not kill instantly. Dee could not help but to think this was not a coincidence.

"As the man was walking inland, towards the mountain, more and more werewolves joined and now a hole pack of werewolves has arrived with the man to a cave by the foot of the mountain. I have seen it with my own eyes, but I am told there are more than a hundred werewolves surrounding this strange man and his silver stone. We call him 'Dances with Werewolves'."

"My ship was carrying an unknown cargo, or at least unknown to most of us. We only knew it was very valuable and there was much secrecy surrounding it. Among us crewmen there was a rumor that the box contained a silver egg. Nobody had seen it, but everybody talked about it as if they had." Tadao added. "I wonder if this man is one of my former crew-mates, and if he, somehow, had rescued the cargo."

Dee almost did not dare utter the words.

"What if it is my brother?"

Tadao looked at her. He wished to say to her that there was almost no chance that it could be her brother. Of all persons on that ship that was lost along the way, and the most likely outcome that the ship was lost at sea, it would be a miracle if it was her brother. But then again, it was a miracle that he himself had survived.

Dee turned to Timboy and Devoras.

"Can you take us, I mean me, to this cave? Does the Sky road extend all the way to the mountain? And how long will it take us to get there?"

Timboy and Devoras looked at each other. Both hesitating to answer.

"Well, we can take you there but…" Devoras was the one to start speaking. "…it is impossible to tell you how long it will take. The distance and the number of steps you need to take is always the same, but for some reason the journey varies in time. The quickest someone has moved from here to the mountains are one day. The longest several weeks."

"I've tried to run the distance once, counted each step, took me five days to reach the last platform. Another time I've walked the same distance and almost the same number of steps, a bit more actually, and it only took three days." Timboy continued.

"That is simply not possible, you are trying to fool us!" Tadao exclaimed.

"I can believe it, but not explain it…" Leola said, with a low voice, almost a little to herself.

Dee looked puzzled, tried to catch Groll's eyes for, but he did not look up, nor say anything.

**Eighty two.**


Grime stood back, filled with horror and fear. It was done, it was completed. All nine bottles of venom, mixed with human blood from the unborn children of the girls and his very own herb tincture, Vampireized of course.

In front of him the Vampire Master agonized. There was indeed a change in his body. Not something that could be seen, but something that Grime could scent into the core of his bones. Chills went down his spine. A part of him was overly joyed with confidence and pride in what he had done, another part of him was terrified of the consequences as to what he had just done. This could very well mean that he sent this world into a darker path. The good thing was that he at least would be on the Master's good side, or at least Grime hoped.

"Bring me one of the girls" the master commanded to one of the guards posted by the doors. And before Grime could utter a protest, his favorite girl stood in front of the master.

Grime was not sure that the change was done already and wanted to urge the master to wait a little while longer before testing it, but from the tension in the room he knew to keep his mouth shut.

He closed his eyes as the master started to circle around the girl, he could hear her terrified breathing, he could hear the master shiver of excitement.

Without opening his eyes Grime could well make out what happened next.

The Vampire Master suddenly attacking the girl, biting her neck and heavily drinking her blood, while her body shivered both from the sobbing and from what happened inside her.

Grime heard himself say, still without opening his eyes:

"If my theory is accurate, you'll need to bleed her body dry. Only then will the human part of her give up its fight and the assumed vampire functions take over."

The Master enjoyed every sip and literally emptied the girl's body on blood. Then, just silence. No movement. Nothing.

Grime refused to open his eyes, he assumed that the master stared right at him by now. His brain started to run wild.

"What happens to a Vampire that is completely dry of blood?" he asked.

"Our body functions are slowed down to almost nothing. Very hard to detect. As if in a deep sleep without breathing."

"Does a vampire die from this deep sleep?"

"No, you can be revived with blood infusion through the mouth. First a few drops in the mouth, then we need to feed by ourselves."

"Try it, feed her a few drops of blood…"

The master bit his own wrist, making a few drops of blood fall into the open mouth of the girl.

What happened next was incredible, and horrible. Grime opened his eyes to see this.

The girl suddenly took a deep breath that seemed to fill her entire body with life. Then, greedily, she grabbed the master's arm with great force and started to drink from the fresh wound.

The expression in the master's face could not be mistaken, he was thrilled! Pleased that he now could create more Vampires.

**Eighty three.**


King Thidas waited in his private chambers. How long would this take? Could they not just hurry up? What took all this valuable time?

He walked back and forth tightly holding his latest addition, the heaven stone.

This most valuable piece, a key to his upcoming success. From one perspective one of seven keys, but from his understanding, the most important key of them all.

The stone itself possessed great strength, but together with the other legendary stones this was the key to link their powers into one. The center stone. The key to the keys.

Alone it would…

King Thidas was interrupted by a hard knock on his chamber doors.

"Enter" he yelled, with saliva flying all over the room.

A military officer entered.

"Yes?" King Thidas said, directed towards the officer, very pleased with his discipline and not speaking until asked to.

"All troops are ready my King. Both those who will defend the strong hold and those who will dispatch to the surface."

"Excellent, proceed at once! Are your orders clear?"

"Certainly, my King! Takedown by force, leave no one behind, no dwarf, no enemy. If anyone tries to intervene, they become the enemy. Once we get there, obtain control of the main mines, assist in completing the tunnel. Then use the tunnel to get all the remaining legendary stones here, followed by the tax collections and other treasures.”

“Excellent. Good. And avoid undead if you can. No point in taking those on, did not seem to work well for the last delegation. But now you are greater in numbers, so I do not assume it will be a problem. And one last thing… The head?”

“Put on a stick in the main hall, my King. You should not expect any other sub ordinance from anybody.”

King Thidas started to wander around his chamber again. As if to gather up his thoughts and see if there was anything else before he sent of the army on its mission.

“That was all! Off you go and bring me back my stones!”

The officer left without uttering any other words, and again King Thidas was alone.

He had a hard time to believe that it had come to this. He had planned everything for a very long time, and even if the preparations and the planning was very solid and detailed, he could not believe that it had started. That he was closer to his goals, that every minute of every passing day brought him closer and closer, fulfilling his dreams. No… His destiny!

He was patient and had waited a long time, but in all honesty, he thought that he would have to wait much longer before his brother would either die of old age, get killed or voted away from the throne. In a way, he kind of wished that it had taken a little longer, so he would have gotten further on the tunnel project, but on the other hand, with so many more men working on it, it would be finished in no time.

**eighty four**

As the delegation member had left, fully loaded with treasures and other valuable artifacts, gemstones and metal pieces, Saculg headed right back to his vault. Now, by law, this was his vault. And he had paid his taxes. All paperwork was in order.

The first thing he did was to reopen the wooden box that he had manage to close earlier, without the delegation member noticing it.

He had to gather his thoughts around this.

The heaven stone. One of the legendary stones. The only one of its kind. Yet here were a few, eleven to be precise. This could only mean one thing. Or two. No, rather three. I will take that back. Four.

The first thing it meant was that all or all, but one was not the real heaven stone.

The second thing it meant was that someone, probably his grandfather, had forged duplicates of the heaven stone.

The third thing it meant was that he may or may not be in possession of the heaven stone.

The fourth thing it meant was that he really had to keep this a secret. A huge secret.

How could this be? What was he supposed to do? He could not destroy all the stones or get rid of a single one of the, since he had no way of telling the copies from the real thing.

As he picked them up, one by one for closer examination he noticed very small differences in each one, but so small that it was hard to tell them apart.

He had to make something out of this. At least one thing was clear. This was the, or at least one of the secrets of this vault. And he had to make sure to keep it that way.

He was certainly not the fortunate one. And yet he was. Other dwarfs would envy him, getting fine living quarters in the old parts of the mine. Getting his very own vault filled with various valuable things, one thing more valuable than the other. And there was still plenty, even if the delegation member had both taxed him and accepted his offer.

But the heaven stones. What to do with those?

Saculg left the vault and took the wooden box with him, with all the stones in it. He sat down by the fireplace, rose again to get a fire started, walked across the room to the well filled bar. He had never touched any liquid with alcohol before, but now he wanted to try, a sign of his newly received status as a grown dwarf, master of his own chamber.

It struck him, as he poured something out of a bottle, now he would probably be a full-fledged member of the Ingm clan, possibly with a seat around the table.

Now he wished he had paid more attention to the internal politics that his father and Veron had discussed.

He took the glass with the strange liquid and walked back to the chair by the fireplace. He put the glass down next to the box. Lifted it again to take a sip but stopped himself when the glass reached his nose. What was this? Smelled awful, like some old wet tared piece of wood put on a fire creating heavy smoke. Was this really drinkable? What if Veron had a bottle of poison in his bar? Not very likely, he took a sip.

Oh heaven, really strong and heavy in taste, but a real pleasure for his taste buds. He could get used to this.

**eighty five.**


Oaks listened carefully to Phidas' short but clarifying lesson of the mechanics of the Dwarf Economy.

"If there is only one of something, it is infinitely valuable. If there are two, it is rare, and very valuable. If there is a lot of something, it is common, then it is worth nothing. So, if I find a new type of gemstone, I will mine one for myself. My stone is now infinitely valuable. Should there be another finding, both the stones would be worth a great deal, but the stone I found first would lose so much value to me, so I would want to sell it, as quick as possible. Should it be me who also found the second stone, then I would hide it away, possible destroy it, so the first would keep its value."

Phidas struggled onward on the sky road, but steadfast kept teaching Oaks the basics.

"There have been occasions where one dwarf has decided to manipulate the mechanics of our economy, and to everyone's despair, it actually works, which has created another balance. Once there was a new finding by a lone dwarf. He found a rich area with many gemstones, called the yellow-mirror-stone. He found at least a thousand pieces of it. But he kept it to himself and showed the rest of us only one. Thus, the stone was infinitely valuable. But in secret, he said to many others, that he had found one more. And sold that one more stone to many others, making a fortune. Then the lie was out in the open, and there were thousand stones out on the market, rather worthless from a dwarf's point of view. Now, given our greedy mindset, no-one blamed he who sold it to the others, we blame ourselves for making bad deals. But the dwarf had counted every stone and kept track of them, and once worthless, he bought each stone back for almost nothing. Then, publicly in the great hall, he destroyed all but 9 stones. And like that, the yellow-

mirror-stone was once valuable again. And valuable is desirable for
any dwarf.”

Phidas ended his short, but precise lesson of the basics of the dwarf
economy.

”Now, young Oaks, tell me, what will you do with this
knowledge?”

”Well, when the sky road has filled its purpose, we are no longer
needed up here, and I want to do something different. Then I
thought to myself that trading with the dwarves is practically
unheard of today, but in the old days before the war it was done. So,
I figured I want to give it a try to pick up the old trade routes
again.”

”Hold on, what do you mean by ’the sky road has filled its
purpose’?” Roy joined the discussion again after leaving it of
boredom when Phidas started his lesson.

”I do not know if I’m supposed to say this, but you are the entire
reason for this sky road, and you have set things in motion by
coming here. Soon, if all goes as it is said that it will, the entire sky
road will collapse but only after having played its parts in the
events to come.” Oaks stopped and looked at them both.

”I am not sure I am following…” Roy said with hesitation.

”Well, there is a prophesy, in a way, that has foreseen this moment.
It is this prophesy that made Vladir and the others build the sky
road in the first place.”

”What does the prophesy say?” Phidas wanted to know.

”I have never heard it, but we all know we are supposed to keep the
sky road in good shape, keep it hidden and gather undead in the far
end until you two arrive. Then it is said that the events will unfold
as foretold.”

"Is that all you know?" Roy demanded to know.

"That is all I know" Oaks reassured.

**eighty six**


"I will take you!" Devoras said after consulting with Timboy.

"And I'll go to central command to report." Timboy said. "But we do not think Vladir will be pleased with our choice to leave this section unmanned."

"Since I am the oldest here, it is my decision, and no shadow shall fall on Timboy for this choice. I have a feeling that this is the right thing to do, and hopefully, I can take you and be well in time for my duties and moving the undead…" Devoras did not look very confident in what he just said.

"But I thought you could not say how long it takes to get there… then how would you know when you'll get back? Can't we just walk in that direction ourselves and eventually end up at the mountain?" Dee asked.

"Yes, you could, but a little longer down the sky road, it divides in to many different paths, like a river delta. Even if we would describe the way in detail, the chances are that you still might get lost, and end up at a different location by the mountain. Then it would be hard for you to find your way to the cave." Devoras explained, still with an uncertain wrinkle between his eyes.

"Very well, then it is decided, thank you for doing this for me…" Dee looked around, "for us I mean… it means a lot! When do we leave?"

"We can leave at once, we should only pack plenty of supplies before we go, no way of telling how much we need. We can resupply along the route as well…" Devoras sounded somewhat more cheerful now and went straight on to the preparations.

Dee looked at Groll. He had gone more and more quiet, and more worried the since they arrived at the sky road. She had a feeling he was hiding something. Given the limited space, she had not gotten any opportunity to take him aside and talk to him. But he remained by her close proximity all the time, so she was confident that it was not something she had said or done that had triggered this reaction. On the other hand, it could be their growing numbers. Groll had not had any social contacts for years, and all of a sudden, he is in the middle of seven other people, mostly humans, but also a dwarf. It could as well be nothing and just social awkwardness.

Come to think about it, it was not only Groll that had lowered his social profile, Leola had as well. Her interaction with the others had been almost zero and she kept mostly to herself. Dee got the feeling that she was occupied with something, not that she could say what it was, but something Leola returned to over and over again.

Dee walked over to Devoras to help in the preparations, both to have something to do, and actually to shorten the time to get moving. She wanted so bad to go find out if the mysterious 'Dances with werewolves' was her brother. Even if she on some level already knew it was, she wanted to get confirmation with her own eyes. To see him, to hug him. This was even more important to her now since their father was missing. She needed Rick now, and she was so scared that her feeling that it really was Rick with the werewolves was only her wishful thinking and that those wishes were so strong that it convinced her mind and body to know.

Come to think about it, if it really were Rick, how would she approach him? Sure, she had survived an encounter with three werewolves and lived to tell about it. But waltz in among a horde of werewolves and go up to Rick and hug him. Something told her that this would probably not be the case. Yet nobody else seemed to think about it. The only focus was to get there.

**eighty seven.**

This was the first time in a very long time that Grime had time to reflect on his past actions. As for his own transformation, he could only congratulate himself. He had harvested the strength and stamina of the werewolf. And for this, his pride felt no limit.

But there was a dark cloud on his sky, or rather, a big gathering of dark clouds.

He had set a side many of his principals and had broken more than one decent code of conduct. There was his manly need and his short coming towards the girls. There was his lack of respect towards creation itself, both when it came to harvesting the power of a werewolf and tampering with the vampire. And of course, tampering with the vampire part itself.

He was well aware that he had unleashed great evil in the world, and had no way of forgiving himself for it, nor expecting anybody else to forgive him for it.

Then there was the revelation from the truth flowers. The actions of his so-called sister. A deception and a great betrayal, but the underlying question was: was it greater than his own recent betrayal of everybody and what were her motives?

He had learned that she had used some kind of magic spells to plant fake memories of a childhood with her as a big sister. She had erased his true memories, which he had not yet regained. But with more serum from the truth flower that could probably be accomplished.

His initial feelings of rage and revenge towards her had faded a little, and a growing curiosity and respect and admiration for her skills within her art form had started to grow.

Was it possible that she needed him to walk this path, covered and embedded in pure lies, to get to this point where they actually could be tremendously powerful together?

If that were true, what was her end game?

He had to get out of here! He had to find her and ask her why? What was going on?

So many mixed feelings. Thrill, pain, regret, anger, remorse, pride, joy.

He had to get out of here. Now! He needed an escape plan. Now it was too late to worry about the girls, now it was just him! Could he possibly use the werewolf somehow? Or was it better to leave it behind? Maybe its corps? What good could a werewolf corps be to the vampires?

Suddenly, time felt short. First escape, then hunt her down. He needed answers. Now, one step at a time. He needed a plan. Get out of the room. Get to the werewolf. Get past the guards. Get out in the open air. Get as far away from this dreadful place as possible in as little time as possible. In what direction? Timing was very clear. Dawn. The sun would be his best, and probably only allied.

Or should he ask the master to be released just like that. It was a possibility. After all, he had held his part of the deal. Then again, the master was not to be trusted, he always had his own agenda.

Grime was interrupted in his thoughts by a guard that entered the chamber.

"The master requests your presence at once!"

**Eighty eight.**

What was supposed to be a rare occasion, had become part of the ordinary for the dwarves in the northern province.

Once again, they were gathered to send a big delegation, no, correction, an army. The only difference this time was that they all were part of the army, and only a few would remain behind. The northern province was down to skeleton crew. This was the first time ever since it was established. Those who remained were well drilled in the protocols of this event, but none of them actually believed that this would ever occur. One thing was different from their practice runs. They had a workforce from the main mines to control and feed. This meant that their work on the tunnel had been replaced with guarding and household duties for those who kept working the tunnel.

King Thidas sat on his throne and had a great view of the ordered chaos beneath him. He really questioned if the none trained military staff would actually follow orders and do everything for the kingdom, but he had great faith in his military command and knew that they were drilled to perfection. They would know what to do in every situation and only sacrifice as many as needed for the greater good. For the kingdom. For his kingdom! For him. Yes, they would do it for him. He, and he alone, was this kingdom. His vision, his strength, his knowledge, his ambition. They all belonged to him and carried out his will.

He imagined that this would be similar of having a child. No, correction, this was probably nothing like having a child. He had seen other dwarves with children arguing with their offspring and complaining that they did not pay attention, did not listen, did not follow their instructions. This perfected machinery in front of him carried out his directions to perfection. Like no child ever would do.

From another perspective it felt very good that it had already started. The final step of his plan to gain absolute control and power over the entire dwarf society. Fulfilling his destiny as their leader. He truly deserved it after all patience he had shown and tolerance towards others in the political game he had played to get where he was now. But soon it would be over. Every dwarf would follow his law, his command and his wishes. And they all should be thankful and grateful for his commitment in their wellbeing and the greatness in the dwarf way of life. He was truly their savior, but most of them could not see it. But to him it was perfectly clear. A vision he had carried with him for many ages. Sure, there were a few around him that shared his views, but most of them feared him and dared not oppose him. Sad that they could not see his greatness. But he was goodhearted and just, he both forgave and pitted them at the same time. They did not understand their own best, and fortunate for them, he did, and carried it out with perfection for all to enjoy and share. Fools that could not see and share this. Well, soon they would come to celebrate with him, the biggest event in dwarf history. The union of the two-dwarf fraction, uniting under one great leader. The dawn of a new era lured in the horizon, and as the sun would rise and shine on him, they would all understand that he was their true leader, their king. They would beg to be part of the greatness, the perfection.

In front of him now, he saw mostly fear and uncertainty in the faces of those who were about to leave their safe haven behind. A good experience and in a way a good way to leave the old and through this be reborn in the new dwarf nation. Sure, it was not guaranteed that everyone would return and have the chance to be a part of it all, but like always, the weakest needed cleansing, and there would always be individuals who would not make it through the cleansing. And afterward, the dwarf society would stand stronger, without the weakest among them, and they could all unite in one perfect harmony. True perfection.

Chills of pleasure went down his spine. It had started! He saw the big mass of dwarf's march to their destiny. To the future.

241

**eighty nine.**

The Ingm-clan was gathered around the table.

"Do we really have to accept him as a replacement for Veron? Is there no other more suited?" One of the dwarves uttered with dismay in his voice.

"It is your son you are talking about…" another replied.

"As head of the clan I have gotten information that is unofficial as of yet, but I want to share this with all of you around this table, before we all make up our minds…" the oldest of them that were seated in the largest chair by the fire spoke.

"As we all know, we are heading into a new era. A shift in regime affects us all. And no one in this room is blind, we can all see it happen. No one knows what will happen her just yet, but I for sure do not like the way it seems to be heading. So it is my opinion that the Ingm-clan must adapt to the new future, even if we do not know what it looks like. We need to embrace it, adapt quickly and benefit from it. Whether we like it or not."

He paused and met the eyes of each member around the table.

"I have heard, from a trustworthy source, that Saculg may be nominated to an official post in this new regime. Should he be selected, it is important that we have already welcomed him with open arms to this table. This may give the Ingm-clan a leverage against the other clans."

"But the boy is stupid as a rock!" Saculg's father spoke again.

"You say so, but I know your brother thought differently. And even the remote possibility that he may be right, and the fact that he could play a part in the new order around here, is reason enough for me. I say we give him a seat around this very table with open arms!

And we all know that even the simplest rock can be turned into beauty, given the right time and hard work…”

”No, I will not allow it. I know him and it would be our undoing. Besides, he does not think much of me either. I am not certain being in the same council as me would be in his interest.”

”But it is in ours, in my opinion. And should we do this, I strongly suggest you be the one to tutor him and rebound with him. I believe that we need him in order to keep our position in these new times. If nothing else, perhaps we gain nothing but a healed family, perhaps we gain our new future. Bear in mind that he does not longer have his uncle to lean on, he will need a new role model now.”

The oldest of them looked at his fellow dwarves again, before continuing…

”But the very first thing, and most important of all…”

He dramatically paused to emphasize his next words even more.

”…we need to make sure that our clans secrets remain hidden inside his vault. And that should be the task of someone who is well familiar with him, and who is not a stranger in the vault…”

The elder turned to the dwarf next to him.

”Are you up for the task while the rest of us vote for the possible replacement of Veron?”

**ninety**

"The castle is about one hour in that direction," Oakes pointed due south east, "and I will wait for you until you get back to lower the ladder to get you up here again. You'd better be careful, even at dawn they keep watch, but in cover of sunlight you are safer than at night."

Phidas and Roy thanked their guardian and started to climb down. The terrain below was difficult to maneuver, especially for Phidas.

Roy was a little tired, he had almost gotten used to sleep during the day and walk the sky road at night. But the adrenaline of being close to the vampire stronghold helped a lot in keeping him wide awake.

He turned to Phidas after they had walked about five minutes since the touched ground for the first time since they had gotten into the house.

"Now that we are here, what are we supposed to do?"

"Well, I have been focusing more on getting here than what to do, but I am sure we think of something… I kind of wish I had planned this and brought a few blast stones with me from the mines…"

"Blast stone, what is that?"

"Oh, it's a rare stone that we use in our mining process on particular difficult and hard parts of the mountain. It is a quick and dirty method of getting forward. See, normally we take pride in doing everything by hand, according to the old traditions. But this stone makes it possible to cut time when the mountain wants to slow us down. Downside being that it powders everything, including whatever findings we could possibly find, which is probably why we do not use it so often."

"And if you had this Blast stone, what would you do with it?"

"Probably attach it to the castle structure and bring the walls down."

"Is it possible to find it here?"

"No, I think not. This is a black stone, buried deep in the mountain, brought to daylight, it would shimmer a bit, almost like it had small pieces of silver in it… The only chance to find it here on the surface would be if someone had carried it here and leave it on the ground."

"Say we had it, how do you set it off? Fire?"

"Yes and no. Fire is the best way to set it off, but not an ordinary fire from wood or coal, it needs to be a fire with greater, far greater heat. So we would also need an iron-coal legation. Equally rare. This far we have only found it in once place a long, long time ago in the beginning of our great mine. Of course, it can be replicated, but not in as good quality. And to be perfectly honest, the findings we have left are of the lowest quality. All the good ore have been used up long time ago."

"Ok, sounds like we need an entirely different plan… From what I have heard, isn't it possible to break solid rock with fire?"

"Yes, it is possible, but you would need a big fire to create enough heat, and since I expect the castle to be built with boulders, it would take a huge fire to heat each and every one of the individual rocks to the critical temperature. We would need a huge fire… and lots of wood…"

"What about water then? Can we do something with water? I am sure there are some kind of water source nearby. I mean, even vampires need to drink, don't they?"

"I am afraid not, son. The only thing they need is blood."

**Ninety one.**


Devoras was surprised. This was the fastest recorded walk to the mountain, only one night. By sunset they left the platform, by dawn they arrived at the last platform by the mountain.

Along the way, they passed several hordes of undead beneath the sky road. The others found it hard to believe that there existed so many undead and was both horrified and astonished by the fact that the sky road guardians had managed to gather them up and keeping them moving to their will. It was an impressing operation. Very well organized and smoothly operated. Planned in the smallest detail. Almost like a crew on a ship, and yet entirely different.

The view on the last platform was magnificent. The sun slowly rising from behind, casting light at the mountain top, and a sharp line of shadow slowly descending towards the mountain base.

Devoras hesitated a little. Should he remain on the platform, as per instruction, always leave at least one behind on the platform to manage the ladders. Yes, he would remain behind. He had already violated several rules of the sky road, best not push it further.

"I will remain here" he turned to the others, "and as soon as you get back here, I can offer you passage at the sky road again, and should you choose another route, I will head back. But no rush, I will remain here a few days if needed. But no longer that five sunrises, on the fifth sunset I am obligated to return the way we came from, regardless if I have heard anything from you or not."

Dee looked at him, almost with tears in her eyes. This could mean goodbye, but she hoped not. She had kind of grown fond of him. Without words, she hugged him and started her climb down the ladder to the ground. It probably was not like this, but when looking back at it, Devoras was sure that as Dee climbed down the ladder, she pushed the darkness away from under her and as she set her feet on the ground it was instantly lit up by daylight.

The others followed her example, but not as majestically as Dee, from Devoras point of view.

When all was gathered with packing on ground level, they turned to Dee, kind of waiting on instructions. After all, this was her expedition.

”Well, let's find the werewolves, and find out the identity of the mysterious man carrying the silver egg.” She turned towards the mountain and started to walk.

”What do you want us to do when we find them?” Tadao asked.

”Well, let's find them first, and hope for the best. When I met Groll I first encountered three of them without getting killed. And they have not killed the man with the egg, so let us hope for the best and take one step at the time, first thing is finding them. Devoras pointed in this direction, so this is the direction I want to walk.”

”May I suggest that we go in this direction?” Tadao pointed towards a ridge ahead. ”I believe it is wise to seek high ground to easier spot the whereabouts of the werewolves, so we do not risk marching right into their nest unprepared and unannounced.” Tadao started walking without waiting for any answer, since he felt this was the only option if they did not want to risk being werewolf breakfast.

”No.” Groll spoke for the first time since they left the platform where they met Timboy. ”If we are approaching werewolves, they need to see us from a distance. Let us take the direction Dee chose, and keep to the lowest track we can find. They will see us.”

”Why? It sounds like suicide!” Leola looked skeptical.

”I have my reasons…” Groll muttered.

**ninety two.**

"Your work is most impressive..."

Grime stood in front of his master in one of the master's chambers.

"...but it is not nearly finished!"

What!? Grime could literally not understand what he was just hearing and was to surprised to think of a reply.

"My offspring cannot continue to reproduce..." the master spoke slow and very quiet, almost like a whisper through his teeth. Was he mad at Grime? He could not tell...

"When she bit one of the other girls, she only satisfied her thirst, the other did not reborn..."

Grime started thinking. Enhanced vampire bites human. Infects human with vampire strength, drain her of her blood, resurrect her with its own blood.

Resurrected human in vampire form, bites human, drain her of blood, the second victim does not get resurrected, despite feeding of blood.

Where is the missing piece of the puzzle?

As if the vampire master understood that Grime was working to find a solution to this delicate problem, the master kept quiet.

A stray thought of escape passed through Grime's mind, but he forced his focus back to the problem at hand.

"I have no guaranteed solution to this, from this point I can only experiment, and as of now, I have two things I can think of trying, both very dangerous and filled with risk. One may cost the werewolf's life, the other one will. Both can cost your life..."

Grime turned to the master and looked him straight into his intense eyes.

”Not if you enhance another and make your experiments on her…” the master answered calmly.

Grime realized what he was asked to do, work with his favorite girl, with a great chance of killing her in the process. He could not help but to think that this was part of the master's plan all along.

Back to the drawing-table.

Step one. Repeat the enhancement to her.

Step two. Cut out the venom producing gland from the werewolf and try to get the vampire body to accept it. This could kill both the werewolf, her and himself.

Step three. Possibly included in step two, depending on what happened to the werewolf, take the heart of the werewolf and implant inside her. This would kill the werewolf, possible her, but post no risk to himself, except the wrath of the master if it failed.

Herbs. He would need to gather more. What species? He needed to go back to his books, right away. And without meaning it, deep in thought, he turned his back on the master and exited the chamber and headed back to his temporary home.

A strange thought. But yes, this had become his home. In a way.

**ninety three.**

They had calculated that they would exit the mountain by sunrise, but someone had miscalculated terribly wrong, it was a thick darkness that hit the dwarf army as it surfaced. The rain lay heavy in the air and the wind drove it through the amours from the side. Clouds covered the night-sky, cutting out all light from the moons and the stars.

Without any visible landmarks or stars on the night-sky the designated navigator was blind. She could not make heads or tails of direction. The military leader was very frustrated and argued that it was better to get moving in any direction than to stand still, but the navigator explained that going in the wrong direction would possibly only add time to their journey ahead. So her recommendation, perhaps based on fear of the dark, remained setting up camp. Or returning to the protection of the northern province and the safety of the mountain.

The military leader liked to keep his head attached to his body and preferred the rain and the open air instead of returning to the mountain, so he ordered camp.

Since everything either already was wet or was getting wet, no campfires was lit that night, and without light it was hard to raise camp and weather-protection, so the camp was not more than groups of dwarves, sitting on whatever they could find, back to back to try and keep warm.

Had there been any dragons around, which there were not, it had been a delicate smorgasbord of dwarves and a fair share of treasures.

But lucky for the dwarves, their only nearby enemy that night was the dark and the rain, and of course, their own fear and their own inner demons, which for most of them was more than enough. Not even the well drilled military commanders and their soldiers were unaffected. So at dawn, when the sun rose and the rain stopped, most of them felt a relief that they had survived the night, even if there had been no real danger or anything to worry about at all. They would all, soon enough, long back to this night, when the mountain was near, their food and water supply filled, and with good spirits.

Their escapade would later be called 'the wandering dwarf army' and be mocked by everybody, even amongst the dwarves themselves. But that would not occur until after their defeat in the coming war. A war that would be the second great war in the history of dwarves and that yet again left the dwarf-kind scattered and few in numbers. Most of them yet again clinging to the main mines for survival.

The first war fought with pride for liberation, the second of madness for greed. But as always, the dwarf-kind is strong and stubborn lifeforms that prevail any external and internal threats.

Next time it rises from the aches it will be in a new form, with a new strong leader. But all this is unknown to the scared and wet dwarf army sitting here in the dark, afraid of their own shadow.

By dawn the rain stopped, most of them were cold and stiff from the night and it was a sad sight as they started to move, slow and aching.

The military commander was grateful that King Thidas was not around to witness this but tried to keep the dwarf pride high and infuse bravery and energy in his almost defeated army. How could he train them to find pride, strength and fighting-skills while marching across the open land? It was clear to him that he could not use fear, since the bigger part of the army was already broken by it. No, he had to find something else, something that would raise their spirit and something they could take pride in. Preferable without trashing King Thidas and backstabbing his orders.

**ninety four**

There was a hard knock on Saculg's door.

He hurried to open it and thought to himself that he had never imagined that having his own quarters would mean answering the door time and again. He had to work out how to expect and treat guests. Both invited and uninvited.

"Mother! Welcome!" Saculg was surprised to see her, he did not expect a visit from her. Maybe his father, but even that was unlikely… Yes, he had expected a delegation member or some other official visit that needed complementing of some tiny detail overlooked at the last visit, or the visit before that. But no, it was his own lovely mother!

"May I come in, dear?" Saculg still occupied the doorway, blocking passage into his new home.

"Oh, yes, I'm sorry mother, come in! Would you like something? What brings you here? Did Papa send you?"

"No, dear, I wanted to visit you in your new home. I want to ask you if you want to bring some of your things from your former room? I wanted to see you! I will miss you, you know!" The warmth in her voice was the unmistakable caring of a mother.

She looked at him with the same warmth and love, then something changed in her eyes and she looked away.

"…and also, I am sent by the table of the Ingm clan to ask you a few things…"

"The table? What could the table possibly want to ask me? I recon they do not fancy me much?"

"Well, actually, they do, in fact, as I left there was going to be a vote whether you should take Veron's seat around the table..." she was still looking away, and it made Saculg uneasy.

"...and what if I do not want his seat by the table?"

"...ehh? Don't you? Why wouldn't you? Of course, you would like to have a seat by the table! It is a once in a lifetime opportunity and will guarantee your social status for all future!"

"Well, I've been thinking about that possibility, and at first it was very appealing, but then I thought that it's not me, it's not my path..."

"Either way, the vote is taking place and I recommend you to rethink. But that was not the main reason for my visit..." she started to walk towards the vault door.

"Have you explored the vault yet?"

"Oh, yes, mother, I have... what nice treasures..."

"Did Veron tell you anything about it containing secrets?"

"Why?"

"Well, the Ingm clan has entrusted Veron with a great secret... and we have to make sure that it stays a secret!"

"A secret in a wooden box?"

"No, silly! No-one would hide a secret in a wooden box... will you let me in so I can inspect it with my own eyes?"

**ninety five.**

As Roy and Phidas got closer and closer they unintentionally lowered both their pace and profile, and pretty soon they crawled along the ground in the general direction of the castle, not that they were sure exactly what that direction was anymore, but they had a good understanding of them being on the right track. And after a long, long time their eyes got to rest on the magnificent castle. It was built by large solid rocks, each rock as tall as Roy and equally wide. They stayed low behind a formation of trees so they would not be detected from the castle.

”This looks even more horrifying than I imagined…” Phidas hope was diminishing. ”Looks impossible to cause any harm at all to this fortress…”

”Didn't you say you wanted blast stones? Black stones with tiny bits of silver?” Roy asked, looking down at a big pile of strange stones he had never seen before.

”Yes, that's right, but it would be impossible to find around here, I'm afraid…” Phidas replied, still with his eyes fixed on the castle.

”So this pile of blast stones would not come in handy then?” Roy asked, picking one up, weighing it in his hand, far heavier than he expected.

Phidas turned and looked at him.

”Great beard and rocks of fortune, it is blast stone! And lots of it too… I do not understand… how…” Phidas could not believe his eyes…

Roy looked a bit ahead to the next possible place to hide from the eyes of the castle…

"Looks like we have more over there..." and he turned to look at other nearby places... "and on several more locations all over..."

"This cannot be..." Phidas was in doubt. "Too easy, and highly unbelievable... How can there be so much of it just laying around? This is very rare under the mountain... a quantity of this has not been found in many years, and I bet it is more than we have in stock in the mines..."

"So what do we do? Gather it up and sneak to the castle and attach it there?"

"Yes, we need to force it in the crevices between the rock all over, or as much as we dare..."

They started to get to work, first very slow and careful, then they realized that on this very area of the castle there were no windows, so to be detected, they had to be seen from above the castle, and the odds for that was minimal during daylight. Even so, they always took a peek at the top before they moved across to get more or get back with new blast stones to force into the body of this dreadful castle of beasts.

As each pile of fine quality blast stones emptied, in the core of the pile they found equally fine quality ore of iron-coal legation.

"This is pretty unbelievable!" Phidas said, several times, as they kept on working during the hours of daylight.

"I think we dare to call it a night soon, and tomorrow, at sunrise, we place the ore all around this wall, piling up the rest of the blast stones here and there, with hopes that they will cause some damage from the outside." Phidas said as they moved over one last time to squeeze in some more blast stones.

As they reached the wall, Roy gestured to Phidas to be still and quiet. He pointed up towards the rim of the great wall they had been working on all day. Phidas tried to look up, but more importantly, listen.

Yes, there were clear movements.

**Ninety six.**

Dee lead the party along the valley bottom towards the mountain. Groll was back up at her shoulder, and Dee had to admit that it felt very safe and comfortable having him there.

Leola and Tadao walked together, muttering in between them, Veron walked alone as a middle party, not knowing who he would bet his money on. Groll and Dee sounded very sure in their opinion, while logic and reason definitely stood on the same side as Leola and Tadao. Well, Veron figured he would find out soon enough.

"This is foolish! From what I've heard the werewolves know someone is approaching from a long distance and will ambush everybody they encounter…" Tadao said with a low whisper to Leola.

"I for one are not too keen on walking into a horde of werewolves… I value my life and do not want it to end by stupidity! Keep close to me if you want to live! Once before I have managed to use my magic to hide from werewolves. I'll do it again if I must!"

Veron noticed that the two behind him whispered as if they made plans of their own, which made him quite uneasy. This is not really how he had imagined a life on the surface, but on the other hand, better to be free and backstabbed by friends than living a lie underground.

They continued to walk for about half a day before they encountered the werewolves.

They stood in the valley between three ridges. The ridge before them lead up to the mountain side. On each ridge, a long string of werewolves with their full attention on their little crowd. The way back through the valley was cut off by a big pack of hostiles, slowly closing in on their position. The once from behind had probably been following them out of sight for some time.

Dee stopped instinctively and Groll demanded to be put down on the ground in a hurry.

”All stay behind me!” he said hastily and this time no-one questioned him, they all formed a perfect line without much space between them.

They stood quietly waiting while the werewolves got closer and closer, rounding them up like predators’ hunts pray.

Groll did not say anything, the others did not dare say anything.

They all just stood there, waiting as the free space around them shrunk. Dee looked around. From her view there was plenty of space between them, considering the space she had on her last encounter. But this time there was not three, more like three hundred or more.

Now they could all start to hear sounds from the werewolves, their breathing, grufling and muffling, growling. At first only silent, but as they came closer the louder the sounds became.

Tadao who was the last person in their little queue dared not turn around, but very soon he not only hears them but also feel their breath down his neck. Each exhale caused chills down his spine and all the tiny hair on the back of his neck stood straight out.

Leola felt Tadao pushing hard against her, and in any other situation, she would have taken this as affection and an invitation to something much more pleasurable than soon to be savagely eaten by beasts.

## ninety seven

He made a careful inventory of what herbs he had already gathered. An impressive stock, Grime thought, but not nearly enough for his next challenge.

Even with a few days of reading through his books he only had a clear picture of step one. Make the enhancements on her. But for step two, much more complicated. So much more complicated. Introducing foreign tissue in a body was not easily done. And to just get the body not to reject it was unimaginable difficult, now he had to get the body to accept the foreign tissue and interact with it and in the end integrate it to its own functions.

This had been done earlier, giving the master the ability to fly. How had that been done? He needed to ask the master about this, see if there was anything left behind from the previous… oh… there had been another before him. Someone who most likely had done well at first, as he had. Then perhaps not so well, and then… maybe not a happy ending… he needed to make himself unexpendable. He needed to get some reassurances. Foolish to think that this could be accomplished, after all, it was the vampire master he was thinking about. A more unpredictable person was hard to find, both among mankind and elsewhere. He had no equal, he saw himself above all other, no matter what race or heritage.

Grime thought to himself that the werewolf he was about to kill for his marvelous and incredible work probably had a higher chance of survival than himself.

How should he maneuver this situation? He had been here before since he was captured. Felt like a long time ago. How long had he been here? He did not know. Only knew it was way too long. Come thinking about it, he would probably have gone mad by now. Kept isolated in captivity. Was he a mad man? No, first sign of madness is the endless monologues the subject has with itself. That was not something he would engage in. No, not the least. He was as sane now as the day he was captured! What was that day anyways? And what was this day? Unclear. Another sign of madness was incoherent thought-pattern. This would mean the inability to keep to one subject and just following associations to whatever next step the mind saw fit, jumping back and forth between various subjects. That was something he would never do. Besides, he had only one thing in his mind, how to perform his next big thing for the master. And yes, escape, not to forget about that, and then of course inventorying the herbs. No, that is right, this he had already done. But what was it more? Something he forgot… The revenge on his so-called sister? No, that was not it. Yes, liberating the girls, but no, he had almost killed them all, at least in spirit. They would not be fit to rejoin the world again, after everything they had been through. The rapes. No, not rapes, it had been their contribution to the project he was working on. But not really voluntarily, but if he had asked them nicely, they would probably have agreed that this was for their own best and would not have protested or taken harm from it. But he had not asked. Foolish when you look back at it, but then again, no regrets. Except for giving the vampire master his new powers… And his own powers! That was it! He had to test his own new strength. What was he capable of doing now that he had not been before? This would need some serious testing and evaluation. Grime, the new Grime, a true genius and masterpiece created by his own doing. Yes, this was worthy of celebration and perhaps…. Yes, a celebration with one of the girls, maybe even the vampire one, so he could get a feeling of her new body and the works of it. On the other hand, no, do not want to piss of a vampire, it needed to be one of the others, either one of them would do. What herbs did he now lack for performing his next step? The inventory suggested that he had what he needed for the first procedure with the girl. But for the second. Back to the books, this needed to be solved right away. And where and when would he gather what he needed? Could he trust the vampires with limited herbal knowledge to get them for him or could he somehow get another tour outside the castle? Another tour outside the castle was needed, especially as he needed to escape. But then he could not complete his work to the master. He, Grime, the one and only! The marvelous. The genius. He should not be denied the opportunity to show the world his true potential!

**Ninety eight.**


After two day straight marching in the open, with the rain as a constant companion the military leader was desperate for ideas to boost the morale of his army. Not only did they march further from home, further into the unknown and potentially closer to danger and the horrors of the surface, they also suffered from the cold and rain. Granted, the absence of the sun was welcome and gave their eyes time to adapt to the open land, but the rain, the wind and the cold was highly demoralizing and at a quicker pace than anyone could anticipate or even relate to. Drastic measures were needed.

The commander ordered halt, for no apparent reason at a random place. He gathered his fellow commanders and started to give orders.

"We need to get out of this horrid rain, we need to get dry, we need to boost morale amongst us. And this is how we are going to do it. First squadron, you will select four trees to mark the corners of a temporary wooden dwarf fortress. Mark them carefully and clear any trees that are within this square. These trees will be used to build our structure. Second to fifth squadron. You are to build a rooftop and a floor four our fortress. Priority roof - floor. We need to get dry. In the floor set fireplaces strategically. Squadron six to fourteen. You build walls. They will protect us from any outside threat. Squadron fifteen to twenty-four, security, keep us safe, set a wide perimeter at first, then slowly shrink the main perimeter as quick as possible to focus on the fortress, should we need to go outside the perimeter for material, squadron twenty-five to  thirty, you set local and temporary perimeters around any workforce that leave the main secure area. Squadron thirty-one to forty, you stay center and fill out any unanticipated temporary needs requested by squadron leader to squadron leader. Rest of the squadrons reinforce permanent needs requested by squadron leader to squadron leader."

He looked out as his men with pride.

"We are dwarves, make this happen as quick and effective as we still were in the mountain. Wood is only a weaker form of rock. Gives us the advantage. For King Thidas!"

The other officers answered unison:

"For King Thidas!"

And so, it started. More dwarves than could possibly meet the eye teemed all over the place and in a blink of an eye trees started falling, fist small trees, than bigger and bigger.

It is easy to compare what just occurred as a huger form of ants building a gigantic formicary.

The transformation was almost unreal, and it happened between two deep breaths. The entire army transferred from rock bottom low lives to an effective and well synchronized piece of machine.

The commander stood in the middle, overlooking everything for a while and found great pride in what he had accomplished in form of changes is mood. It was still raining, but in every face surrounding him he saw focused determination. Time to get to work.

"Squadron leader forty-seven, I fall in under your command for the duration of this escapade. Use me as workforce."

The Squadron leader of the forty-seventh squadron welcomed the commander and immediately handed out work tasks.

**ninety nine.**


Saculg's mother entered the vault and walked straight pass many things to a corner where the vault walls were uneven, and no shelves were crafted. She rapidly started to move her hands over the naked wall.

"A vault inside a vault? Clever!" Saculg exclaimed.

His mother did not pay much attention but kept working on the hidden vault door to open it. As it silently opened and revealed it's secret Saculg could not help himself and forced his way to see what it was.

The small compartment contained two things. A blade, beautifully carved in a dark metal, and an odd black stone, emitting some diffusely iridescent light.

"What is that?" Saculg asked.

"Nothing for you to bother about, until you are one of the selected members around the table." His mother said and rapidly closed the vault again.

"I expect that someone will come and get these items and transfer them somewhere else." She continued, while turning around and exiting the vault, heading straight for the door.

"But if they are in my vault, they have been given to me, and they are my responsibility!" Saculg protested and followed his mother all the way to the door but did not leave with her. She did not say anything else, just left, probably heading back to the table.

A vault in a vault… cleaver… was this the only one or could there be any more?

Saculg walked back in, regretting not paying better attention to the opening sequences… He looked around. Five potential places for a vault like the one he just saw. Two for even smaller vaults.

He started to feel around the potential hidden doors, on three of them he was pretty sure that there were vaults, one uncertain and one most likely nothing. The two smaller vault-doors was easy to open, but unfortunately, they were empty.

The blade and the stone, what were they? He tried to remember any fraction of story or rumor he could grasp. Nothing came to mind. But clearly something very valuable and very important. Veron was its guardian, it was something that belonged to the Ingm clan. Something not commonly known. A blade. From the war? No, did not seem right. Weapons from the war was typically not something that was kept hidden, they took front seat and was widely bragged about. No this was something else. A weapon of power? What power? The dwarves had no official enemy, nor did Saculg remember any great enemy of the past that would need any specific weapon. A blade. Something ritual? Possible. A symbolic relic? Possible. And the stone. Almost glowing. What could that be. What could cause glowing? He had never heard of any stone that was glowing. But could it be that it was reflecting the light from within the vault somehow? No, it had been rater dark and it definitely lit up the interior of the small compartment.

The discussions by the table was interrupted by the return of Saculg's mother. She looked pale.

"It is still there! And the stone is glowing…"

A cold silence spread in the room. Even the fire seemed affected by it.

**one hundred.**

By a miracle they had stayed undetected from sunset to sunrise. They both pressed as hard as they could to the solid wall behind them. Both tired form a hard day's physical work, nervousness during the day that escalated throughout the night, and of course, the lack of a nights well needed sleep.

Several times Roy had to poke Phidas when he was about to fall asleep, so they wouldn't be revealed by Phidas' snoring.

During the night, the moons had kept them company on a cloudless sky, casting two faint shadows of animals passing outside the castle. Roy had tried to count them all, but he lost track.

At one time he reflected on that the piles they had destroyed and moved was not visible from where they were standing. And it was a good chance that they were not visible from the top of the castle wall either. If they had been, the vampires probably should have sent out patrols to investigate the changes on the ground around their castle. But there had been nothing of this sort, even if they had heard the activity of the guards above throughout the night.

At another time he was thinking that it was very lonely standing next to Phidas all night long without being able to speak or move. Just stand still, keep Phidas awake and nothing more.

They had waited until the sun stood above the treetops before they dared to move. And should anyone has seen their stiff walk across the field, they would have found it very laughable, but lucky for them, no-one saw them.

Neither of them spoke until they had cleared the tree-line.

"Fire" Phidas said.

"We need wood and fire…"

"Wood is the least of our problems…" Roy answered looking around, expecting to find something to make fire with. After all, everything else they needed was just laying around so why not something to create fire?

"What do you create fire with?" He asked Phidas.

"Flintstones" Phidas answered, also looking around, probably thinking the same as Roy.

"In fact, these Flintstones!" He said with a smile cracking his tired face. "Let us gather wood, go over one last time, set the thing on fire then head back towards the sky road."

"Another days hard work… Let us get to it" Roy said, with an equally tired face, split by a smile.

But he was wrong, it was not another day's work, just a few hours, and by midday they had light the fire and was well on their way back to the sky road as the silence of the forest was filled with huge explosions.

"Good thing it exploded in daylight! If the blast did not kill them the sun must have helped!" Phidas said to Roy with a sad expression in his face.

"I regret not having planned this better, now I can only believe I have made harm to the vampires, logically expect that I have, WE have done harm to them, but impossible to know. And by nightfall I think the woods will be crawling with angry vampires, so by then I hope we are long gone from here…" he continued as they reached the ladder that Oaks had lowered for them.

"Great fireworks - well done!" Oaks greeted them as they came up through the hatch.

**one hundred and one**

Grime tried to stand up. It kept ringing in his ears, he knew he coughed, but he could not hear it. It was dust all over the place. It was a struggle, but eventually he stood on his feet. He slowly walked towards the door. So much light. As he reached out to open it, it fell and revealed… Un comprehensive… He expected to see a dark corridor in a stone castle, instead he saw blue sky and treetops in a distance. The corridor outside his door did not exist anymore. Where the floor had been there was only air.

He moved closer to the edge, but as he took a step the floor disappeared beneath him, taking with it the walls and he had to throw himself to the back of the room and press himself hard against the wall only to witness the wall, big parts of the floor and roof falling down just in front of his eyes.

What had happened? How could a huge stone castle just fall apart? Grime could not believe what his eyes were telling him, yet it was gone. One step in front of his feet the floor seized to exist. In front of him a huge pile of big stones along with pieces of various object that could have come from his own room and others above, next to and beneath his room.

If he just took a leap from the edge, it would be a fall of two man heights and then he would land on top of the pile, and with a little luck he would be able to climb his way down to the ground. Then he could run to the trees.

The sun would hopefully protect him from any hunting party, at least until sunset.

And if the castle looked like this, would they have time and manpower to hunt him down? Hopefully not!

The master… was he alive, or was it possible that he lay dead in the ruins? …and the werewolf? What had possibly happened with it? Was it dead? Set free?

The more he kept thinking, the harder it was to take the leap. But Grime closed his eyes. Forced his feet to the edge without looking, then, still coughing and with his eyes still closed, he did it. He took a leap. And what felt like forever, he fell, and fell, like Alice down the rabbit hole, and then he stopped. A hard stop that made every bone and muscle in his body ache. He tumbled. Fell once more, but just a short fall this time. Then stopped. He lay completely still a while before he dared to open his eyes.

Then slowly, still without being able to hear anything, he opened his eyes. Directly in front of him was a big rock, blackened from fire. It probably came from somewhere above his room. He moved his arms and legs, to find something solid to hold on to and try to rise again.

All around him was debris from the castle. Nowhere did he see anything that looked like a vampire or a vampire body. Of course not, stupid. There would not be any vampire bodies in the sun.

He slowly descended to the ground level and moved out on the open field towards the ridge of the wood.

Just before he reached it, he stopped to turn around and see the extent of the devastation.

The castle was nearly annihilated and there were still fires here and there among the ruins. Only the one tower remained, and from it, parts of two great walls stood in angle to each-other, both heavily damaged and as if the remaining walls embraced the big pile of stone in between them.

A sight that Grime knew he never would forget.

There was no sign of movements except from the scattered flames and the smoke who slowly reached for the sky. He turned and continued his steps as a free man. A free enhanced man.

**one hundred and two**

They were surrounded entirely by the werewolves by now. Should anyone think to reach for one in either direction they all, including Groll, would have been able to touch them, but neither of them tried.

Dee found it strange that they did not attack. They had no apparent reason not to. And when Groll started to walk ahead, the others followed. To Dee's surprise the werewolves opened and let them through, without any hostile moves.

"This way, stay close to me!" Groll said over his shoulder, as if he was speaking to Dee's knee, but they all heard him and dared not do anything else but to follow him.

Slowly, and in a very spasmodic way, the little strange gathering of a troll, a human, a dwarf, a wizard and a human moved their way through an endless mass of werewolves.

Dee did not experience time, the situation just started, kept on going infinitely, and then, suddenly, without a warning, it stopped.

They stood in front of a dark entrance to a cave. The werewolves stood on each side of the mountain walls and behind them, like an ocean they had split up in front of them. They had wondered through the werewolves unharmed, and each step they took the werewolves opened a little, just enough to take that step. And as soon as the last of them moved the last foot, they closed behind them as if there had never been space, they could possibly have walked on.

Dee looked down at Groll, as if to ask permission to enter the cave.

But Groll just stood there looking into the dark.

"Well, now it seems like we need you, wizard. Can you chase away the dark in here?" Groll said out loud without taking his eyes of the darkness in front of them.

Leola closed her eyes, mumbled something and made some gestures with her hands and arms, and then, some kind of glowing started between her palms, and it slowly grew and hovered in front of her. It took the form of a sphere and floated midair about twice as high as Groll was tall. Leola commanded the orb to move forward and Groll followed it, the others followed Groll.

A few steps into the cave the orb was attacked by a werewolf paw, but it seemed to be made of nothing else than light, so the paw just went through it as if striking air.

The orb revealed another wall of werewolves, and Dee realized that if she had entered alone, she would probably not have been alive. They needed the protection of Groll, he needed to be there with them.

Groll seemed to know what Dee was thinking and hurried up to the orb and stood right below it, the others hurried to follow him and placed themselves in a half circle behind Groll and the orb.

For each step Groll took, Leola pushed the orb further in and the growls and howls of the werewolves was amplified by the massive walls of the cave and if possible there were twice as many werewolves on the same space as it had been outside. Or at least that is how it felt to Dee.

Another infinity started once they entered the darkness of the cave, but when she looked back at it later, it could not have been more than a hundred small steps into the dark cave.

Then all of a sudden, they had walked past all the growling and howling, and the cave opened up in a small compartment. There in a nest, the small light from the orb reflected in the surface of a rather large silver egg. And next to it someone was sleeping. Not just anybody. Dee immediately recognized Rick!

Saculg's mother tried once more. She knocked hard on the door to her son's quarters. It remained as still and quiet as before. She could not understand where he possibly could be. Only the table members of each clan were allowed to leave their quarters at will and could move freely in the two main living areas and the routes that connected them. All others were confined to their living-quarters for the time being. Only the delegation and their soldiers were allowed to walk around freely. So either Saculg did not answer his door, or he had been requested somewhere by the delegation.

She was desperate. Two things were decided by the table of the Ingm clan. Saculg was to be asked to take Veron's seat around the table, and it was time to move the blade and stone. And she needed the stone, the survival of the entire main mines could very well depend on it.

Why, oh why didn't he open?

As she stood there, banging on the door for the somethings time, she had lost count, her attention was directed elsewhere. A gathering of dwarves was moving towards her and hurried passed her. Then another, and another.

"What is going on?" she asked one of the by-passers.

"Have you not heard? We are all called to the main hall for an important announcement. Our presence is required. They gather all of us."

She did not want to abandon her task and decided to stay longer. Or at least as long as she could.

Groups kept passing her, and soon she figured she was the last person in this area, and to confirm her thoughts, a squad of soldiers rounded the corner of a corridor and walked straight at her.

"Please move away from the door, your presence in the main hall is required." One of the soldiers addressed her.

"But I need to see my son, he lives her, but he won't open…"

"Saculg is already in the main hall, so get moving!"

"You know Saculg?"

"We all know Saculg, and from today, so will everybody!"

Saculg's mother did not know what to answer and at first, she did nothing, but when she realized that the soldiers had stopped and had no intention of moving before they made sure she was heading towards the main hall.

What did they mean? How could everybody know Saculg after today? Had he done something and was about to be punished in public? Had he tried to trick his way out of taxation somehow?

For each step she took towards the great hall, the center of dwarf society, her heart started to beat faster, and she got more and more worried. Her motherly instinct told her that nothing good would come out of this. And soon she found herself running towards the main hall, leaving the squad of soldiers far behind her.

She had to get there, she had to know. She had to see, even if it would be painful. Her Saculg, what had he done now?

**one hundred and four**

Oaks led two very tired beings back along the sky road. They were not very unlike the undead at the moment, and as of the blast, the night rule had been obsolete. They walked for the remainder of the daylight on the day of the explosion, and by nightfall the arrived at the strangest part of the sky road, the dwarf saver passage.

Oaks, who often walked a little ahead to see that everything was clear signed to the two tired beings to be quiet. As they stood all three with their heads so close that they could whisper to each other, Oaks pointed down.

"The ground is filled with dwarves. I do not know exactly what they are doing, but it seems like they are building something in that direction. They have taken several trees and from what I can tell, they are not done yet. Is it only me or is it an odd coincidence that the ground is crawling with dwarves just beneath the dwarf saver?"

They all looked down at the febrile activity below for a while, and Phidas could not help but to feel a certain amount of pride. The dwarves were hardworking and well organized. Almost like a mining expedition when exploring a new part of the mountain.

At a moment of lower activity below, they started to cross the roped passage, Oaks first, then Roy and Phidas last, since he did not want anybody behind him to push him forward, he needed to make this in his own pace.

Oaks and Roy crossed quickly and undetected. Phidas took his time. He was so exhausted from the previous day and night and was uncertain if he really could continue forward at all. For each agonizing step Oaks and Roy worried that he would be detected. Even if the dwarves beneath were busy they looked up every now and then, as if the evaluated trees.

When Phidas was about halfway, the dwarves on the ground started to chop down a tree pretty close to where they were standing. Phidas did not seem to be aware of it and no matter how much Roy gestured with his arms Phidas just did not move any faster.

If they were unlucky, the tree would fall in their direction, and that could be a very big problem. But as it seemed now, Phidas was moving faster than the dwarves on the ground worked, so with a little luck they would be long gone before the tree fell, and it would not matter in what direction.

In the middle of all the excitement, Roy thought about the poor dwarves that would be stuck below at nightfall, and the possibility that a wave of furious vampires would flood the very ground that surrounded the poor souls. They sure needed any and all protection they could manifest.

Roy was interrupted in his thoughts by the sudden movements of the tree the dwarves worked on. It would soon fall, and Phidas was still struggling on the ropes, one foot in front of the other.

Roy and Oaks could only watch without the ability to intervene. The tree started to fall in the direction of the rope bridge. At first Roy though it would hit Phidas, but as it turned out, it fell just behind him. The force of the falling tree was a lot greater than the ropes could withstand, and they snapped rapidly one by one letting the big tree loose and fall to the ground where the dwarves started to work on it immediately.

Roy dared not look over the edge of the platform. But Oaks did and turned to Roy with a smile.

"Look!" he said pointing down.

Had it been a wooden bridge, like the rest of them, it would have scattered and anyone on it would have fallen to the ground only to meet death. But this part was built by rope. The Dwarf saver. And it worked. Tangled in the ropes was one dwarf who had not fallen to the ground to meet his death.

**one hundred and five**

In the great hall everybody was gathered. Soldiers stood guard as a barrier to the throne and on it Achim looked over his humble subjects with an expression of contempt in his face.

It took time to gather all, and since the soldiers took up a lot of space, it was more crowded than usual.

Achim waited until all had gotten quiet before he rose to speak.

"I have been here for a while, and among you I have only found greed and lack of trust. You are loyal only to yourselves and the traditions of old. When taxed you have cheated, lied and have, without consideration to your own honor, tried to scam your way out of it with as little personal loss as possible."

His face wrinkled in dismay as he continued.

"One of you, and only one, stood up, tried to negotiate and find new terms, beneficial to both parties of the table, and not forgetting the third part by the table."

He paused dramatically.

"Yes, I speak of personal bribes to the delegation-member in charge of the taxation."

The entire audience gasped unison.

He turned and pointed towards Saculg who stood between two guards with his head hanging low.

"This individual bribed our delegation member, he convinced an old accountant to look the other way while both himself and our great King lost in treasures while our delegation member got himself a personal gain in the deal."

Achim looked out over the filled hall.

"What do you say to this? Is his behavior appropriate and acceptable?"

His question was met with silence.

"Do you agree with the actions of this young individual or should we punish him?!"

Still silence.

"Dare no one speak up? Are you loyal only to yourselves or to each other? Is there something higher than yourselves? Are there something true and just?"

As he spoke wildly and energetic, saliva burst out of his mouth in small showers that landed on the floor in front of him.

"What should we do with this young dwarf? Say I left his faith in your hands, what would be appropriate in this situation?"

The head of the Ingm-clan was the first to speak.

"Punishment! Outrageous behavior!"

Soon the entire hall was filled with words and suggestions of a suitable punishment.

When Saculg's mother heard the word 'decapitation' she buried her face in her hands and tried to shut the masses out and wished she could sink through solid rock.

**one hundred and six**

Dee still got tears of joy in her eyes hours after her cry woke up Rick and seemed to scare away the werewolves who all moved closer to the cave opening.

Leola had placed the orb above the silver egg, and they all sat down in the half circle, facing the egg and orb as if it were a fireplace. None worried about the werewolves. If the werewolves wanted them dead, there had been plenty of time to arrange that by now.

Rick and Tadao told their story from the events on the Glory until the night of the storm, and then Rick continued to tell his strange story.

"At first it was the one werewolf that herded me, and each time I took a step in an undesired direction or tried to put the egg down it howled and growled and threatened me with its claws or teeth. It was very clear in its directions.

I was not allowed to stay and sleep, nor put the egg down to rest, just walk and walk. But as other werewolves joined, they started to force me to rest, gathered food for me, mostly raw meat, and even provided cover for me, after I put down the egg safe. I have never in my life felt so safe as when I traveled with them. Every day their number kept growing and now I can even pet them as I please and when I please. It's like I have got a very big pack of really strange dogs."

Rick took Dee's hand and continued while Groll laughed a little to himself and muttered 'strange dogs'.

"They prefer that I sleep in the cave next to the egg, but they let me go outside during daytime. And I get fresh meat twice a day. I never thought I would see another human face again! They won't let me wander off to far from the cave."

Rick looked at the others.

”…and believe it or not, but they have never tried to harm me in any way! At most, they gather up as a wall in front of me and drive me back to where they think I should be.”

Then Dee shared her story, and Tadao his, and as an end twist to his story Tadao asked:

”What is this silver egg anyway, and why is the werewolves so obsessed with it?”

After a silent moment, Leola answered, with intense eyes resting on Groll.

”According to legend, the silver egg is made up of life essence from the creators. And the werewolves are created to guard it but are prohibited from touching it. They themselves lack life essence in their body, and are drawn to it as a vampire is drawn to blood. But this is only legend. Nobody knows for sure, and most doesn't even think it exists.”

Dee looked confused.

”Life essence? What is that?”

Leola continued.

”It is said that most life are made up of three things. A body, a soul and life essence. If you believe the old stories, the silver moon represents the life essence in us, the blood moon our body, and the sun our soul. But to most, that are just ancient stories. I personally find it appealing and very poetically beautiful.”

**one hundred and seven**

They others helped Phidas back up to the platform. His face had both turned red from all the blood flowing down to his head from the up-side-down-tangled-in-a-rope-routine, and pale from the shock of the same.

The rest of the journey back to Vladir and Yena was without incidents, and the celebrations o their mission success was just about to start when Phidas overheard some of the others.

"What did you say? Another dwarf on the sky road?"

"Well, yes, on the mountain side. In companion with two humans, a wizard and a troll. Quite the strange party, wouldn't you say?"

"Well, not stranger than my own alliance with Roy!"

Phidas turned around looking for him and it took a while to find him.

"Roy! We need to leave, right now! No time to lose!"

"What do you mean? The party is about to start, we can't leave now, it would be very rude of us, turning down hospitality like this!"

"I have two pieces of information that states we need to move right now! First of all, there are another dwarf on the sky road, by the mountain, and second of all, the party includes dismounting the sky road for good, which prevents me from finding my kin."

Roy did not seem to comprehend what Phidas was saying, so he repeated himself.

"I need to find the other dwarf, it is very important. And we need to get moving right away, otherwise it will be too late."

"Yeah, I heard you! I was only thinking… when you find the other dwarf, what will you do then?"

"Well, it all depends on who it is, but I have my suspicions of who it might be. We have a dwarf army on the surface, which is an awfully bad sign in itself. And this army did not consist of ordinary military trained dwarves. I did not recognize either one of them, which means that they are from the northern province, sent by my brother. Everything in this is sad pieces in a puzzle that by themselves is alarming. And together they are part of something bigger and darker. I feel it is my duty to try and prevent it, as I have tried to eliminate the vampires. Succeeded or not, I feel I need to focus on my own kin to try and put things back in order."

"What will happen to our companionship when you find the other?"

"Well, dear Roy. You will always be my friend and I will always be grateful for our time together and remember everything we have been through with a smile and warmth in my heart. But these dark events in the dwarf society calls upon me, and I fear that it is not very likely that I will survive it all. And should it be so, I do not want you to be in harm's way, nor even close enough so you can see the danger. It pains me, but this is what needs to be."

"Well, no time to loose then, my friend. Let us go and find your kin's man." Roy had often wondered if this friendly dwarf was really capable of leading the dwarf society. Now, after this little speech and everything they had been through, there was no doubt in his mind.

They said farewell to Vladir and Yena, and started their journey towards the mountains, leaving the party and destruction behind.

## one hundred and eight

”Enough!” Achim’s voice echoed in the big hall.

”You should all be ashamed! While you all thought only of yourselves, this young man thought of himself, our great King and the hardworking man in the middle. This is creative new thinking, something we all need in a time of changes.”

Again, the silence in the great hall was unnatural.

”You are all stuck in the past, resisting change. And the consequence of this is that I need to dissolve all old hierarchies. Here by, all clans are obsolete, and no former clans’ members may ever hold any official position in the new order from our great King. All clan meetings are hereby banned and will be punished with imprisonment or death when caught. And we have eyes and ears everywhere, so you will get caught if you attempt to have meetings in secret.”

This caused a little mumbling among the gathered crowd, but nothing that stopped Achim.

”This exemplary young man, Saculg, is an honor to both his parents. An honor they do not deserve and perhaps not understand. Saculg, and Saculg alone, will be your representative in all questions where either me or our great King needs your opinion.”

Now the sound level was intense, everyone was discussing with the one standing beside them, and from the rising intensity of the volume to judge, they did not like it.

”And a word of advice. Saculg will be your official. And as your official he will be put under my protection. Please him and you will have a chance to get your voice considered. But Saculg has got clear instructions to NOT let him be affected by your simple opinions and wishes. He has a sharp intellect, and we ask him to use it wisely. He has the ability to think and act in new ways that will benefit us all. Treat him well. He is your only way to me, and I am the only way to our great King."

The last words of Achim brought back the awkward silence and it was not until he left the throne and resigned along with Saculg that the crowd began to speak again.

Saculg's mother was both horrified and relieved. The ways of old had been brutally scattered. A shift in power that was intensely dangerous for their way of life. Indeed, the beginning of a dark era for the dwarves. An era that would benefit her son, for as long as it lasted. And should it for some reason change, her son would most likely not benefit from the change. How can any mother relate to that?

It took time for all the dwarves to leave the great hall, and as they did, they all passed strategically placed guarding post in all tunnels. Perhaps their confinement to their homes would be lifted at some point, but it did not look like they would be free anytime soon. Their prison would only grow slowly.

Saculg's mother thought of the glowing stone. She thought of the secrets the Ingm clan was guarding, and what the other clans could possibly holding secret to the others. She had a vague feeling that King Thidas did not fully understand the purpose of the clans and saw them only as political alliances. He could not be more wrong if he thought so. The clans had always been a solid part of the dwarf society, to keep balance, to protect the great mass from different threats. In the Ingm clan, it was their secret duty to keep watch for the stone-worms and slay them if necessary. But now there was no Ingm clan and they could not get hold of the two things they needed to fulfill their secret duty.

**one hundred and nine**


Vladir and Yena stood together on the platform above their house. The party had been a success, but it was a shame that Roy was not there to share this with them.

"Amazing that it worked! He was really stubborn about the dwarf saver passage. And now it has played it's part in all this."

Vladir turned to Yena and held both her hands.

"I never thought we would meet him from the time before. It was hard not to say anything."

"Yeah, I know, I constantly waited for him to reveal the joke but I think it really was him from before."

"It makes sense that Phidas would be with him now, so I guess it is right what you say, but I really also was expecting him to crack up in a laughter any time, giving him away…"

They stood quiet looking down at their hands. Yena was the one to break the silence.

"You think we'll see him again?"

Vladir hugged his loved one.

"I assume I will, giving my condition. And I hope you will too, my love…"

"I hope so too…" Yena sighed with her face pressed against Vladir's shoulder. "You know, tomorrow we will start the destruction of the sky road towards the sea. Then as the undead has passed, we will destroy it towards the mountain. What do we do then?"

"Well, strangely enough I have not thought about it. I have been so consumed by the sky road for so long, so I have not really thought about the time after the sky road…"

"How do we know that it is the right thing to destroy it? What if he is wrong in that?"

"…I have to say that he has not been wrong once, even if I have had my doubts at times… so I see no reason to doubt this either… but of course he could be wrong… but we would probably never know, because we are going to start the destruction mechanism tomorrow. It will destroy everything towards the sea. Then, on cue, we will start it towards the mountains… we need to do that, we owe him that much… then I guess it's just you and me, perhaps some of the sky boys… but I figure they will follow their own road to their own destiny… no point in staying behind…"

"You are probably right, love, but it feels like we're breaking up the family…"

"Yes, we are…" Vladir paused "…indeed we are…"

"What will happen to us after it is destroyed?"

"I do not know, my love, I do not know… but as long as we are together, I am sure we'll think of something…"

**one hundred and ten**

Rick and Dee sat on the sunny slope of the roof to the cave where the egg was kept.

Groll had used his strange gift and pushed the guarding werewolves back so they had the entire cave and a large opening in front of the cave. To compensate, the werewolves surrounded them everywhere in all directions.

Groll had been very clear, he seemed to know a thing or two about the egg and the werewolves. No one could touch the egg, except for Rick since he had already carried it so long.

Tadao and Leola could not be seen from where they were sitting, but Groll wandered back and forth, mulling to himself, looking back the way they came from. Dee had gotten to know Groll a bit by now, and she could tell that he was either worried or impatient.

Veron was standing by the mountain wall, inspecting it as if he read a book.

Without warning there was a loud noise from within the cave and Tadao flew out of it, as being pushed by an explosion and landed on his back on the ground outside of the cave.

In an instant the werewolves swarmed all over and filled the cave from every possible direction. There were only two islands in the werewolf ocean, where Tadao lay on the ground, and where Groll made his way through the emerging chaos.

Soon they heard screams from Leola, but it was not screams of agony or fear, it was rather rage and madness. The werewolves kept coming and her raged screams seemed to move closer to the cave opening.

At the same time, the moving island that was Groll was also moving closer to the cave opening.

Both Rick and Dee stood on their feet without really understanding what was going on, all peace and quiet one moment, all chaos and mayhem the other. Dee could not help but to relate to the attack of the undead, except this time it was werewolves who moved like the ocean, and not the undead.

When Leola's screams and Groll's moving island collided in the opening of the cave Leola unleashed her great fury and turned it from the werewolves, who up until now had been slaughtered in great numbers and held back in greater numbers.

Groll on his hand also seemed to attack, even if he just stood there with his eyes focused on her. The werewolves kept attacking her, and whatever growing things that was nearby, grass, bush, roots from small trees nearby. Everything was growing to a tangled mess, who seemed to enclose Leola fully.

But her rage flashed with lightning and fire and tiny pieces of rock that was thrown like small spears in the air towards Groll.

The werewolves closest to him put themselves in harm's way, but Dee got a bad feeling as the events started to slowly unfold in favor of Leola.

She continued her slaughter of the werewolves but had changed direction in the ocean of werewolves and was heading away from the cave and away from the valley they came through. All the while haunted by the werewolves.

When the werewolf ocean followed her up the slopes towards the mountain, they left an empty battlefield with missing werewolf bodies, Tadao looking up confused and Groll laying wounded on the ground.

Dee ran straight to Groll and the others joined her. He was in bad shape, and Dee could see he had lost a lot of blood already.

As Tadao joined, he mumbled to the others:

"Great creator, she tried to take the egg, I said she shouldn't, but she tried anyway…"

**one one one**


Saculg visited his new official quarters. They had, until recently, belonged to one of the heads of clan. Saculg was uncertain of which but did not care the least.

The quarters were very exclusive with a great deal of fine things, all his to do as he pleased. It would take him a while to get used to this, to his new role, to being a part in the political madness that had rained down on them all.

Enough for now, he walked to the door and as he opened it, the guards that were posted outside saluted him. Two of them remained to guard the quarters, and two followed him as he walked through the halls to his own private quarters. There were also two guards stationed. Saculg was not sure it was only for his protection; it was most likely also to monitor him and his visitors.

Once home, behind the closed door he could be alone with his thoughts. So much had changed in a short time. He let his mind wander. He knew there was something he had overseen. An unspoken thought that teased him.

He walks inside the vault, walked around at random. He stopped in front of the hidden vault his mother had opened. He tried to reopen it but was not successful. But he discovered something new, another hidden and well-sealed compartment, containing only a little note.


*To whomever finds this.*


*Hidden inside these walls are the last blade of the fallen knights, and the warning beacon they used to detect the presence of the stone-worms. We invaded their world, took their home. We think we have slaughtered them and have chosen to forget them. But there is a prophesy that foresees their return. Keep them safe. When the rock starts to glow, they are near if it shines bright, they are here. Then it is too late.*

Saculg could remember the stone, it looked as if it were glowing. Did that mean that there were stone-worms nearby? And what was a stone-worm? He had never heard about it. Nor had he ever heard anything about the fallen knights.

His first thought was to talk to his mom about it. But when debating it internally he thought it would be best to tell Achim about it. On the other hand, that could lead to something dangerous to his mother, since she was the one who opened the small vault. If only he could open it himself, then he could keep her out of it. Then again. What evidence did he have that all this was real?

Maybe it was just an old piece of text from an old book, something that was dear to uncle Veron, or maybe a strange joke from his part.

He decided to keep it to himself, for the time being. And to keep trying to open the safe. Maybe it would be that once he opened the small vault, he would find that the stone was not glowing, but was just an ordinary stone, hidden along with some kind of blade.

No, wait and see. Should it be real, and the stone would shine, then it would not matter. Besides, maybe it would not be to terrible if all this would end. This nightmare.

**one hundred and twelve**

When Roy and Phidas reached the last platform, they found Devoras waiting, anxiously looking towards the mountain. Since the others went down the whole valley in front of him had filled up with werewolves, out of nowhere. And they had closed all possible escape routes back to the sky road.

Once Roy and Phidas had arrived Devoras knew it was time, even before they had delivered the message from Vladir. He instructed Roy and Phidas how to lower the ladder, then asked them to say relay a message to Dee, if they would find her, and then he left to unleash the undead.

Roy and Phidas stayed on the platform, uncertain what to do next. It seemed like a bad idea to lower the ladder and walk towards the werewolves.

As they sat quiet waiting on inspiration, they heard a faint bang, almost like a delayed echo of their escapade by the vampire castle.

At first it did not seem to have had any impact, but pretty soon the werewolves moved longer into the valley and the wave moved slowly towards the hills, beyond their sight. The movement accelerated rapidly and in an instant, the valley was completely empty again. Almost as if there had never been any werewolves. Only the dust that had not yet settled again was the only sign on the drastic change that just had occurred in the landscape.

Phidas insisted to follow the werewolves to see what happened, but Roy hesitated. Despite all he had been through, it was still werewolves they were about to follow. One werewolf is bad enough, and what they had just seen was a horde.

But somehow, they agreed on following the horde.

The climb down was the hardest Roy had done, yet it was
something inside him was driving him forward. As if he was meant
to be here, meant to follow the werewolves. Even if he did not
believe in destiny, he was almost tempted to use that word. He felt
destined to find out what was in the end of the valley.

Phidas seemed to be distracted by the proximity to the mountain.

”Do you miss the mountain?”

”Huh? Well, yes… and no, I do not know… mostly I’m worried.”

”About what?”

”Well, I fear that since I left our great mines, a lot has happened. It
seems like my brother has launched an army that marches straight
to the main mines. He has always been hungry for power, and now I
suspect he reaches for it.”

Phidas thought for a while before continuing.

”And the fact that there are another dwarf outside the mines, that
just happens to be at the sky road at the same time as me, it has to
be more than a coincidence. And if I am right, it is an individual
that I would benefit greatly from having by my side at this moment.
He has a free mind and that is something will need in order to gain
control of this puzzling situation. Perhaps I need to prevent a civil
war among the dwarves, perhaps I need to fight off an invasion…”

”Who do you think the other dwarf is?”

”I hope it is Veron of the Ingm clan. But I do not expect you to
know who it is…”

Roy laughed.

”No, not really, you are the only dwarf I have ever met. But it looks
like I might be about to meet another, look up at that hill. Do you
see the cave opening?”

Phidas looked up. There was indeed a cave opening, and the werewolves had passed it and their wave continued to move up the slopes behind the cave and over the edge of this part of the mountain. But it was too far away for his eyes, and he could not make out if there were anybody by the cave.

"What do you see up there, Roy?"

"I see a gathering of a small group, gathered around something on the ground. Hard to say what it is. One of them are running to the cave, entering it. The others stay outside."

He paused and kept looking as they slowly moved forward towards the scene.

"Now there is someone coming out of the cave, carrying something. Looks shiny. Rather big. Could be something round. Maybe black or silver, hard to say…"

**one hundred and thirteen**

"Thank you, Rick!" Groll said with great effort.

"Since you have carried this egg, affected by its power you have been, and live an unnatural long life you will. You can die from blood-loss, but not from hunger or lack of breath."

He gestured to Rick to put the egg down beside him. And then he put his hand on it and took a small piece out and put it on the ground next to him.

"This little piece is to Roy, if I ever will meet him again. If I die before I do, you will need to destroy it. Toss it on the fire and leave it burning until it has vanished."

He turned to Dee.

"Close your eyes."

He lifted the silver egg with one hand, as if it were made of air. He held it in front of Dee and started to push the egg inside her chest. Dee felt a warm sensation in her heart that spread to every part of her body. When Groll was done pushing, the egg had vanished completely and had been absorbed by her body.

"Now, Dee, I have given you all the life essence except for Roy's piece. Use it well. It will give you great powers, learn how to control them. Your first task is to…"

Groll had to pass and catch his breath.

"Your first task is to relieve the world of the werewolves. Their task was to guard the life essence. It is no more, and never will be, so they are no longer necessary."

Groll kept losing blood, and his voice got weaker and weaker as he spoke.

”It is an important task, and Rick can help you. They will not attack you since they feel the life essence in you.”

Dee got tears in her eyes.

”I am counting on you. They were never meant to run free among the creation. They were sealed up. I think Leola released them. But she could not have known. She is after the life essence. She is your enemy now. Be aware of her powers. Never underestimate her. Dangerous she is. Much to learn she still has.”

Rick, who still stood with his back towards the cave opening from when he ran to get the egg noticed that there were two people approaching their position. The did not move very fast. One of them was probably a dwarf. Perhaps one of Veron's friends? Either way, they were headed towards them, and soon enough they would arrive, so Rick ignored them for the time being and focused on Groll again. It did not look to good. He was still bleeding heavily.

Dee could feel the warmth in her entire body, something was going on, and at first, she could not understand where the silver egg had disappeared, but she realized that it somehow had to be inside her now. All that was left of it was the small piece Groll had saved.

What had Groll meant with all this? What would it mean to her to have the silver egg inside of her?

”Filthy human!” Groll looked at Dee with a smile on his face. ”You took me out of the sorrow. Showed me life again. Keep it up, show everybody life!”

## one hundred and fourteen


Roy and Phidas were close now, they had both seen a little being pushing the object inside of a girl.

Phidas had recognized the one of his own kin, Veron. The one dwarf he hoped to meet.

As they arrived at the small group the little creature spoke before they or anyone else had a chance to say something.

"Ah, Roy! At last! I was wondering if I ever would see you, and if it would be in time. Never thought it would be like this…"

"I am sorry, do I know you?"

"Yes, and no! Consider you an old friend I do, and still, it is the first time we meet, from your perspective. Last time from mine. Roy, old friend. My name is Groll. Pleasure to finally meet you again!"

"I do not understand… please explain…"

"No time, come, kneel next to me!"

Roy did as requested of him by this little creature.

"I can see you are hurt and in pain…"

"No time, close your eyes!"

Groll took the remaining life essence and pushed it inside of Roy's chest, as he had done with Dee.

"Now Roy. You live forever. If you choose to, and I know you will. You can die from blood-loss, but not from hunger or lack of breath."

"What do you mean with live forever?"

"Live, as in not dying… I do not remember you as slow… you will catch on eventually!"

Groll got weaker by each breath. Even if Roy and Phidas did not know what had happened or how long ago, they could tell it did not look good for this little creature.

"Tell me how you know my name and how others seemed to have known me as you do, even if I am certain I see them for the first time! I need to know!"

"You will, eventually, old friend! You will!"

Groll had a hard time breathing by now and Roy dared not ask more questions.

He could see from the look on the faces of the others, including Phidas, that this was not the time to ask questions, rather the time to respect this little one and leave him be, to die in peace and harmony.

Neither spoke for a while. They all just stood there around Groll.

**last one**

There was no chance of stopping the bleeding, and Dee feared for Groll's life.

Soundless, and from nowhere, an old man appeared on the top of the hill.

Roy recognized him as the man he had seen coming out of the house that day when he met Phidas for the first time. Now he appeared as the house had done that time.

By the look on the others, this was an extraordinary event, but somehow, Roy saw this as completely natural, given everything he had been through so far.

The old man walked towards them, did not pay any attention to any of the others, except Groll.

He kneeled beside him.

"Goodbye, old friend. Thank you for everything!"

He took Groll's hand, put it in his and closed his eyes for a while. Then, as if this were nothing special, he just rose, turned around and started walking up the hill again.

Roy hurried after him.

"Hey, wait up! Who are you? I am curious about the house that appeared, and why you came out of it…"

Roy did not have time to say anything else since the old man disappeared again, and after a breath or two, Roy also vanished, in thin air.

Dee cried out in fear as Roy vanished. Tadao grasped. Rick, Veron and Phidas just stood quiet.

Roy was gone!

Groll coughed and everybody turned their attention to him again.

"Who was that?" Dee asked, "and do you know where Roy disappeared?"

Groll swallowed, clearly in pain.

"A wizard of old. My creator." Another burst of pain shot through Groll and he had a long pause before continuing. "Created me and Rueen he did."

The others did not know how Rueen was.

"Lost in time Roy is. That is what she does not know, Leola. Time is the factor she is missing; magic does not work without time."

Another long pause. Groll was getting weaker and weaker.

"The wizard of old hid a house in time, here in the valley. Causing time rifts and strange time waves… Roy was probably caught in one…"

Groll gasped again. Closed his eyes.

"Dee. Hold my hand!" Groll asked, and Dee took his hand in hers.

"Use your gift to do good. You are the last. No body after you. Can never be. The last White Witch..."

He opened his eyes for the last time, looked directly at her, intense.

Dee said nothing, only looked back at him with tears in her eyes, somehow knowing this was it.

Groll closed his eyes and whispered:

"I'm coming Rueen… my love..."

Then he was no more.